The Brightest Star

Books by Fern Michaels

No Way Out
The Brightest Star
Fearless
Spirit of the Season
Deep Harbor
Fate & Fortune
Sweet Vengeance
Holly and Ivy
Fancy Dancer
No Safe Secret
Wishes for Christmas
About Face
Perfect Match
A Family Affair
Forget Me Not
The Blossom Sisters
Balancing Act
Tuesday's Child
Betrayal
Southern Comfort
To Taste the Wine
Sins of the Flesh
Sins of Omission
Return to Sender
Mr. and Miss Anonymous
Up Close and Personal
Fool Me Once
Picture Perfect
The Future Scrolls
Kentucky Sunrise
Kentucky Heat
Kentucky Rich
Plain Jane
Charming Lily
What You Wish For
The Guest List
Listen to Your Heart
Celebration
Yesterday
Finders Keepers
Annie's Rainbow
Sara's Song
Vegas Sunrise
Vegas Heat
Vegas Rich
Whitefire
Wish List
Dear Emily
Christmas at Timberwoods

The Sisterhood Novels:

Bitter Pill
Truth and Justice
Cut and Run
Safe and Sound
Need to Know
Crash and Burn
Point Blank
In Plain Sight
Eyes Only
Kiss and Tell
Blindsided
Gotcha!
Home Free
Déjà Vu
Cross Roads
Game Over
Deadly Deals
Vanishing Act
Razor Sharp
Under the Radar
Final Justice
Collateral Damage
Fast Track
Hokus Pokus
Hide and Seek
Free Fall
Lethal Justice
Sweet Revenge
The Jury
Vendetta
Payback
Weekend Warriors

Books by Fern Michaels (Continued)

The Men of the Sisterhood Novels:

Hot Shot
Truth or Dare
High Stakes
Fast and Loose
Double Down

The Godmothers Series:

Far and Away
Classified
Breaking News
Deadline
Late Edition
Exclusive
The Scoop

E-Book Exclusives:

Desperate Measures
Seasons of Her Life
To Have and To Hold
Serendipity
Captive Innocence
Captive Embraces
Captive Passions
Captive Secrets
Captive Splendors
Cinders to Satin
For All Their Lives
Texas Heat
Texas Rich
Texas Fury
Texas Sunrise

Anthologies:

Home Sweet Home
A Snowy Little Christmas
Coming Home for Christmas
A Season to Celebrate
Mistletoe Magic
Winter Wishes
The Most Wonderful Time
When the Snow Falls
Secret Santa
A Winter Wonderland
I'll Be Home for Christmas
Making Spirits Bright
Holiday Magic
Snow Angels
Silver Bells
Comfort and Joy
Sugar and Spice
Let It Snow
A Gift of Joy
Five Golden Rings
Deck the Halls
Jingle All the Way

Published by Kensington Publishing Corp.

FERN MICHAELS

THE BRIGHTEST STAR

ZEBRA BOOKS
KENSINGTON PUBLISHING CORP.
www.kensingtonbooks.com

ZEBRA BOOKS are published by

Kensington Publishing Corp.
119 West 40th Street
New York, NY 10018

First Kensington Books Hardcover Printing: October 2020
First Zebra Books Mass-Market Paperback Printing: November 2021
ISBN-13: 978-1-4201-5034-6
ISBN-13: 978-1-4201-5035-3 (eBook)

10 9 8 7 6 5 4 3 2 1

Printed in the United States of America

Prologue

October 2016
Santa Maria Island, Florida

Lauren Montgomery opened her second box of tissues and sneezed into the cushiest brand she'd found at the drugstore; she'd been dealing with a nightmare of a cold for the past three days. *All the snowbirds must be bringing extra germs with them this year*, she thought. She hadn't felt this rotten in ages. Probably not since she was four, fell off the slide, and broke her collarbone. "No, this is worse," she said to herself as she poured another glass of orange juice.

Taking her glass outside, she sat at the small table and chairs on the balcony of her beachside condo overlooking the Gulf of Mexico. It was early, yet the beach was already filled with tourists toting beach chairs, brightly colored umbrellas, and the bags of paraphernalia one required to spend a gorgeous winter's day on a Florida beach.

Lauren had just finished writing a biography on one of the hottest stars of social media, Albert Grossman, CEO and founder of Shout Out. If she had to be honest with herself, she hadn't been taking good care of herself during these past two months as she finished work on the manuscript. She put heart and soul into her work and, in doing so, often neglected her own well-being. Lauren told herself that as soon as she was over this cold, she'd get back into a stable routine. She enjoyed tinkering in the kitchen. She'd make pots of homemade chicken-noodle soup and freeze them, just in case. This was the start of the cold and flu season, so it couldn't hurt to be a bit more prepared.

She downed the last of her juice and went inside. Lauren liked the relaxed lifestyle that came with living on the beach and was grateful she didn't have to deal with snowstorms and other such weather-related issues that sent the snowbirds flocking to the Sunshine State every winter. Her life was peaceful, and she liked it that way.

She thought about Eric, and their relationship, which had gone sour. With a wry smile, she knew she'd done the right thing when she broke it off with him. He wasn't the one for her, and she was okay with that. At thirty-two, she knew the years were passing her by, and she did want to settle down one day, get married, and have a family. But no way was she going to settle for just "so-so" in a relationship. She'd rather be alone than with someone she did not love with all her heart and all her soul.

Deciding a hot shower was in order, she put her juice glass in the dishwasher. She was sitting on the side of the tub in the master bathroom about to turn on the water when her cell phone rang.

This was a critical time in the publication of Albert Grossman's biography. It could be her editor needing some sort of change or other.

She answered with a cheerful, "Hello."

The voice on the other end was familiar. There was no "Hello," no "How are you, honey." Not from her mom. Her mother never stopped to think how her words affected someone, anyone, even her one and only daughter. Nope. Good old mom just went full bore. "Lauren, it's your dad. He's been diagnosed with a rare disorder. I need your help right now," her mother blurted shrilly. "I need you to come home. *Now!*"

Jolted back to Fallen Springs, North Carolina, Lauren knew her time on the beach had just ended.

"I'll be there as soon as I can, Mom."

The next phase of her life had just begun.

Chapter 1

Black Friday, 2019

Lauren Montgomery's eyes blurred as she viewed the day's final sales figures. Try as she might, there was no way she could deny the results. She'd added, subtracted, and multiplied the numbers a dozen different ways and could come to no other conclusion: this was it. If sales didn't improve in December, there would be no choice. Razzle Dazzle Décor would have to file for bankruptcy.

Razzle Dazzle Décor had first opened its doors way back in 1935 when her great-grandfather, Alfred Montgomery, was a mere twenty-two years old. At the time, it was called the Montgomery General Store. Centrally located on the main street of Fallen Springs, North Carolina, West King Street, MGS, as it had been called by the locals, started out as just what its name implied. It generally supplied a little bit of this, a little bit of that, and everything in between. From potbellied stoves to Big Chief tablets, as her father and grandfather used to say. Anything one would have generally needed to run a household at the time.

During the sixties, as big-box stores started to fulfill shoppers' every need, the prospects for basic general stores essentially disappeared. So her grandfather, Alfred Montgomery Jr., decided to shift focus and begin to sell holiday décor, which led to an abundance of Christmas decorations that "sold like hotcakes." As the years passed, holiday items comprised most of their inventory, hence the name change to Razzle Dazzle Décor.

Lauren could hear her grandfather and father saying, "I'm razzled and dazzled every time I walk through these doors." Both were still alive but no longer active in the day-to-day operations of the store. Her grandfather was now living in a fancy-dancy assisted-living facility, and her father had been diagnosed with a severe form of crippling arthritis at age fifty-eight. The past three years had taken its toll on both her father and her mother, who was her husband's constant caregiver. Lauren didn't know how her mother managed, but she knew that something had to change, and soon, or her parents' source of income would dry up. She felt sure that they had some sort of retirement plan. What she did not know is whether or not that plan included the loss of income from Razzle Dazzle. She needed to know the specifics of their personal finances but dreaded telling them why she needed to know. Maybe she could find a way around the problem with the store.

One last time, she went over what should have been record sales for the day, since it was, after all, Black Friday, and again, the numbers just didn't come close to where they should have been. Disgusted, she tossed the calculator aside and looked at her watch, a Rolex given to her by her father when she'd sold her first biography. It was almost midnight, and her parents would be asleep when she got home.

She had been thirty-two when she moved from Florida back to Fallen Springs after her father was diagnosed with severe rheumatoid arthritis. It had never been in her life plan to return to Fallen Springs, but family was more important than living in her beachside condo. She sold her place quickly, making an indecent profit, which allowed her to give up her work as a biographer and run the family store. She had written four biographies of giants in the business world, all of which had been best sellers, something she was quite proud of.

It had been over three years since she'd done any writing at all because everything that running the store entailed required her full attention. Perhaps she could have made time for another book if a publisher had asked her to write one, but no one had come begging for another, so Lauren worked from sunrise to sunset to keep her family's retail legacy alive.

And I am doing a crappy job, she thought. A few locals had come in to browse, but the resulting sales came nowhere near the amount needed to remain solvent. They'd sold four wreaths she'd taken on consignment from her mother's craft group. Most of that money went back to the crafters. Other than that, she had sold one artificial tree and a few boxes of handblown ornaments, to make her Black Friday truly a dark day.

Lauren turned the store lights off with the remote on her desk that had been included when she'd purchased them during an after-Christmas sale last year at one of the big-box stores in Asheville, then did a quick walk through the aisles in order to tidy up. Red, green, and white twinkle lights framed the storefront window, where an artfully arranged pile of decorated boxes lay just so around the faux-fir tree, which had ornaments from the store tucked neatly inside and around the branches, the price tags discreetly hidden. The uniqueness of their stock should have brought shoppers from across the state, as it had done in the past, but, sadly, that pipe dream fizzled out as fast as the gas logs in the fake fireplace, where handmade red-and-gold stockings, again from her mother's crafting group, hung from the mantel. If she were a stranger and happened upon a store as Christmassy as this, she would've spent a good portion of today perusing the shelves, but she'd grown up with beautiful, unique items such as these, and it was all in a day's work to her and her parents.

She often wondered if her choice of colleges had something to do with the fact that Florida just didn't seem like a place where one would surround oneself with Christmas things. She'd been wrong on that front, too. Floridians took advantage of the warm weather and overdecorated their front yards and lanais. Hot-pink flamingos wearing red Santa hats were seen on lawns, and sometimes even on rooftops. Santa's sleigh was pulled by seahorses, dolphins, and, now and then, gators, in honor, she supposed, of her alma mater. Sand replaced snow. In Florida, hot toddies were replaced by frozen margaritas, totally the opposite of what she'd been used to. Her college choice had been so long ago, she truly didn't remember when the idea to attend the University of Florida had hit her. Lauren had always returned to Fallen Springs for the Thanksgiving and Christmas holidays, and a few other times throughout the year.

When she returned to her birthplace, she'd adapted as well as any grown woman could have, and so far, she had no regrets.

Until today.

She'd been sliding through the days, weeks, and months as though there would be plenty of time to think about the store's finances, and now, here she was. It was the busiest shopping day of the year, and all she had were a few sales from locals who had yet to buy into the online-shopping craze.

And that was the problem. She'd realized it long before her return to Fallen Springs. Brick-and-mortar stores are in a race for survival, she'd explained to her father and grandfather. They needed to step up their game if they were to survive. Open up an online version of Razzle Dazzle Décor. Or at least join a website where people from across the globe would be able to purchase what they had for sale.

Again and again, her father wouldn't hear of it. He gave her his usual spiel about the business, how it had been handed down from one generation to the next. It had provided for many and would continue to do so. "End of story," he always added.

Not just story, she thought. *End of business.*

She left through the back door, locking up behind her, then rummaged through her purse for her car keys. She unlocked the door with the key fob and slid behind the wheel of her ten-year-old Honda. Turning the key in the ignition, she almost cried when all she heard was a clicking sound.

"Damn," she said loudly. "This car needs a tune-up, and I can't . . ."

Even run the family business properly.

Those were her thoughts as she pulled the latch on the hood. She left her purse on the passenger seat, then raised the hood, using the metal rod to ensure it stayed up.

She tugged on the battery cables, but they seemed okay. She used the light on her outdated iPhone to see if there was anything loose or out of place. "Like I would know if there were."

No way was she calling her mother at this hour of night. Fallen Springs' closest garage, Jimmy's, had closed hours ago, and besides, even if they were open, they wouldn't be able to do anything until tomorrow, maybe not even then. It was a holiday weekend, and most normal people were snuggled in bed beneath a warm blanket after a day of shopping online in the comfort of their own homes. Which is precisely where *she* would be, if given the choice. Sighing, she knew she didn't have the luxury of a choice at that moment. Her only option was to go back inside the store and spend the rest of her night on the sagging sofa in the office.

She shivered as she reentered the store, having lowered the thermostat to sixty-three degrees in order to save on the heating bill. But tonight she'd make an exception. She bumped the temperature up to sixty-eight, then found the pillow and blanket she stored in the office for times such as this. She hadn't spent too many nights in the store, but there had been times when it was necessary. Stock orders that needed to be organized, displays that required her full attention, no customers, things of that nature. A broken-down vehicle was a first.

The forecasters were predicting an extremely cold

winter this year, and so far they'd been spot-on. It was in the low thirties, and she felt chilled to the bone. She made up the sofa, took off her shoes, and tried to get comfortable. She was bone-weary tired. She had arrived at 4:00 A.M. to make sure everything was ready for what was supposed to be one of the busiest days of the year. She had opened the doors at 6:00, preparing for the early shoppers to arrive, despite the fact that no one was lined up at the entrance, as she'd hoped.

As she lay there with nothing but her thoughts to occupy her, she thought about her father and his illness. He remained in such high spirits and always had a positive attitude, and she knew that she had to do whatever it took to keep the store open. If that meant delving into her own funds, then so be it. She didn't have the heart to deliver the news to her parents, especially at the beginning of the holiday season. She would call her financial adviser Monday morning. Lauren knew he would advise against this, but she didn't care. It had to be done. Family was such an integral part of her life. Even though she'd been an only child, she hadn't been spoiled. Lauren had worked for her family since the seventh grade and had started saving her pennies even then. The Montgomerys were a tight-knit bunch, and that meant a lot to her.

After punching the pillow numerous times in order to get comfortable, she finally gave up and decided to make a cup of tea. She took a bottle of water from the refrigerator, poured it into the all-glass teakettle she kept at the store, zapped it in the microwave, and ten minutes later sipped her favorite chamomile tea. It was just after two. She wasn't going to sleep, no matter how tired she was, so she let her thoughts drift where they might.

Until shortly before returning to Fallen Springs three

years ago, Lauren had been in a very serious relationship with Eric Porter, her polar opposite. He came from a large family, had relatives spread throughout the States and abroad, and cared little for his siblings or his parents. While Lauren hadn't liked this aspect of his personality, she'd accepted it as his history. She'd never met his parents, and maybe Eric had had good reasons for his feelings. The few times she'd brought up the subject, he'd become angry, so she would let the topic rest, giving him the benefit of the doubt. They had been an item for almost three years when she started to realize that the parts of his personality that had amused her during the early stages of their relationship had begun to turn her off completely. Soon, they began to spend less time together, and when they did, she realized she couldn't wait to get back to her condo and her life.

He was a bit arrogant, too. She came to realize all of this as their relationship faded. He'd always questioned her about her finances, and that was just one more thing to add to her ever-growing list of discontents. When seeing him became a chore, she broke it off and felt as though she was free to live life on her own terms again.

It was soon after this that her mother made the fateful telephone call asking her to return to Fallen Springs. Lauren was devastated by her father's diagnosis and immediately prepared for the changes it would bring.

At first, she didn't see her father's illness as debilitating. He was able to continue with his normal routine but tired easily. She had thought her mother might have exaggerated the extent of his disability until she saw firsthand how debilitating his condition was.

When he became unable to walk, her mother had called the ambulance, and he'd been admitted to the hospital for infusions that seemed to help for a few weeks. After several episodes, he became even weaker, and Lauren realized that her mother truly needed her. She was thankful she'd had the freedom and the financial wherewithal to help her parents when they had needed her most.

At 5:00, she finally fell into a fitful sleep, only to be awakened by the business phone.

"Hello," she said groggily.

"Lauren, why are you still at the store? I've been worried to death," her mother asked.

"Mom, I'm sorry. My car wouldn't start. I didn't want to wake you. I'm okay."

"Well, thank goodness. I was about to send the police to the store."

Lauren smiled, knowing her mother would have done just that.

"Go back to bed. I'll have my car towed to Jimmy's tomorrow, today." It was already tomorrow, she realized. "I think it's just a wire or something." She had no clue, but she knew her mother was a worrier in every sense of the word.

"I can have Maggie bring you a change of clothes and a hot breakfast," her mother offered. Maggie had been her mother's best friend since first grade. She was like family.

"No, I'm fine, really. I'll wash up here and send out for something later."

"If you're sure?"

"I am. Everything okay with Dad?" she asked.

"He's in bed. I didn't want to wake him, but for the most part, he's had a decent day. This cold weather isn't ideal, but we'll get used to it."

"Then I'll catch up with you later. Try to rest, and if I need a ride home this evening, I'll call Maggie." She didn't want her mother anywhere near the store at the moment. All the extra stock she'd ordered in anticipation of Black Friday remained on the shelves throughout the store. Her mother knew the store's inventory as well as she did and would see that sales hadn't even been close to what they'd been in previous years.

"All right, Lauren, but you make sure and get a hot breakfast. I can call Ruby's Diner."

Knowing her mother meant well, she patiently said, "I'm really not hungry. I've munched on cookies all night, but thanks. I'll get something later, I promise." She would, too. It might only be a cup of coffee, but she was always true to her word.

"Then I'll talk to you later, dear. Don't be afraid to call me. I'm awake most nights anyway," her mother added.

Lauren's heart broke for her. She and her father were both young and vibrant, at least he had been. Her mother had retired from teaching elementary school when she'd turned fifty and spent her time at the store and involved herself in so many activities that Lauren would get exhausted just hearing all that she had on her calendar. Crafts, her passion; the church choir; tutoring the occasional student. And now, her days were spent caring for Lauren's dad. Her father would have done the same for her mother had the situation been reversed. They loved one another, and the more time she spent with them as an adult, the more Lauren realized that their relationship was truly quite rare. The total devotion, understanding, and commitment they shared was an example of true love. She thought of her relationship with Eric, which, in her own words, had turned out to be a real dud. Grateful she'd had the sense to get out of that relationship, she had long ago decided that she would not settle for just any guy. At thirty-five, she'd started to think about her biological clock. She had always wanted a family, maybe two or three children, and still did. Time moved quickly the older she got, and she knew she had a limited amount of it in which to fulfill her goal. But if she didn't, that would be okay. She wasn't going to settle just because she had a vision of what she'd planned. Maybe she'd stay single, footloose, and fancy-free. She'd had several casual dates with Brent Ludmore, the local sheriff, but she'd known him since she was four and couldn't imagine him as a life partner. Nope, she would wait until the right man came along, and if not, then so be it. It wasn't as though Fallen Springs had an endless supply of eligible bachelors. She'd thought about checking out the online dating sites but had never had the time to devote to searching for a date as she only had access to the Internet at the local coffee shop, the Daily Grind, or at the pharmacy next door.

You do now, the voice in her head reminded her.

"What the heck," she said as she booted up the computer, her personal laptop, which was used exclusively for her writing. *Right*, she thought as she waited for the Internet browser to load. The pharmacy's owner, Wilbur Davis, was her father's best friend. He'd given her his Wi-Fi information for when she needed to use the Internet; he too knew how much her father refused to even take a peep into the twenty-first century. After she logged on, she searched the most popular dating sights, skimmed through the requirements, and decided this wasn't for her, at least not yet. She viewed a few bios that were interesting but not so much that they took her mind off her current situation. She logged off and sighed.

Something had to give, and right now, the only giving "thing" was her. Deciding this was the best move for now, she set the alarm on her phone with a reminder to call Roger Riedel at Sun State Bank and Investments in Florida. She needed to find a good firm locally, or at least in Asheville, but keeping her current financial adviser worked for now. Making that change was just one more decision she continued to put off.

It was 6:00 A.M., and she needed a jolt of caffeine if she was to get through the day. Normally, the store closed in the early afternoon on Saturdays. She'd made the decision to stay open both Saturday and Sunday on the holiday weekend, in spite of her parents' objections. Sunday, they reminded her, was a day of rest, a time to spend with family, go to church, renew and rejoice. Normally, Lauren agreed with that philosophy, but again, desperate times called for desperate measures, and though she hoped that her parents would remain unaware of the state Razzle Dazzle's finances were in, she convinced them this was a chance to draw in new customers who might have made the trek to Asheville to visit the grand Biltmore Estate. During the holidays, it was a place to be seen by all—at least that's what most Carolinians believed.

She smiled, remembering her very first trip. It had seemed so huge, a castle unlike anything she'd imagined, and it was, but now that she knew its history, she put all things Biltmore into perspective. It was a must-see, she would never deny that. But the idea of it generating overflow traffic to Razzle Dazzle was nothing more than a pipe dream. Besides, it was at least a two-hour drive away, and that was during good weather and light traffic. Somehow, she'd made it seem like a real possibility, and her mom and dad acquiesced.

She would open the doors promptly at 7:00, just as planned, so she needed to freshen up and prepare for whatever the day might bring.

She washed her face and brushed her teeth in the small private bathroom in the office. She brushed her long blond hair and took a few minutes to do a fishtail braid. She had a tube of lipstick and some blush in her purse, touched a bit to her lips and pale cheeks, then added a bit of mascara to her light-blond lashes. She always carried a tube of black mascara with her since otherwise it looked as if she did not even have eyelashes. She located a stack of hand-painted sweatshirts created by one of the many local artisans and took one into the office so she'd look pulled together even though she wasn't. Thankful that she had worn jeans to work, the top was all she needed for a change. This one was red, with a smiling Santa face beautifully hand-painted across the front. She felt that it was a bit young for her, but decided it would most likely be the last of the lot to sell, if it sold at all, so she'd keep it for herself.

She glanced at her image in the mirror. "It'll have to do," she muttered. Knowing Ruby's Diner would be in full swing at this hour, and especially on a Saturday morning, she grabbed her purse, locked the back door, and stepped out into the brisk morning air. Chilled, she ran the two blocks down King Street. She'd get something to go.

As she entered the diner, she heard a din of voices, shouts from the kitchen, a glass shattering from somewhere, and the heavenly scent of coffee. She was a tea drinker, but she occasionally needed the kick from a robust cup of coffee, and Ruby's brew was certainly that.

"Hey, girly," Ruby called from the kitchen when she saw her slide onto a barstool.

She waved. "Morning, Ruby."

Louise, Ruby's sister, slapped a light-green pad down on the counter. "What's it gonna be, kiddo? We've got the sausage gravy on special today. Three biscuits, three eggs, and three big ole' heaps of gravy. You game?" Louise asked. "You sure need some meat on your bones."

"Sure. Why not? I'll take it to go, though. We're keeping the store open today. You know, the biggest shopping weekend of the year." Lauren glanced around the restaurant. It was buzzing with customers, and a line had started to form at the entrance. Good thing she'd gotten there early.

"Give me five minutes, kid. You want a coffee while you wait?" Louise asked.

"Yes, and one to go as well. Need the caffeine."

Louise placed a giant mug of coffee in front of her. Without any urging, she took a sip and sighed. This was good stuff. She needed to get a Keurig and bring it to the store. There was no rule that said she couldn't have that as well as her microwavable teakettle. It wasn't like she had a boss telling her what to do. Taking another sip, she thought that at the moment, that wouldn't be a bad thing. A boss took responsibility for all. Unfortunately, she was the boss and did not like it one bit. Running a retail store was not as easy as writing a book. If she said this out loud, people would look at her as if she had lost her mind; but for her, it was a fact. Writing was her forte, and she told herself she would get back to it. She had recently pushed her literary agent to find something for her. She could run the store and write during the quiet times, which, lately, lasted the entire day.

"Anything else?" Louise asked, bag in hand.

"Ah, no. This smells good. I can't wait to dig in," she said, and placed a ten-dollar bill on the counter.

"Nope, not today. This is on the house. All local business owners eat free."

"Louise!" Lauren said. "You can't . . ."

"Don't you recognize half the people in here?" she said as she handed her the bag of food and a Styrofoam cup.

Lauren gazed around the diner. Yes. Many of Fallen Springs' business owners were filling the booths and tables. "Then thank you. This is a real treat."

"All right, kiddo, get outta here, and get to work." Louise sounded harsh, but she was as sweet as sugar. When Ruby's husband, George, had passed away, Louise, who'd never married, moved in with her sister, and together they'd kept the diner running like clockwork. The food was excellent, and the prices were just right. Giving away free breakfasts to the local businesses was a great idea.

She hurried back to the store so she could eat before the doors opened. Back in her office, she scooped half of the giant amount of food onto a paper plate and zapped it in the microwave, as it had cooled off during her quick walk back to the store.

Sitting at her desk for the next fifteen minutes, she allowed herself to enjoy the meal. She rarely treated herself to such an unhealthy breakfast, but today she felt she deserved it. She was tiny, barely reaching five feet, and weighed exactly one hundred pounds, but she'd always been somewhat of a health nut and prided herself on preparing healthy and tasty meals for herself.

In college, she'd been very popular during football season as her tasty tailgate treats always drew in a large crowd. She'd enjoyed making her friends and acquaintances happy. So when she'd returned to Fallen Springs, she'd taken over in the kitchen when her mother was too tired. Her mother was a tough cookie when it came to her kitchen, but whenever Lauren could force her to sit down and take a break, she did, and Lauren too enjoyed puttering around in the kitchen. She'd researched her dad's illness, found that there were many anti-inflammatory foods that might be of some help, and tried to prepare meals with that in mind when she was doing the cooking. She knew that both her mom and dad were beyond grateful for her and what they always called her "great sacrifice," but Lauren didn't think she'd sacrificed that much. Yes, she'd had to sell her condo, but considering the profit, that was no hardship at all. And when the time was right, if she chose to do so, she could always buy another one. It didn't have to be on the beach in Florida. North Carolina had beautiful beaches if she wanted beachside. For now, she was content to live in the home that had been in her family for three generations. It was a giant of a place, with mature trees scattered on the property and the Blue Ridge Mountains as a backdrop. Who in their right mind would complain about such surroundings?

The leaves had reached their peak, and they were a sight to behold. One of the most colorful mountain ranges, extending into eight states, the Blue Ridge boasted the longest-running fall leaf season in the world. The reason, Lauren knew, was the many varied elevations. The jewels of color began at the highest elevation in early October, working their way down to the lower elevations in the early part of November. She'd enjoyed every minute of the view she'd grown up with; it never got old. Today, she could have used some cheering up, something to kick up her Christmas spirit, but with sales sinking to record lows, she doubted there would be much to get all cheery-eyed over, unless today's and tomorrow's sales broke all prior records.

She finished her breakfast, which was divine, drained the last of her coffee, and prepared to open. Surprised when she saw a few women gathered at the door, she quickly pasted on a smile. "Please come in, I hope you all haven't been waiting long," she said as she allowed them inside. She sneaked a glance at her watch. No, she was fifteen minutes early.

Three women, who appeared to be close to her mother's age, smiled and entered the store. One, who was wearing a camel-colored jacket with an evergreen scarf, shivered as she entered the store. "Brrr, this North Carolina weather is absolutely treacherous."

Lauren smiled. "We are having an early winter, but today isn't too bad. Can I make you a cup of hot tea or cocoa to warm you up?"

"Oh, no, ma'am! I'm a Floridian, and cold weather just isn't my cup of tea," she replied. "No pun intended."

The other two women laughed.

"We're just here to do a bit of leaf peeping while our husbands play golf."

Golfing in the winter was a bit odd, but she knew there were die-hard golfers who played in all kinds of weather.

"It's beautiful this year," Lauren said, as a way of promoting the state she loved so much.

One of the women, who was clad in purple leggings

with a short black jacket, added, "You should see Florida in the winter. You have no clue what you're missing."

The third woman laughed in a smug way.

Three snobs, Lauren thought. *Just what I need.*

"I received my bachelor's and master's degrees from the University of Florida. I've spent many winters in your state. I just prefer a change of seasons." She paused, then just because she felt slightly miffed, she added, "We are offering a senior citizen's discount this weekend. I'm sure we have a decoration that you won't find in Florida." *There*, she thought, and inwardly grinned.

"I'm not so sure," said the woman in the purple leggings.

"Have a look around," Lauren said. This was exactly the type of customer she didn't need today. She was already frustrated, tired, and cranky. Not wanting to take it out on prospective customers, even if they were a bit snooty, she said, "If you see anything you're interested in, I'll be in the office." She motioned to the back of the store, where a sign on a door clearly stated OFFICE.

Leaving the three women to browse the aisles, she sat down in her chair and sighed. If this is what she had to deal with today, she had little hope of making a sale. Bored women with nothing better to do. She'd encountered many in her lifetime and knew that it was best not to get upset. Not that she was upset, but she was miffed, definitely. She was very protective of North Carolina. There was so much the state had to offer, and occasionally, she would get a bit defensive if the situation called for her to, and it had just then. At least she felt that it had. She wasn't going to sacrifice her pride just to make a sale to people who didn't appreciate what they were buying. Well, yes, she would if she absolutely *had* to, but not to that group of women.

It was not a good way to start her day. Taking a deep breath and forcing herself to focus on the here and now in a positive manner, she reminded herself of all she had to be grateful for. Her parents were still alive. She was healthy. She was sharing her childhood home with her mom and dad and was totally okay with it. While she wasn't a millionaire, she was in very good financial shape, which meant she had the means to keep the store up and running throughout the Christmas season. And that was all she needed for now.

A tapping at the door drew her away from her thoughts. She swiped her hands across the Santa sweatshirt, then opened her door. "Yes?" she asked the woman in the purple leggings. "Is there something you need help with?" She stepped out of the office into the store's main aisle.

"This," the woman said, holding up a small glass angel. "Do you truly expect me to pay this awful price?" She dangled the glass angel by its tag.

Lauren was so taken aback, it took a few seconds before she could reply. "Please," she said, taking the fragile ornament from the woman, "these are very delicate, and yes, I do expect you to pay what's shown on the tag. These are one-of-a-kind pieces. Made by well-known artisans across the state." She couldn't believe how crude these women were. "Perhaps you might find something more to your taste and pocketbook at a . . . flea market."

The look on the woman's face was worth the loss of a sale. "Well, I do believe you are one rude clerk." She turned around so quickly that Lauren felt an actual gust of frosty air.

Lauren prided herself on being, cool, calm, and collected. Most of the time. But this was not one of those times. She whirled around and walked toward the front door. When she yanked the door open, a gush of icy cold air surged throughout the store. She pointed at the women. "I'd like for you all to leave. Now."

Seeing the shock on their faces, she almost laughed, just managing not to.

The three objectionable females marched toward the exit like three blind mice.

Purple leggings said, "I am going to write a review of this . . . place on Yelp, and it's not going to be a good one."

The other two nodded their agreement.

Once they were out of the store, Lauren closed the door and locked it, then placed the CLOSED sign in the window.

Back in her office, Lauren took a deep breath. She could not believe how she'd reacted to their pettiness. What she needed was a break from all the stress the holiday season was generating.

Wait. The holidays were just getting started. She couldn't throw in the towel, no matter how much she currently felt like doing so. *This, too, shall pass.* She'd had a terrible Black Friday and then these catty ladies today. Lauren wouldn't let this get her down. She could not afford to. The least she could do was to give the entire month of December a chance.

Before she completely forgot, she dialed Jimmy's. His brother, Johnny, answered, "Jimmy's," in such a Southern twang, Lauren smiled.

"Hey, Johnny, it's Lauren over at Razzle Dazzle. I think I need a tow," she said, and went on to explain what had happened the night before. He promised her they'd pick the car up before noon.

That's progress, she thought. At least she had that problem temporarily taken care of.

Chapter 2

Sunday, December 1, 2019

Lauren was in a much better frame of mind. Her car had needed a new battery and a tune-up, nothing major. She'd made a few decent sales late on Saturday, enough to give her hope and put the crabby ladies out of her mind. If they came back into the store, which she sincerely doubted, she'd show them the exit again. While her father, his father, and his father prided themselves on excellent customer service, it was her personal belief that the customer was *not* always right.

She hadn't discussed the women with her parents last night, not wanting anything to upset her father that evening, as he seemed to be having a good day. Her mother had prepared a pot of vegetarian chili with homemade corn muffins. They'd had a relaxing meal, and when they'd lingered over tea and coffee, her mother had asked her about her sales at the store.

Not wanting to lie, she'd said, "They could have been a bit heftier, but it was so darned cold yesterday, there weren't a lot of shoppers willing to leave the comfort of their homes."

As she thought back on the night before, she knew she hadn't fooled her mother; but her mother, being the kind and graceful woman that she was, hadn't called attention to the conversation.

She had high hopes for Sunday. After a good night's rest, she'd adjusted her attitude, and there she was, back at Razzle Dazzle Décor. It was almost 7:00 A.M. Time to open the store.

As soon as she unlocked the door, several tourists entered. They seemed kind and interested in what the store had to offer. Ringing up sale after sale, she had a renewed sense of hope that Razzle Dazzle might just make it after all. When lunchtime approached, she did a mental tally of what they'd taken in and was pleased.

Most of the special-order decorations had been picked up by the customers who placed such orders each year, so she didn't really count these as new sales, but nonetheless, they were sales. And now every single sale mattered.

Lauren was refolding several tree skirts when the door opened, bringing another burst of cold air inside. She looked over her shoulder, and a smile came to her face. When she saw that it was none other than Brent Ludmore, out of uniform and carrying a brown bag from Ruby's, her heart lurched. And not in the way Brent probably intended. He wasn't going to give up easily, she'd give him that.

"Hey, Lauren, thought you could use a bit of lunch," he said, holding up the brown bag.

She was hungry, so she shot him a genuine smile. "Perfect timing, too. I was about to see what I could rustle up from the fridge."

Brent was a true hunk, in the traditional sense. Six-foot-two, a perfect two hundred pounds of solid muscle, dark brown eyes, and ink-black hair that he wore short, given his position as Fallen Springs' sheriff. Lauren wished she felt something other than brotherly friendship toward him, but sadly, she still remembered him as he'd been in preschool and elementary classes, then high school. They were tight. They were close. But what they weren't and never would be was a couple. Much as Brent tried, it just wasn't there for her. She truly cared for him, always would, but not in the way he wanted.

He came up behind her, and she caught a whiff of his aftershave. Woodsy, manly. She liked his scent, as it was very comforting. Something like a favorite blanket, something you could always rely on. She'd never voice those thoughts to Brent, but it was what she felt. Comfortable, reliable, no need to be anything but herself around him.

"Hey, I'm a mind reader," he said.

"We're a bit slow now. Let me lock the door and put up my 'out to lunch' sign. Hang on," Lauren said, walking to the door, locking it, then hanging her sign. While this wasn't going to entice new customers, most of those who shopped here frequently knew she'd be back in a flash. "Follow me," she directed, heading to the office.

In the office, she cleared her desk. Brent opened the bag, and delicious smells wafted throughout the room.

"Yum, whatever it is," Lauren said as she took paper plates and plasticware from the shelf that held her supplies.

"Today's special. Roast chicken, with potatoes, carrots, and those danged yeast rolls Ruby makes to entice people to kiss their diets good-bye." He winked at her. "She's trying to fatten up the entire town, and Louise encourages it. Threw in a couple extra rolls for you, she said to tell you."

She laughed. "Louise and Ruby always give me extra food. I'm small by genetics, and she just doesn't get it, but I do love those rolls."

Brent doled out the luscious food, and Lauren was truly grateful. "You're a prince for this," she said between bites.

"Didn't see you at church this morning. Saw your mom, and she told me you were open today," he said, letting his words hang in the aromatic air.

"No, I thought I'd give the Black Friday weekend my full attention. Sales haven't been what I'd like this year."

Brent stopped eating and took her hand. "You're going to be okay, right? I mean the store. This place is an institution in Fallen Springs."

She shook her head. "I hope so. Brick-and-mortar stores are becoming a thing of the past. I've asked Dad to consider going online, but you know how he's totally against change."

"That surprises me. Your dad's been a great influence on so many around town; even Ruby's has an online menu now. Grubhub deliveries, too. Why do you think he's so against it?" Brent asked.

"He tells me his father, and grandfather, et cetera, et

cetera, ran this place quite successfully without the help of some Internet that he can't even *see*, and there is no reason he's going to change his mind."

"Have you told him you all might need the extra sales to keep the doors open?" Brent asked.

"No, and I haven't told Mom either, but I suspect she knows since she sees the bank statements every month." She wasn't going to tell Brent that she was planning to subsidize the store if needed. That was way too personal.

"So, you're planning to open on Sundays then?"

"I thought just this weekend, I'd try, but frankly, as you can see, people aren't beating down the doors. I'm in a bit of a pickle, but I'm sure we'll make it through another season. We've got the unique decorations, and I just don't . . . well, I do know. Our clientele is local. Our products are made by Carolina's best artisans. Maybe I should come up with a brochure, something I could mail throughout the state. Place more ads in papers. I don't think Dad would object to that type of promotion. It's certainly an idea, but I don't know if it's too late to even get that going. It would take several days to get a brochure printed, and, of course, I have to have permission from my artists to do so." She shook her head. "Seems kind of hopeless when I say it out loud. You have any ideas?" Brent was smart and savvy, plus her dad adored him and had tried to bring them together since as far back as she could remember.

"You want me to talk to him? I'm free this evening. I could stop by."

If she asked him to do this, would he and her father take this as more than just a friend helping a friend? She'd decided to dip into her own funds, but a few ads placed in some of the state's local papers wouldn't hurt.

"I think Dad will be okay with newspaper ads. He's done it before when he had something unique. I don't think I have enough time to pull off a brochure, though."

"You're avoiding my question, Lauren," Brent said.

"Oh, well, sure, stop by. It can't hurt, plus Dad would be thrilled with some male company."

"What about you?" he asked, his tone suddenly serious, the voice he used when he was in his "are we ever going to get serious?" tone.

This was not the topic she cared to discuss at the moment, but she knew that if she put it off, his feelings would be hurt. *What will it take for him to realize that I just don't feel* that *way about him?* If there were someone she could set him up with, she would, but no one came to mind. She suddenly had an idea. "I always enjoy seeing you, Brent, you know that. We've been friends forever."

"And you don't want us to be anything more, right?" he asked, his tone hurt.

Crap, she thought. She hated when he put her in this position. "I can't lie to you, Brent, I care for you, just not in the way you want me to. It would be cruel of me to let you believe otherwise."

The hangdog look on his face broke her heart a little bit more, as it did each and every time the topic came up.

He sighed, stood, and took their empty plates to the garbage can, dumping them inside. She knew he was trying to regain his composure, laugh this off as nothing more than a guy trying, but it still saddened her. She wished she were able to fall madly in love with him. They would make a lot of people happy if she did. Unfortunately, she would not be one of them.

"Brent, we've been over this, and I know how you

want me to feel." She could feel tears welling up, and she didn't want to cry. Not that day. She had more important issues, but then she reminded herself that his friendship and his feelings were equally important. What to say? "We're friends now, and that's all I can give you."

Should she tell him that she'd actually perused a few online dating sites looking for a date? No, that would be too hurtful.

"And I'll accept that, Lauren. You know that, but I'm not getting any younger. I thought I'd have a couple of kids by now, you know? A wife, too," he added, a sad smile softening his features.

She wanted to tell him that if he'd focused his attention elsewhere, he might have achieved his goal already. He'd had girls crawling all over him in high school and pushed them away. She'd gone to college and was sure he'd done some dating, and who knew what more, but in Brent's mind, he wasn't going to accept the fact that she wasn't the one for him. He needed to get her out of his system and move on. She just wished Brent could adopt this attitude. Maybe she would call Madison, her best friend, tonight and see if there was someone she could fix Brent up with—of course, without his knowing she'd been behind the hookup. Another thing to add to her list.

In high school, Madison had always loved a good matchmaking challenge, and she did even now, after she'd married Scott Murphy ten years ago. They had been college sweethearts, and one only had to watch them together to know they were still madly in love.

Wanting to steer the conversation elsewhere, Lauren said, "I think life tosses us in so many directions, it's impossible to predict where we'll be tomorrow." She took a drink of her tea and stood. "Lunchtime is over, that much

I do know. It was so sweet of you to think of me," she added.

Brent nodded. "Well, you can't blame a guy for trying. So what about tonight, do you want me to stop by the house? I don't have any plans, unless there's a bank robbery or something, and we both know the chances of that happening here in Fallen Springs are slim to none." He smiled.

"Yes, I'll call Mom. Have dinner with us. I'm sure Dad gets tired of all the female chatter at the table. Seriously, I'd like for you to come over, too." She really liked his company, but as a friend. "We can play cards if you want," she added, knowing how much this would please her parents.

"Name the time, and I'll be there," he said.

"Sevenish?" She'd have to call her mother and make sure whatever she'd planned for dinner would be enough for Brent, too. He was a big guy and consumed loads of food. If not, she'd stop and grab pizzas on her way home.

"I'll see you then," he said, standing aside as she unlocked the door.

"Sounds good," she replied, forcing enthusiasm into her tone of voice.

When he left, Lauren breathed an actual sigh of relief. There was no way she would lie about her feelings for him. That would be dishonest and unfair to both of them. Brent deserved better, which reminded her she had a couple of phone calls to make.

First, she called her mother. "Hey, I know this is last-minute, but I invited Brent over for dinner and cards if you all are up to it. I wasn't sure if whatever you're making will be enough to feed him, too. You know what an appetite the guy has. I can grab a couple of pizzas if you want."

"Having Brent over is a wonderful idea! Your father is feeling good today, and I've made a pot roast with all the fixin's, so I'll get busy," her mother said, her voice filled with joy.

"I told him sevenish. Is that okay?"

"It's perfect."

"Thanks, Mom. I'm closing at five, so I'll be there to help out."

They said their good-byes, and before Lauren got busy and forgot, she dialed Madison's number.

"Hi, stranger," Madison's cheery voice said. Caller ID canceled out all surprise phone calls these days.

Lauren laughed. "Stranger?"

"I didn't see you at church this morning, and you haven't called me in nine days. The way I look at it, that makes you a stranger."

They both laughed.

"I'm sorry, I've let the store occupy all my time. It's that time of year once again, and you know how it is," Lauren said. "I promise to take you to lunch as soon as I can, but I called to ask a favor," Lauren explained. "Brent was in the store today. Brought us lunch from Ruby's."

She gave Madison a couple of seconds to absorb her words.

"And that means what?" Madison asked.

"This sounds so silly at my age, but I was wondering if you knew of anyone who's available for, you know, a date. For Brent."

Madison laughed out loud. "Someone other than you, you mean?"

Lauren couldn't help but laugh. "Exactly. The guy can't

get it through his thick skull that I'm not interested in him, at least not in the way he wants. From what I know, he doesn't even try to date anyone."

"He doesn't."

"What did he do when I was away in college and living in Florida afterward?"

"Oh, he did some casual dating. But nothing serious that I know of."

"So, do you have any ideas? Some kind of hookup? Anyone? I'm desperate, Madison. I just can't break his heart. Every time the topic of a relationship between us comes up, and I tell him I only feel friendship toward him, he gets all sad. And then I feel sorry for him. I don't want to hurt him. I wish I felt the way he wants me to; heck, my parents would be thrilled if I married the guy and had a couple of his kids, but it's just not there."

"Well, there is Barb from the library. I'm not sure if she's ever even had a date," Madison said. "She'd probably pee herself if Brent asked her out."

Again, Lauren giggled. "Madison, that's mean, and you know it."

"Why is that mean? She's single, local, and works at the library. She's super smart, too," Madison added.

"I'm serious, here. I don't really think that Barb is Brent's type, that's all."

"Or you just don't think she's all that attractive?" Madison asked.

Lauren blew a loud breath into the phone. "She's just not his type. I know what you want me to say, and I am not going there," Lauren added.

"Then I will. She's two hundred pounds overweight, has an overbite that would rival a horse's, and it's common knowledge that she's smelly."

More laughter from both of them. "Maybe you should take her under your wing. Give her a few lessons in all things beauty. I'm sure she'd be open to it coming from you." Madison was a total knockout. Tall and thin, straight black hair with the lightest blue eyes ever, she'd done some part-time modeling in high school and college. If anyone knew a few beauty tricks, it was Madison.

"If I thought she were the slightest bit interested, I would. We both know all she thinks about are books and more books."

"That's true, but seriously, I wish he'd find someone. He's a great guy, beyond good-looking, built like an oak tree. There are so many women who would fall over in their slinky heels if a man like him showed them any attention."

"You're just not one of them, right? And who in Fallen Springs, especially this time of year, wears slinky heels?" Madison asked.

"Madison, that's why I called *you*. You're a known matchmaker, so I thought for sure you'd at least have an idea of someone you could fix Brent up with."

"I *am* quite the matchmaker, but honestly, I can't think of anyone single, other than Barb. I'll think on it, though. I promise. I'll ask Scott if he knows anyone."

Her husband was an IT guy for one of the largest gaming companies in the world. He did most of his work from home via the Internet. "How's that supposed to work? He rarely leaves the house, and when he does, it's to go to another country." Lauren stated what Madison already knew.

"Yes, I know, but a few of his gaming buddies come into town now and then. I'll ask if they have any sisters or ex-wives," Madison said.

She was serious, Lauren knew. "All right then, but try and steer clear of ex-wives. You know Brent is . . . well, I don't think he's the type for seconds, if you know what I mean."

"Lauren Elise Montgomery! That's a terrible thing to say. So, I'm to steer clear of widows, too?" Madison asked.

"Oh, stop, you know what I meant. Brent's just so . . . clean-cut, and . . . wholesome."

"I'll set my radar to single, innocent, and *virginal* women in their late twenties to early thirties with no ties ever and see what I can come up with."

"Come on, you know what I mean. I just think he deserves someone who has the same values as he does," Lauren explained. "No one is perfect; I'm not that naïve."

"True, but at our age, I doubt if there's someone out there for either of you with a superstellar background," Madison said. "I'll poke around and see, but no promises."

"Thanks, Maddy. I have a lot of faith in you. Now, I have to get busy. I've invited Brent over for dinner and cards tonight. I told Mom I'd help her in the kitchen."

"Wait, wait, *wait!* You just asked me to fix Brent up with a date, and now you've invited him over for dinner?"

"I know, but I felt sorry for him. As I said, we'd just been through our usual song and dance, and I thought it might cheer Dad up. Brent too. He needs a bit of male company, and you know how Dad likes playing cards with Brent. It's nothing more than that, I can assure you," Lauren said.

"So you say," Madison teased.

"Come on; you, of all people, know me. I adore Brent,

just not in a romantic sort of way. We're nothing more than friends, and never will be anything but friends. How many times am I going to have to say that?"

"I know, but I do love teasing you," Madison replied. "Okay, I need to go. I'll catch up with you if I locate any worthy, unattached females. And don't forget you promised me lunch."

They said their good-byes and promised to stay in touch.

Lauren busied herself in the store, hoping, praying for an after-lunch rush of new customers. She shined, polished, and dusted items that were already sparkling, but she had to stay busy. Standing around would drive her crazy.

As she was about to return to her office to make a cup of tea, a group of teenage girls entered the store. They giggled, and Lauren recognized them as locals.

"Hey, there. If there's anything I can help you with, let me know."

"I'm looking for something for my mom. She's in the hospital, and I thought she could use some cheering up," said one of the girls, who was wearing a heavy purple sweater over a thin jacket.

"Lee, Charlotte's mom, adores your store," said another.

"Thanks. Would I know your mom?" Lauren asked.

"Lee Hessinger," Charlotte said.

"Yes, of course, I know her. I'm so sorry she's in the hospital. She adores just about everything we have. Want me to help you choose something?" Lauren asked. She'd gone to high school with Lee, who had married right after graduation. Lauren knew that Lee had a daughter but didn't realize she was in high school. Time flies, she thought.

She could have had a child in high school had she found the right guy. Well, maybe not high school, but elementary school at least.

"Thanks, I'll look first, and if I don't see anything, you can help me out, if that's okay?" Charlotte said.

Lauren got the feeling Charlotte wanted to pick the gift out herself and understood completely. "Of course, it's okay. I'm here if you need help." She let the girls wander up and down the aisles while she continued to make sure everything was in its place.

"Excuse me," one of the girls said, and motioned with her head to Lauren to step into an aisle away from the other two girls.

"I'm Lacey, Char's friend. She doesn't have a lot of money, and I have some saved, so if she doesn't have enough to pay for whatever she buys, would it be okay if I secretly paid the difference? If there is one, I mean. Her mom is really sick and all."

Tears welled up in Lauren's eyes. "Of course, but let's do this. Whatever Charlotte chooses, I'd like for her to allow me to give it to her. Free of charge. As a get-well gift. Since her mother is a good customer, and in the hospital. Do you think that would be okay with Charlotte? And just so you know, I think Charlotte's very lucky to have such a good friend." This was so much like her and Madison at that age that, again, she had to fight back the tears.

"You'd really do that?"

"I really would," Lauren said with a smile so big her cheeks hurt.

This is what Christmas is all about, she thought. *Giving, sharing, and caring for those in need.*

But, she reminded herself, *I have to keep the store up*

and running, no matter what else I have to do. Still, a little generosity isn't going to make or break the place, and it feels right.

For the next half hour, the girls perused practically every item in the store. When Charlotte chose a handmade scarf with a matching afghan, it was all she could do to keep from crying. Her mother had knitted that last season with the finest wool, and Lauren had wanted to keep it for herself but knew it would find a good home in the store this year. Silver-and-gold threads sparkled in the late-afternoon sunlight as the girls brought the items to the register. Lauren knew there was no price tag on these two items. She'd held back in hopes that if they didn't sell, she'd add some cash to the till, and they would be hers. Now, however, she was thrilled they were going to a very special home.

"Mom is so cold all the time, I think this is perfect," Charlotte said as she placed the items on the counter. "They feel really nice."

"I think your mom will love these, too. Would you like for me to wrap them, or would you prefer to do that yourself?" Lauren asked, not wanting to assume too much.

"If you could wrap them in pretty paper, I'll pay extra. Mom loves unwrapping, and, well, we don't really have any fancy paper at home."

"This is what we have," Lauren said, motioning for the girls to follow her to the wrapping area in a small alcove off the office. She'd set up the special wrapping area when she'd returned to Fallen Springs, and was thinking of hiring someone to do the wrapping when they were busy. So far, that someone had turned out to be her, and she found that she actually enjoyed the task.

"Wow, this is awesome," said the one girl whose name

she didn't yet know. "I'm Kiley," she added, apparently reading Lauren's mind.

"Nice to meet you, Kiley. I'm Lauren. Sorry for not introducing myself before."

"Your parents own the store, right?" Charlotte asked.

"They do, and I work here." She was really getting a kick out of this trio.

"Before I pick out the wrapping paper, I better make sure I have enough money to pay for this," Charlotte said. "I didn't see a price tag."

Lacey caught Lauren's eye.

"I'd like to give this to you to give to your mother as a Christmas gift. If you don't mind. My mother made that last year, and I fell in love with it, but she insisted I bring it to the store to sell. Now I think it's found the perfect home, if you'll accept my offer," Lauren said, again, with tears in her eyes, though this time she didn't bother trying to hold them back.

"Wow," Kiley said.

Silvery tears shimmered down Charlotte's face. "I don't know what to say."

Lacey spoke for her friend. "Say 'yes' and 'thank you very much.'"

They all laughed, and Lauren couldn't believe how good she felt, how wonderful it was to give rather than receive. She knew this was not the way to run a business, but at the moment, it was how she chose to operate. "Then let's get these wrapped so you can get them to your mom as soon as possible. What paper would you like?" Lauren asked.

"The gold, the one with the shimmery stuff, if that's okay. And maybe a matching ribbon?"

"Absolutely, and a bow, too?" Lauren asked as she

began the task of carefully boxing the scarf and afghan. She added silver tissue paper, then sealed it with the store's logo seal, a sparkly silver snowflake. She wrapped the heavy, gold, shimmery paper around the box, careful to make sure each corner was precisely folded, a perfect crease. When she finished, she added gold ribbon and a glittery-golden bow. She tucked a blank name tag beneath the ribbon. "Give this to your mom, Charlotte, and tell her I said 'Merry Christmas.' "

"You're the best, Lauren. I know Mom will be so happy with this gift, and warm, too. Is it okay if I tell her you gave this to me?"

Lauren grinned. "I think that can be your secret. You decide what you want to tell Lee. My lips are sealed unless I hear otherwise."

When the girls finally left, Lauren saw it was after five. She hadn't had any more customers, and just then, she was perfectly fine with that. Undecided if she would tell her mother what she'd done with the afghan and scarf she'd knitted, she figured that if the topic came up, she would simply tell her the truth. That had always been her way with her parents and friends—at least, it used to be.

She knew she was deceiving them, in a sense, at least as far as the store's sales went this Black Friday weekend, but she'd call her bank first thing in the morning and have some funds transferred to the store's checking account. When her mother questioned her about it—as she knew she would, because she examined the monthly bank statements—she'd tell her it was her way of . . . investing in the family business. That had the virtue of being the truth, too.

She rushed around the store, making sure the gas fireplace was turned off, then went to the office and turned the rest of the lights off with the remote she kept on her desk. Only the lights in the front window remained on. She turned the heat down several degrees, knowing she'd be freezing when she returned tomorrow morning, but she'd dress warm.

Jimmy's had also tuned up her car, and she was grateful when she turned the key and the engine came to life. "Nothing like a purring engine," she said, her breath visible in the freezing temperature. She checked the digital reading on her car's panel. Twenty-eight degrees. She felt every bit of it, too, as she waited for the engine to warm up so she could turn the heater on. Once she flipped the switch on to HIGH HEAT, she delighted in the warmth as she directed the vents toward her hands. She'd left the house this morning without gloves. Knowing the temperature was predicted to be well below freezing, she'd try to remember to stuff her gloves in her coat pocket before she left the house in the morning. Along with a note to herself to remember to place a call to Roger Riedel to set up a bank transfer to Razzle Dazzle's business account.

She drove down the long drive leading up to the house. Looking at her watch, she saw that it was almost 6:00. Unsure how the time had gotten away from her, she hurried inside and was greeted by the sumptuous smell of her mother's pot roast.

"I'm home," she called out as she headed upstairs to change. When she'd moved back into her childhood home three years before, she'd returned to her childhood room, and with her mother's help, they'd redecorated it in cool grays and whites, a décor that a thirty-five-year-old woman was comfortable with. While she appreciated her mother's keeping her room as it had been, she couldn't imagine living in her former girlish room after living on her own since she had left for college. They'd packed the memories away, and Lauren had thought at the time that maybe someday she'd share the mementoes with her own daughter. But at the rate she was going, she'd be too old to remember them herself. Smiling at her own silly thoughts, she undressed and took a hot shower. As the water slid down her back, easing the stiffness in her muscles, she felt the tension of the day wash away. She hadn't washed her hair, but she did re-braid it in a long French braid. She didn't bother with makeup but added a touch of mascara to her blond lashes.

She put on a pair of soft, faded jeans with a worn Florida Gators sweatshirt and a pair of thick socks. She hadn't realized how tired she was and, for a moment, wished she hadn't invited Brent to dinner. But reminding herself how this would make her father's evening, all traces of "poor me" were wiped away with the thought. Dad spent most of his days in the house, and given his limited mobility, having a visitor was a big deal to him.

Downstairs, Lauren joined her mother in the kitchen. "Yum, I'm starved," she said as she peered through the oven's glass door.

"I am too," said her father as he made his way to the table in the center of the large farmhouse kitchen.

"Hey, Dad, how are you feeling?" Lauren asked as she gathered plates and flatware for the table.

"I'm pretty good today, despite this chilly spell we're having." He sat down, and Lauren knew he was in pain from the look on his face.

Once a towering man at six feet, he'd appeared to have lost a bit of height a few months after he'd been diagnosed. His features were still that of a handsome, middle-aged man. Despite his illness, he remained hopeful, and never, at least that she knew of, allowed himself to go into a dark, depressive place. His dark-blond hair still smelled of Prell shampoo, and she knew he still used Mennen After Shave. Smiling to herself, as she thought of these features of her father, her dread of the evening ahead vanished.

"What are we drinking tonight?" Lauren asked her father.

"I'm sticking to the hard stuff," he said, and pointed to the pitcher of water her mother was bringing to the table.

"Don't say I can't read your mind," her mom told him, then winked at Lauren.

"I know better than to get involved in this conversation," Lauren said, filling a glass with ice and placing it on the table in front of her father.

They went through a similar routine almost nightly, and Lauren knew this was their way of trying to keep their lives as normal as possible under the circumstances. It broke her heart, yet she was amazed by the strength of character they exhibited by refusing to wallow in self-pity. Her parents were good people. Hardworking and tough. She wished she could just convince her father to step into the future. Another time, she would touch on the subject, but not now. She would stick to her father's method, place as many ads in newspapers as she could, and hope that they would reach a few new customers before the season was over.

"Lauren, can you get that?"

"What?" Lauren asked, then she heard the doorbell. "Oh, sure." She'd allowed her mind to drift into the what-ifs again and hadn't even heard the doorbell.

She took a deep breath, plastered a smile on her face, and opened the door. "You're right on time," she said, glancing at the clock in the foyer.

"Sevenish is seven, right?" Brent asked.

She laughed. "If I said no, then what? You're late? Too early?"

"Regardless, I'm here, and I brought this." He held up a bottle of wine. "Red."

"Perfect, it's beef night," she said, and took the bottle from him. "We're eating in the kitchen. Family-style," she said. They always had their meals in the kitchen, except on holidays. Then she and her mother would decorate the formal dining room, and she really enjoyed those occasions. It was akin to playing dress-up, only rather than clothing, they used the many cherished decorations that had been handed down from one generation to the next, plus each year they chose a few pieces from the local artisans and added them to their collection. Lauren enjoyed the prep, and the big finale, the meals that she'd had a hand in preparing.

"Ilene, Al," Brent said as he entered the kitchen. "Thanks for the invite. It smells awesome."

Lauren spoke up. "It does. Here, I'll chill this," she said, placing the bottle of wine in the bottom section of the new high-tech refrigerator that would cool the wine to a perfect temperature within minutes. She could remember what it had taken to convince her parents that if they had to get a new refrigerator when the old one gave up the ghost, it should be something with the convenient features their old one had lacked. She sometimes thought that, given their own way, they would have settled for a nineteenth-century icebox.

"I'm glad you came, Brent," her dad said. "These two, well, they are about to step on my last nerve with all the attention I get." Her father laughed. "Nice to have another man in the picture." Her dad winked at her. He seemed to forget she wasn't sixteen anymore.

Brent took four wineglasses from the cupboard, just one more detail that made him feel like family. A brother. "You all okay with a sip of wine?" he asked as he placed a goblet in front of each place setting.

Lauren rolled her eyes. "We're all of legal age, Sheriff," she replied.

"Of course you are," he said. "It wouldn't help my reputation if word got out that I was serving minors."

Lauren thought the comment a bit off and decided to go with it. "Is there much underage drinking these days? Here, in the paradise of Fallen Springs," she added.

After her mother filled bowls with mashed potatoes and green beans, Lauren placed them on the table.

"It's everywhere, unfortunately, Fallen Springs included. Sadly, it's not always booze that attracts kids these days. Now we've got meth, opioids, pot, you name it. Alcohol is too easy to come by now."

"Here? In Fallen Springs?" her father asked. "Surely not. We've always held our youth to the highest standards."

Lauren couldn't believe how old-fashioned he was! He wasn't even that old himself. His ideas were so antiquated that she wanted to shake some sense into him. *Not now. Let Brent tell him what the real world is like, and here in Fallen Springs, too. He would be more likely to listen if it came from Brent.*

"Sadly, it's true. We've got a problem, for sure. Not as bad as in the larger cities, such as Charlotte or Raleigh, but it's still here. It's not always made public, but I've arrested more than my share of addicts who were barely old enough to drive."

Lauren took the bottle of wine from the refrigerator and the corkscrew from the drawer next to the sink. She carefully inserted the corkscrew, then slowly released the cork. She probably should have allowed Brent to do the honors since he had brought the wine, but she was too enthralled as she listened to him fill her father in on the life of teenagers in the twenty-first century. Maybe this is just what he needed. A dose of reality. Show him how the world was changing. Sadly, it wasn't the most upbeat topic, but she was glad. He needed to hear that Fallen Springs wasn't immune to the ways of the world.

"Then why aren't we reading about this in the paper?" In print, the *Daily Banner* was only a weekly publication now, yet they had a daily version online, which her father had no knowledge of since he didn't have a computer or access to the Internet.

"The arrests are usually reported in the paper if they're of legal age, but since many of these kids are still minors, we can't put their names in the paper," Brent explained.

Lauren poured wine into their glasses, curious to hear her father's response.

"I'm sure it's not that bad. We're a relatively small town. It's not like New York City or Los Angeles." Her father's refusal even to acknowledge the *sheriff's* facts was almost borderline crazy. She looked at Brent and raised her eyebrows.

"I have to disagree, Al. We're not the small-town Fallen Springs of your generation, and I don't mean to insult you in any way, but it's simply a fact. We've had to add four new officers to our narcotics squad, and I'm hoping next year's budget allows us to hire more. It's an epidemic."

"Oh, it can't be that bad, Brent," her mother added. "I never saw any drug use when I taught school."

"You taught second grade, Mother," Lauren reminded her. "And you've been retired for a few years, remember? I've heard Madison talk about the drug use in high school. She's been teaching in the system a while, so I know she's aware of what goes on."

Lauren hated this topic for Sunday-night dinner, but it was all true. Her parents couldn't continue to live in their Mayberry-type bubble.

"I still find it hard to believe," her father said, then took a sip of wine. "This is excellent, Brent. You do have good taste in wines."

That was her father's way of saying, enough. He was going to change the topic of conversation. End of story.

"Thanks. A friend recommended this. It's from the winery at the Biltmore." He swirled the dark liquid in his glass, then took a sip. "Good stuff. In moderation."

Lauren couldn't help but wonder if the friend was female. She wanted to ask but decided she'd keep her thoughts to herself. She took a small sip. It was okay as far as wines went; she wasn't much of a drinker, so they all tasted pretty much the same to her.

"Remember the time we took a tour of the winery at Biltmore?" Brent asked her.

She couldn't help but laugh. "I do. I think we thought we'd be allowed to drink wine all day. Being underage hadn't even been a consideration," she said, and recalled the weekend in her senior year of high school, when she and Brent, along with Madison and some guy she'd been dating at the time, decided to take the wine tour at the estate and see if they could get drunk for free. They hadn't even considered that they would be asked for identification.

"Why am I just now hearing about this?" her father asked, a grin on his face.

Her mother placed the platter of sliced pot roast in the center of the table. "Let's say grace before this gets cold."

Saved, Lauren thought, and she bowed her head and closed her eyes while her father said the blessing. It was an unwritten rule that he always said grace, and if anyone at the table chose to add something after, he would give them the opportunity. Lauren waited for her mother or Brent to speak, and when they didn't, she raised her head, and saw Brent staring at her. His gaze said all that he felt. She quickly focused her attention on the food. "Pass those potatoes, I'm starving," she said.

For the next half hour, as they ate, their conversation centered around the food and her mother's skill in the kitchen.

"I've made a cobbler for dessert. Apple."

"My favorite," Brent said.

Lauren knew that, her mother knew that, and so did her father. What was she trying to do? Keep him here all night? Dessert and coffee at the Montgomery house could last until midnight.

"I'll pass, Mom, but save me a piece for tomorrow. I'm so full now, I'm about to bust."

"Of course I will. Now"—her mother stood and began gathering the empty plates—"Lauren and I will get this mess cleaned up. Al, get the cards ready."

Again, Lauren wished she hadn't added the card invite but decided that she would play a couple of hands, then excuse herself.

Once they'd cleared the table and put the dishes in the

dishwasher, she brewed a pot of decaf and filled their cups, while her mother served dessert.

For the next hour, they played crazy eights, war, then blackjack. She yawned and decided it was time to call it a night.

"I hate to break up the party, but I'm wiped out." She stood and gathered the dessert plates and added them to the dishwasher. "I'm calling it a night."

Brent stood, too. "I've got a long day tomorrow myself. Ilene, Al, the food was terrific as usual, the company even better." His eyes met Lauren's as he said this. "And I hope we'll do this again, soon."

"You know you don't need an invitation," her mother reminded him. "We usually have dinner between six and seven."

"I'll remember that," he said. He shook hands with her dad, gave her mom a kiss on the cheek, then looked at Lauren. "You want to walk me to the door?"

No, she thought, but it wasn't as if she had much of a choice. She didn't want to make a big deal out of anything Brent asked.

"Sure," she said, and led him to the foyer. He stood at the door, hands in his pockets, a faraway look on his face.

"Is something wrong?" she asked, hoping he wouldn't try to continue the conversation they'd had at the store earlier.

"Not really. I'm just worried about your dad. He's stuck in a time warp, and I . . . well, it's not a good thing."

She breathed a sigh of relief. "I know. He's so stuck in the past that it's starting to worry me, more than I let on."

"Do you think this has anything to do with his illness?" Brent asked.

She gave a wan smile. "No, and if that were the reason,

I think I'd be better equipped to deal with this fantasy world he lives in. You know how old-fashioned he is."

"He is that, for sure. Have you discussed this with anyone, besides your mom?"

Was this Brent's way of saying her father needed to speak with a professional? She didn't totally disagree with that assumption, but she felt guilty for even having such thoughts.

"Just you and Madison."

"He's in denial, and it concerns me."

"What are you trying to say?"

"I'm not sure, just that he worries me, his lack of belief in what's going on in the real world. Has he ever been checked for Alzheimer's? Damn, I hate saying that word, but it's crossed my mind more than once."

Lauren truly hadn't even given that a thought, but now that Brent had raised the possibility, she knew she would have to convince her mother to consider asking their rheumatologist about this, and maybe for a referral to a neurologist.

"I'll mention it to Mom. He doesn't seem abnormal—I mean, his memory is excellent," she said, but he did live in the past, and she knew that was a characteristic of Alzheimer's disease.

"Good. I've wanted to tell you this for a while, but the timing was always bad. I hope you're not ticked at me for bringing this up."

"Actually, I'm glad you did. I'll talk to Mother, see what her thoughts are. She spends more time with him and would know, I assume, if Dad wasn't . . . right," she said.

"Okay, I'll check in with you later in the week," he said, and gave her a peck on the cheek.

"Thanks, Brent," Lauren said, and closed the door the second he stepped out. The frigid air had gone straight through her, and she couldn't wait to snuggle beneath the down comforter in her room.

But before calling it a night, she returned to the kitchen, where her parents had started a new game of crazy eights.

Wouldn't her father's ability to play a simple game of cards be hampered if he had Alzheimer's? She wasn't sure. Tomorrow, she'd go on the Internet and look up the symptoms before bringing up the subject with her mother. She needed to check her e-mail tomorrow anyway.

"I'm calling it a night, folks. I'm beat," Lauren said, and gave her father a hug and kissed her mother's rosy-red cheek. "Dinner was excellent as usual, Mom," she said. "I'll make dinner tomorrow night, give you the night off, if that's okay."

"Yes, of course, it's fine, Lauren. Anytime you want, this old kitchen is all yours," her mother said.

"Then I'll plan on it."

As she made her way upstairs, thoughts of tomorrow's dinner plans were replaced by concern about her father. Was it possible he had some physical or even mental disorder that forced him to live in the past? Unsure, she knew she'd have to do whatever it took to find out.

Chapter 3

Monday, December 2, 2019

As soon as Lauren entered the store, she bumped the thermostat up to seventy degrees. It was the coldest day of the season, according to the local weather report. Twenty-one degrees. She used the remote to turn on the lights and started the sound system so she would have Christmas music playing in the background. She never turned the music on until the first day of December. To her way of thinking, December 1 was the official beginning of the Christmas season. A personal quirk of hers.

She filled the kettle with water and turned on the gas fireplace. With any luck, it would warm up the store in no time. The building was old and rickety, and took a while to get warm when the temperature went below freezing.

She made herself a cup of tea, then carried it with her as she walked up and down the aisles, checking to make sure everything was just so before she unlocked the door. She'd thought about opening at 7:00 again but decided to stick to their usual hours of 9:00 to 5:00 since the biggest shopping weekend of the season was over and opening early hadn't made all that much difference.

Convinced that there wasn't much left to do other than unlock the door, she did so and went back to her office. The bell she had hung over the door would alert her to customers, so she felt free to get down to work.

First, she called Roger Riedel and explained what she wanted him to do.

"Lauren, this isn't a sound investment. I would advise against it," he said, when she explained why she wanted funds transferred to Razzle Dazzle's business account.

"Probably not, but it is my money," she countered. "And the store is mine in every sense of the word. My parents are retired, and I know for a fact that the store will go to me when . . . when they're no longer here." She didn't like saying the words aloud, but it was a reality, and unlike her father, Lauren didn't see the world through rose-colored glasses.

"Of course, but remember I'm advising against this. Take out a small business loan instead, Lauren; your credit is excellent."

"No, I won't do that." It was against her rules. Period. She was not going into debt, nor would she put the store in debt. She'd close the place first. Knowing she sounded as stubborn as her father, she didn't care. Even though her dad lived in the past, she agreed with him when he'd talked about being debt-free.

"Then I'll make the arrangements as soon as we're through," Roger said.

"Good. And thank you, Roger. I know you don't agree

with me on this, but it's something I have to do, with or without your approval."

She ended the call, took her laptop out of her bag, and logged onto the Internet. She really needed to install Wi-Fi at the store. Her father wouldn't know if she did, and it was a bit embarrassing when she had to use the pharmacy's account.

She typed the words SYMPTOMS OF ALZHEIMER'S DISEASE into the search engine. Hundreds of links came up. She scrolled through several before finding an article from the National Institutes of Health. The article listed several symptoms. Mental decline, difficulty thinking and understanding, confusion in the early-evening hours. *That's odd*, she thought. She read on. The inability to create new memories, unable to do simple math. Aggression, agitation, meaningless repetition of words, inability to recognize common things. Anger, depression, and hallucination, loss of appetite. The list was lengthy, yet Lauren could not match a single symptom to her father's refusal to believe how the world was changing. Just as she'd always thought—he was just stubborn, bullheaded, and insistent upon doing what he wanted in his own way.

Relieved, but still concerned that his behavior could have dire consequences where Razzle Dazzle's future was concerned, she knew her decision to add to the store's bank account was the correct one. Lauren would talk with her parents when the time was right. Her plan was to get through the month of December and reassess their finances after January 1.

She checked her e-mail and saw one from Angela Winters, her literary agent. She opened the e-mail and read through it, then read it a second time, and even a third time.

"I'll be danged," she said out loud. Before she replied, she read through the entire e-mail once again, hardly believing her eyes.

Angela had asked her to call as soon as she'd read her message. Without another thought, Lauren dialed her agent in New York, knowing she'd be in her office.

"I take it you read my e-mail," Angela said when she took her call.

"Yes. I read it four times just to make sure I was reading it correctly."

"And?" Angela said, never one to waste time on words.

"I'd like details," Lauren said.

"I don't need to tell you who John Gerard Giampalo is," Angela stated.

"Not if it's *the* John Gerard Giampalo of Global goods.com, the largest online retail operation in the world, no," Lauren said. "This is the person you're referring to, right?" she asked, just to make sure she wasn't dreaming.

"The one and only," Angela said. "He contacted me personally and asked if you were available. Said he knew how successful your biographies were."

"Okay," Lauren said. She knew she'd have to pull the details from Angela because this was a big deal, and Angela loved it when she had super-good news to tell her.

"There are terms, as you know, especially when it's someone of his caliber."

All of her biographies had terms, and she knew that Globalgoods.com's would be as strict as they could be, given who John Gerard Giampalo was in the business world. He was probably the richest man in the United States of America, if not the richest person in the world.

"And what would those terms be?" she asked, no longer calm enough to play Angela's guessing game.

"First, and foremost, he wants you to come to Seattle and meet. He wants an upbeat, positive story, and here is the kicker—he wants the first draft in six weeks."

Six weeks?

"That's not a lot of time, given the man's life." Lauren said. "He's . . . a phenomenon in the business world. Is six weeks enough time to even begin researching his accomplishments?"

"He believes it is. Remember, we are dealing with a man who rarely sleeps, a man who is a genius, and a man who most likely expects the rest of the world to be on his intellectual wavelength."

Lauren didn't know what to say.

"So, you'll do this, right?" Angela probed. "I've compiled a lengthy list of facts about him in a pdf that I'll send you as soon as you decide."

"As soon as I decide? Do you actually think I'd turn this down? I haven't written in three years! I'd be a fool to walk away from this," she announced.

"Lauren, you haven't even asked about the financial benefit. Do you want to know?"

Her heart rate increased. "Of course, I want to know. I just . . . well, I'm still in a bit of shock that he wants me to do this. Why me? Surely, there are others he is considering."

"No, Lauren, you are the only one he's interested in. He said if you didn't come on board, then he'd just forget about it entirely. And, Lauren, this is a biggie. The biggest deal of my career," Angela said.

She was almost afraid to hear the figure. "Go on, tell me what the offer is."

"Three-point-five million," Angela said, enunciating each word slowly.

Lauren could not believe her ears. She was so flabbergasted that she didn't know what to say, so she said nothing.

"Lauren?" Angela asked. "Are you still with me?"

"Wow, that is a lot of money. I don't know if . . . I'm not sure that anything I write is worth that much money."

"Of course, it is. He wouldn't have made the offer if you hadn't already proved that it is. You have quite the reputation, you know."

No, she didn't know. Yes, she'd written four very successful biographies and made a lot of money, but this? Three-point-five million dollars for one book?

"Send me the rest of the details. I have so many things to consider before I decide to accept this offer."

"What! Tell me you're kidding? There is nothing to consider; this is the opportunity of a lifetime! You have to do this." Angela raised her voice several octaves and was practically shouting into the phone.

"No, I don't have to do anything. What I have to do, and what I am going to do, is look at the terms very closely. As you said, this is the biggest opportunity I've had as far as my writing goes. I want to make sure I have what it takes to complete the assignment."

"You do, Lauren. He wouldn't have chosen you if he didn't think you were qualified. You have to do this."

"Send me the pdf, let me look it over, and I'll get back to you. As soon as possible, I promise."

"All right, but remember, you'll have six weeks to come up with the first draft. And that six weeks starts today; he made it clear that as soon as I presented his offer to you, the clock was ticking."

"You can't be serious? That's beyond . . . well, it's crazy."

"I agree, but it's six weeks. You've had tough deadlines before. You've always managed to meet them. This is important, Lauren. For me, and the agency."

"I get it, but I still want to . . . know what I'm getting myself into. I'm running the store, as you know, and it's the start of the Christmas season. I don't want to make a commitment that I won't be able to keep, no matter how much they're offering."

"Oh, Lauren, you know as well as I do that you can crank out a first draft in a few weeks. And you can still take care of your family's business."

"You're giving me way too much credit," Lauren insisted.

"No, I'm not. If I didn't think you were capable of doing this, I wouldn't have accepted the deal on your behalf."

Chapter 4

"What?! Are you telling me you've already agreed to this proposal, without my even having read the contract?"

Lauren had been with the Winters Agency since the beginning of her career. Angela was always up-front with her, totally honest. There had to be another reason for Angela to agree to a deal without her approval.

Lauren heard Angela's intake of breath. "Pretty much."

"So, you want to tell me why? I think I'm entitled to an explanation." She was ticked; no, beyond ticked. She was pissed off. This was a huge deal any way you looked at it, and Lauren wouldn't compromise her career for the sake of money. She had to know going in that she'd be able to complete the work and that it would be her best work. She did have a few scruples.

"Look, Lauren, the agency hasn't had a decent deal

since your last book. We need this contract in order to keep our doors open."

Nothing like being under pressure, and on the spot, too. Unsure what to say, she said nothing.

"Lauren, are you with me or not?" Angela asked. "You know as well as I do that you're capable of writing this biography, more so than anyone else. You know that I believe you can. I believe in you."

Why did she suddenly feel like the weight of the world was on her shoulders? First, it was Razzle Dazzle's finances, and now her agent's? Could she really do this *and* keep the store open? She'd just transferred enough money to get the store through December, and most likely January and February. She'd had an idea in the back of her mind, a way to save the store, but now she wasn't sure she could do that and write the biography of the CEO and founder of the biggest online retailer in the country and do either justice. It was true that when she hadn't believed in herself, in her capabilities, Angela had. But it was wrong of Angela to make this commitment without her approval.

"Do you want to call me back after you've read the files I'm sending now?"

"Why didn't you ask me first? That's what I want to know." She'd trusted Angela with her career. They were good together. At least she'd thought so—until now. She felt betrayed and wronged, yet she would be a fool to pass up this opportunity, and not just because of the money. Anyone in their right mind would jump on this.

"I thought this would be the highlight of your career. Remember when you asked me a few months back to put a few feelers out there? You wanted to get back into writing?"

Yes, she had asked Angela to do that, and apparently she had. "Yes, I remember, but we've always been up-front with one another. I guess I'm feeling a bit blind-sided."

"I'm sorry. As I said, I'm in trouble. I'll send you the PDF, you can read through it, and maybe you'll call me back."

Lauren heard the desperation in Angela's voice.

"Send it, and I'll get back to you ASAP," was all she could say. She knew this was the opportunity of a lifetime and that she would be a fool to pass it up, but she still liked making the final decisions as far as her writing career was concerned.

Lauren had barely clicked the END button on her cell phone when the e-mail alert dinged, letting her know that Angela's e-mail had arrived.

She downloaded the file and began to read through John Gerard Giampalo's list of accomplishments. It was a very long list, too.

He was seventy-two years old, had one son, and his wife had passed away when the son was just five years old. He'd started his career working in finance. When the World Wide Web started growing at what seemed like the speed of light, he knew it was the time to invest in the early stages of the online phenomenon. While he'd studied economics, he had also been extremely drawn to the literary world. Hence, the beginning of Globalgoods.com. He began selling books online and followed this with music and videos. Having a genius-level aptitude for his e-commerce endeavor, he reached out to the world of book lovers and sent out questionnaires, asking what consumers would buy online if it were available. Within a short period of time, Giampalo's economic brilliance led to consumers being able to purchase practically anything they desired online.

Lauren leaned back in her chair. The man had changed the way the entire world shopped. She'd used Global goods.com to purchase books, but that had been a few years ago. As a biographer of giants in the business world, she knew a bit of Giampalo's story, but she hadn't realized how much of the retail world he now controlled.

And this is what bothered her. It was his displacement of retail stores across the globe that had forced many small businesses either to come aboard or close up shop.

While Globalgoods.com wasn't entirely at fault for Razzle Dazzle's losses, it was somewhat responsible. She thought of her father's complete and total refusal to step into the twenty-first century and, in all honesty, knew that, in reality, it was his decision that was the main reason the business was failing. Many retail stores that had created online venues were thriving, and Razzle Dazzle Décor, with its unique set of products, could do so also. She knew it.

She skimmed through the lengthy list of retailers that had climbed on board with Globalgoods.com and their unmitigated successes, and weighed the pros and cons of what she'd just read.

Angela was wrong to assume she would jump on this assignment, but she'd also planted the seed of a new idea that just might change her family's situation. Before she convinced herself to ditch the entire idea, she picked up her cell phone and called Angela back.

"I'm in," she said the second Angela picked up the phone. "There is a condition, however," she added.

"That was fast; I wasn't expecting to hear from you so soon. What's changed your mind? And what condition?"

For the next fifteen minutes, Lauren discussed the details of the assignment but added a new twist that was not part of the contract.

"If you can't add this in, then I am going to pass on the deal," she said, convinced she was making the right decision.

"I'll call Mr. Giampalo now and get back to you. Give me an hour or two," Angela said.

Lauren heard the renewed enthusiasm in her agent's voice. Maybe this wasn't the right way to approach this project, but all she had to lose was $3.5 million, minus Angela's ten percent fee. Yes, this was a fortune, but Lauren had scruples and wasn't going to toss them aside, even for a gigantic paycheck. If it was a mistake, then she had only herself to blame.

Right after she disconnected from Angela, she heard the bell ring and realized that, no matter what was going on with her writing career, she still had a business to run. She left the office and greeted an elderly couple. Both were white-headed with rosy cheeks, and each wore a smile as bright as sunshine.

"If I can help you find something, please let me know; otherwise, please feel free to browse."

"Thank you," the elderly man said. "We've been invited to a Christmas-tree-trimming party. We have to bring an ornament, and your place was recommended by our neighbors. We drove from Asheville, so I'm hoping you have just what we're looking for."

"I think I have the perfect ornaments," she assured them. "Give me a minute," she added and hurried to the back of the store and opened the box from Jenny Farrow. She was known throughout North Carolina for her ability to make unique, delicate, glass-blown ornaments. She was sure the couple would agree when they saw what she took out of the box that had arrived via FedEx on Black Friday; she'd had to force herself not to open the box until today, a day after her personal start of the Christmas season.

Carefully, Lauren took a few of the angel ornaments from the box and placed them in what she called her egg-crate carrier, something her father had devised years ago, a way to display fragile ornaments without actually handing them to the customer.

"What about this?" Lauren asked the elderly couple, who'd waited outside her office door.

"Oh, my, these are stunning," the woman gushed when she saw the pair of angels. "Henry, I think we need this set for our tree this year. Do you have any more like these?"

Lauren beamed. "Yes, and I have others from this artist." If she sold just three sets of these ornaments today, she would reach the weekly sales figures she'd hoped for, and a little extra, even after Jenny's commission.

Before they changed their minds, Lauren took the set of four snow people, the set of stars, and the last two angels from the tightly packed box, not bothering to place them in the egg-crate carrier. Instead, she placed them on a felt-covered tray she often used when displaying delicate items. Like a jeweler, she'd told her father once.

"This is the rest of the set of angels. The artist calls them a family of celestial beings." Lauren took what she thought of as "the baby angel" and allowed the elderly couple a close look.

"Exquisite!" the elderly gentleman said.

"Jenny's work is perfection, if I say so myself. She's been supplying our most unique pieces for at least twenty years," Lauren said, as they scrutinized each angel in the set of four.

"I would like the entire set," the woman said. "I'm going to keep these, never mind just buying one for the tree-trimming party." She turned to look at her husband. "Henry, get out your credit card. I have a feeling we're going to earn ourselves an airline ticket or two once these are tallied up."

Lauren laughed. "They are pricey, but they're one of a kind. As far as I know, Jenny has never duplicated any of her Christmas pieces."

"Henry, I'm fearful you'll break these."

"Ellen, I was thinking the same thing about you," he said, a smile on his face. "Dear Ellen is as clumsy as a kitten tugging on a kite string. Has been since the day I made an honest woman of her fifty-odd years ago."

Lauren laughed out loud. "I can have these delivered, but I can't guarantee they won't get broken," she said.

"Henry, you'll drive slowly through the mountains, no speeding, no spinning the tires, is this understood?" Ellen said to her husband. "Since he got that new Porsche, he thinks he's a NASCAR driver."

Again, Lauren chuckled, thinking the couple's humor was a good start to her day. "A Porsche? I'm impressed."

"It's his third-childhood vehicle. A red Mustang, then that black Corvette, and now this Porsche. The darned thing is so small you can barely put a few bags of groceries in that space they call a trunk." She said this with a smile, and Lauren had a sudden thought: she hoped she was this vibrant and full of spunk as this couple when she reached their age. She didn't have a clue how old they were, but their lightheartedness with one another was infectious.

Lauren's day had started out as normally as one could expect for the time of year. But then she'd had the conversation with Angela in which she was offered the opportunity to write John Gerard Giampalo's biography for an almost unbelievable amount of money, and the day had become one of the most momentous in her life. She could barely contain her excitement. Meeting this couple and making an enormous sale was an added bonus.

She directed Ellen and Henry over to Ruby's for breakfast while she spent the next thirty minutes carefully packing the angels, the snow people, and the set of four stars, the largest and most delicate representing the Star of Bethlehem. When she was satisfied the package was as secure as she could achieve, she added up the sale, so that when the charming couple returned, their purchase would be ready for them.

An hour later, they returned, their cheeks flushed a bright pink from the brisk temperatures. "It's so cold out today, I wouldn't be surprised if that white Christmas they're forecasting doesn't hit us this year," Henry said to Lauren.

"I heard that on the news this morning," Lauren said. "It's certainly cold enough."

"Henry, give the young lady the credit card," Ellen said when she saw the large package on the counter.

"Yes, dear," he said, taking his wallet out of his pocket.

Lauren swiped the card through the old-fashioned machine that made a carbon imprint of the card's number, then gave it to Henry for his signature. "It's been a while since I've seen one of these old-timers," he said, eyeing the outdated contraption.

"Yes, it's a dinosaur, for sure, but my father—he owns

the store—refuses to get one of the modern machines because we'd need an Internet connection to use it, and he's totally against anything connected to the twenty-first century that makes things a bit easier." Lauren wasn't sure why she felt the need to explain this to the couple, but they had at least twenty years on her dad and were driving a Porsche, and she'd seen that both had the latest version of the iPhone.

"You gotta keep up with the times," Henry said. "Right, Ellen?"

"Yes. I couldn't imagine life without my techie gadgets," she responded.

"I wish my parents thought that way, but I have a feeling things will have to change because it's the way of the world now." She took the credit-card slip and gave Henry his copy. "Merry Christmas," she said. "Let me take this package out to your car, it's a bit heavy."

"You're a sweetie," Ellen said, "I'll make sure we tell everyone we know about you and your store. It's been delightful."

"Thank you," Lauren said as she carried the box to the front of the store. Henry held the door open for her. A blast of icy air took her breath away as she stepped outside. She saw a brand-new white Porsche parked in front of the store.

Henry hit the fob unlocking the doors, then opened the passenger door. "Ellen can hold the box," he said.

"Of course, I can. It's not like we have anywhere to store it, certainly not in that thing you call a trunk, and in the front, no less."

Ellen slid into the passenger seat, and Lauren placed the large box on her lap. "Hang on to this, and I'm sure you'll make it to Asheville without any trouble."

"Thank you, dear. I will do just that."

Henry slid into the driver's seat, cranked the engine, and slowly backed out of the parking spot. They both waved as she stood in front of the store, and she waved back, then hurried inside.

"It's colder than a frozen fish," she said to no one, remembering how she used to say this when she was a kid.

In the office, she nuked the water in the kettle, then added an Earl Grey tea bag to her mug. When the water in the kettle came to a boil, Lauren poured the water into the mug. Warming her hands on the mug, she took the tea to her desk, and for the second time, she read through the file Angela had compiled on the founder and CEO of Globalgoods.com. If she were to sign this contract, she would have to have an Internet connection at the store and the house. She would run the idea past her mother, and if she was totally against it—she knew her dad would be; no, worse, she knew for a fact he wouldn't allow her to do it—she'd have to figure something out because there was no way she could take on such a project without access to the Internet.

Or she could just do it. She was thirty-five years old. She didn't need their approval. As a matter of respect, she had thought she'd ask, but now she wasn't sure. This was such a silly issue; she truly didn't think at this stage in her life that she needed their permission or their approval for something as important as this. So with that thought in mind, and before she had a chance to change her mind, she called the local cable company and arranged for Internet service for both the store and the house. She would have to hook the boxes up herself if she wanted service by tomorrow, but they assured her a five-year-old could do it, so it shouldn't be a problem. All she had to do was stop at the cable company, sign the required forms, and pick up two boxes, with instructions.

"Okay, now all I have to do is hope that Mr. Giampalo accepts my counteroffer," she said to herself.

She took a sip of tea and, again, reviewed the pdf file Angela had sent. She would have to go to Seattle as soon as she signed on the dotted line, meet Mr. Giampalo, and get started. Of course, all of this was contingent on his accepting the terms she'd asked Angela to present to him. If not, she'd just have to cross that bridge when she came to it. She knew this was the opportunity of a lifetime and would hate to pass it up, but she felt that, given Mr. Giampalo's requirements, she might have the power to negotiate a few of her own.

Lauren looked at her watch; it had been almost two hours since she'd spoken to Angela. Fearing the worst, she used the pharmacy's Wi-Fi and logged onto the Internet again. She pulled up her Facebook page and saw the little green dot by Angela's name, showing that she was online; Angela was always online. She typed out a short message.

She waited a few seconds, then saw the gray dots blinking, indicating that Angela was responding to her message.

Angela: CALL YOU IN TEN MINUTES.

Lauren: WAITING IMPATIENTLY!

She heard the jingle on the door—another customer. She quickly logged off the Internet and stepped out of the office. She liked to greet customers, even if they were most often locals just browsing. It was her father's policy and one she actually agreed with.

The three girls she'd given the afghan and scarf to. What were their names? Lee's daughter was Charlotte, and the others she couldn't recall, but that didn't stop her from acknowledging them as though they'd been friends for ages. Weren't they in school on Monday?

"So glad you all came back. I was hoping I'd hear from you. How is your mom doing?" she asked, directing her gaze to Charlotte, who lingered behind the two girls whose names she couldn't remember.

Both girls turned to look at Charlotte.

Chapter 5

Suddenly alarmed when she saw tears in the girls' eyes, Lauren gathered the three of them close to her and led them to the office.

"Please sit down." She motioned to the sagging sofa.

They did as she asked.

"Charlotte's mom is in a bad way," said one girl. "You remember us, right? I'm Lacey, and this is Kiley."

"Of course, I do," she said, crossing her fingers behind her back to cover her little white lie. "What's going on?" Lauren asked, genuinely concerned.

"It's really bad," Lacey said. "Charlotte's mom, Lee—well, they don't have very good insurance, and she's really sick, but the hospital says she has to go home today."

"What? I don't understand. How can they send her home if she's ill?" Surely the girls were mistaken?

Charlotte scooted to the edge of the sofa and wiped her eyes with her shirtsleeve. "Mom has leukemia."

Oh dear Lord, Lauren thought. This is not a happy visit for sure. Taking a deep breath, she said, "Tell me exactly what happened. Who told you this?"

She knew it wasn't her place, but these girls had come to her, and she wasn't going to send them away with a few words of comfort and forget about them. That wasn't her way.

"Mom told me. She needs a bone-marrow transplant. We've got insurance, but it's not all that good—my mom says, cata-something. They say that her policy won't cover the procedure. What's even worse is I'm a match, and, well, they're just sending her home to die because we don't have the money." Charlotte broke down then, and Lauren squeezed onto the shabby sofa beside her and wrapped her arms around her. The girl was bone-thin, and the coat she wore, if you could even call it a coat, wouldn't keep the bitter temperatures at bay.

"Your mom probably means catastrophic insurance, which means it . . . only covers a certain amount." She hoped she was right, but went on, nonetheless. "Is your mother still in the hospital now?" she asked.

Charlotte nodded.

"They're sending her home this evening," Kiley said, finally speaking up.

"Okay." She would handle this. Some way. "I'm assuming her doctor and the hospital staff know you're a donor match?" She held up her hand. "And you are willing to go through this procedure? You have your parents' permission?" Where was Charlotte's father? She racked her brain again, trying to remember if any of the three girls had even mentioned his name, but she was clueless.

"Yes, they tested me last year when she was first diagnosed, but Mom didn't want me to do it. She got better for a while, and then she got sick again, which has happened a lot, but this time, well, I guess the insurance people are tired of her." More tears from Charlotte, and Lauren's eyes swam with tears.

"My dad always told me there is a solution to every problem, and I'm sure there is one for your mom. We just have to figure out what it is," Lauren explained, her mind going a million miles a minute. "Your mom worked at the post office, right?"

Charlotte wiped her nose on the sleeve of her skimpy coat. "Yeah, she still has her job, but the thing with the insurance, well"—she sniffed—"I don't understand it. I think she pays for it and all."

Lauren grabbed a box of tissues from her desk and handed it to Charlotte. "Anyone for a cup of instant cocoa while I put my thinking cap on?" She took the teakettle she used in the microwave and filled it with bottled water. "I don't have marshmallows or whipped cream," she said, a sad smile on her face. She was simply borrowing time, but the girls didn't need to know this.

"That's awesome," said Lacey. "You're the coolest older woman I know . . . well, besides Charlotte's mom."

Lauren laughed. "Thanks, I think."

Charlotte smiled and leaned back into the sofa. "She doesn't mean to weird you out, it's just her way."

"It's perfectly fine. I remember being your age. I thought someone my age, which, incidentally, is thirty-five, was ancient, and now that I'm ancient, it's really not that bad." She emptied three packets of instant cocoa mix into three mugs, then filled each with steaming water. She stirred the chocolate powder, then carefully handed each girl a cup. Lauren was stalling because she truly had no idea what her next move should be.

Think, Lauren, think, she said to herself.

"Aren't you three supposed to be in school? Not that it's any of my business if you're skipping. I'm just curious." She could have texted Madison and asked, but she didn't.

"We just had a morning session today; there's teachers' meetings for the rest of the day," Kiley offered. "That's why we're here, plus we wanted to tell you about Lee."

"Okay, well that's a big relief. I didn't think you three were skipping, truly, but since I'm old, I had to ask." She was saying whatever came to mind, anything to give her a few minutes to come up with a substantive answer, anything that might help Charlotte and Lee. "I think I might have skipped a couple of times in my senior year, but I was lucky; I didn't get caught." At that moment, her cell phone rang.

Crap!

"Excuse me for a sec," she said, then answered the phone.

"He said 'no,' " Angela said into the phone. " 'No' as in no deal. Take it or leave it."

"What?" Lauren shouted, then, remembering the girls, lowered her voice. "Are you serious? If you're teasing me, I don't think it's funny. I have a very"—she turned her back to the girls and walked toward the back of the office—"delicate situation here, and I'd appreciate it if you'd cut the crap." Lauren didn't need this. Not now, when she had a life-altering problem on her hands.

"I'm not kidding, Lauren. He said no. Take it or leave it, his exact words. He'll give you until six o'clock tonight, which is three in the afternoon Pacific time, for you to change your mind. If not, he said he'd forget the entire project."

Lauren took a deep breath, releasing it slowly. "Okay, so this isn't a joke?"

"No, it's not. How many times do I need to repeat myself?"

"None," she said. "Call him back and tell him I'm sorry to be so pushy, and that I would be honored to write his biography. Do it, and call me back." Lauren pushed the END button on her phone. She cleared her throat. "Sorry, girls, that was a personal call. Now, your mom, Lee. We need to figure out a way to keep her in the hospital, at least for another day or two."

Expecting three teenage girls to brainstorm a solution with her was an invitation to disaster. They'd come to her, maybe not to solve her mother's health-care issues, but they'd trusted her enough to confide in her, and for that reason alone, she had to do something. "Charlotte, is your mother at Appalachian Regional Hospital?"

Charlotte nodded. "But they would have to transfer her to Chapel Hill for the transplant. It's a special hospital for bone marrow and stuff."

Of course, Fallen Springs wasn't without good hospitals, but larger cities would be more equipped to deal with this. "I think I may have a plan."

Lauren took the old-fashioned phone book from her desk. All three girls stared at it as though they'd never laid eyes on one. Maybe they hadn't. Quickly, she found the main number for Appalachian Regional. As soon as they answered, she asked to be connected to the nurses' station on the second floor; she knew that that was the floor for cancer patients.

"Second floor. How may I help you?" a pleasant female voice asked.

Good question, Lauren thought. She was going to wing it and hope for the best. "I'm calling about my friend, Lee Hessinger." She paused. "She's supposed to be released this evening."

"Hold, please," said the woman on the other end.

While Lauren was on hold, she tried to recall what little she knew about leukemia, and it wasn't much, but she knew the immune system was in play, and you had to avoid infections, people with colds or flu.

"May I have your name?" the pleasant woman asked when she returned to the phone.

"Lauren Montgomery."

"One moment, please." Lauren was placed on hold again.

"Hello," a soft voice said, and it wasn't the nurse. "Charlotte?"

"Lee, this is Lauren. From Razzle Dazzle," she said. "Charlotte and her friends are here at the store."

"Oh, yes, she said she'd personally tell you thank you for the afghan and scarf. It's lovely, Lauren. Charlotte told me that you gave this to her, and I'm so appreciative. They keep the hospital so cold. It seems I'm cold all the time now."

Lauren could tell that Lee was short of breath. "Charlotte told me about the leukemia, and I'm so sorry. I can't begin to imagine how you must feel."

"I've had better days," Lee said, a defeated note in her tone, one Lauren identified as hopelessness.

"You're leaving the hospital today?" Lauren asked.

"I am," Lee replied. "I need to be home for Charlotte.

She's been staying with Kiley and Lacey off and on. I know it's hard on her, especially this time of year."

This was terrible. The girls forgot to mention this. "What about Charlotte's father? Is he unable to care for her?" She knew this wasn't her business, but she needed to know in order to help Charlotte and Lee.

"He was never in the picture much. We divorced when Charlotte was a baby," Lee explained. "It's been just the two of us ever since."

Lauren glanced at the girls, who remained on the sofa sipping their cocoa. She wanted to ask more questions but could tell that Lee was struggling with each word. Before she gave it too much thought, she said, "Charlotte can stay with me if she wants. My parents are home during the day, and that old house is huge." She stopped. She didn't want to make Lee or Charlotte feel like a charity case.

"Oh, well, I guess you'd have to ask Charlotte. I know your mom and dad, but she doesn't. It's okay because I'll be home this evening."

"I don't mean to . . . interfere," Lauren said, lowering her voice. "The girls told me about your situation, and I might be able to help." She had an idea simmering but couldn't reveal it just yet.

"I can't let you do this, whatever it is. I'm fine, truly."

Lauren wanted to say she knew better but didn't want to say anything that would hurt Lee's feelings. "It's probably not a good idea for you to leave the hospital yet. Charlotte told me about the bone-marrow transplant. I don't know much about that, but I think I know a way that will allow you to stay in the hospital a few more days."

She waited for Lee to respond.

"Lee?" she asked, her tone a bit anxious.

"Sorry, I get short of breath."

"I'll let Charlotte say hi, and as I said, I might know a way to keep you there if you want to stay. I didn't ask. I'm sorry."

She was digging herself into a hole, with no idea what she was doing. She was giving false hope and knew that was wrong. She did have an idea but couldn't speak of it until she knew she had the proper information.

"I'll speak to Charlotte for a minute. Thank you, Lauren, but I've come to terms with this . . . situation. I'll be fine," she said.

Lauren could hear that Lee's drawing out of each word was an effort. "I'll let you talk with Charlotte then." She gave her cell phone to the girl and motioned for Kiley and Lacey to follow her.

"I thought Charlotte could use some privacy," she explained. "This must be a nightmare for them."

"Char cries at night. She tries to act all cool, like she can handle it, but she doesn't have anyone but her mom. I don't know what she'll do if, well, you know Lee doesn't get better," Lacey said. "We're fifteen, all three of us."

Lauren had guessed them to be around fourteen or fifteen. At least, they knew they were young and unable to make decisions for Charlotte.

"Has Lee asked either of your parents to take legal responsibility for Charlotte, if God forbid, she doesn't make it? I don't like asking this, but I need to know."

"Both of our parents have signed some kind of paper that if something happens to Char, they have permission to take her to the doctor, but that's all I know," Kiley explained.

Lauren nodded. "It's very kind of your parents to do this."

"They've known Char since we all started kindergarten. We're like sisters," Lacey said. "I don't think Lee has plans to give her up for adoption or anything, though we could ask our parents." Lacey looked at Kiley, who nodded in agreement. "But I can ask my parents as soon as possible. They don't tell me everything."

Lauren smiled. "That's the role of a parent. It's tough to have responsibilities placed on you when you're young. From what I can see, you all certainly have your act together. Your parents should be very proud of you."

"Thanks," the two girls said at the same time.

Charlotte came out of the office with more tears streaming down her face. "Mom says it's okay if I want to stay at your place, Lauren, but I'm good at Lacey's and Kiley's. She said to thank you again for being so concerned. So what plan do you have to keep my mom in the hospital tonight?"

Chapter 6

Charlotte wiped the tears from her cheeks. "I didn't tell her that I want this, too. She doesn't want to be a burden," she said.

When Lauren had left the house this morning, she could not have guessed in a million years how the day would unfold.

"I promise you I don't think helping you or your mother is a burden. People are supposed to help one another when they can. I'll have to make a few more calls to get things rolling." Just then, another brilliant idea hit her. "Can I ask you all a huge favor?"

They all nodded.

"Can you girls watch the store for thirty minutes? No, never mind. I'll just close early—"

"No, we can help out; we want to," Charlotte said.

"I'm sure we can manage for a bit. I'm good with math," she added.

"Okay, it's a deal. I need to show you a few things, then I'll run out, and I shouldn't be more than half an hour or so."

She took the girls through a run of the items in the store, showed them how to use the cash register, then had to show them how to use the ancient credit-card swiper. They were shocked to learn she didn't have Wi-Fi here or at home. They were quick studies. Lauren said that, if they ran into any problems, to tell the customers she would take care of whatever they needed the minute she returned.

Lauren left through the back door, making sure to lock it behind her. She wasn't expecting any large deliveries that required using the back entrance, and if FedEx had any deliveries, they would have to use the public entrance. She cranked the engine over, again thankful Jimmy's had tuned up her aging Honda.

She hoped this crazy idea she'd concocted wasn't a waste of time. Driving as fast as she could without breaking the speed limit, she parked in the parent pickup area at Fallen Springs Elementary. She shivered as she made her way inside; she'd been in such a hurry when she left the store that she hadn't bothered putting on her coat. She wore a thick wool sweater, but it wasn't enough to fight the dropping temperatures. She popped into the main office and saw Cheryl Stanton, another high-school friend, who was the elementary school's secretary. "I need to see Madison. Can I go to the classroom, or can you ask her to come to the office? It's important, and I don't have a lot of time."

"Go on to the classroom. I think it's art period. There are twenty-plus second graders, and there's no telling what they'll do if left on their own," Cheryl said.

"Thanks," Lauren said, and raced down the hall to room 207. She peeked through the small glass opening in the door, saw that Madison was talking with a student, then tapped on the door.

Madison looked up and, seeing her, motioned for her to come in. "I'm not even going to guess why you're here. Are your parents all right?"

"Yes, they're fine. Listen, I have a bit of a problem, and I need your help."

"Okay, what gives?" Madison said.

Lauren knew she was really pushing it, but when times were desperate, desperate measures needed to be taken. One couldn't get more desperate than Lee. "Does James have hospital privileges at Appalachian Regional?" Dr. James Crawford and Madison had dated for several months during their senior year in high school. James had attended the University of North Carolina in Chapel Hill. He'd gone on to study medicine at Duke University. Lauren had lost track of where he'd interned but knew he'd set up practice in Fallen Springs as a neurologist.

"I'm sure he does. Please don't tell me you're ill and need his services," Madison whispered, while keeping a close eye on her students.

"No, I'm fine. Do you remember Lee Hessinger from high school?"

"Of course," Madison said.

"She's in the hospital now; she has leukemia, and crappy insurance. She needs a bone-marrow transplant, yet the hospital plans to release her today, said her insurance provider wouldn't cover the cost of a transplant. Her daughter is a donor match." Lauren stopped to gather her words. "I need someone to make sure she stays in the hospital."

Lauren could tell by the stunned look on Madison's face that she couldn't have been more surprised. Her eyes were as wide as saucers.

"Start from the beginning, and tell me how you came to be in this position," Madison said.

Lauren told her what Charlotte and Lee had told her, then went on to explain. "I'm not a doctor, but I know leukemia patients have little or no immune system strength. She can't leave the hospital if she's to have this transplant."

"You said Lee's insurance wouldn't cover a transplant. I'm missing something here."

"I'm getting to that part," Lauren said. And this was such a big *if*, she almost backed out, but remembered Charlotte's tears. Taking a deep breath, Lauren said, "I'm going to make sure there are funds available for the transplant."

There, it was out. This crazy idea that had skittered through her brain was out. Details of how she'd fund this, and how she'd manage to keep Lee in the hospital, were just that. Details. Sort of.

"Do you know how much that is?" Madison asked.

"That's, uh . . . part of what I need to ask James."

"And the other part? You could google the approximate cost, Lauren."

"I know that, but I need it from a professional, and I need a professional to see to it that she stays in the hospital while I figure out a way to cover the cost of a transplant." She had six weeks to write a book and earn a few million, but that wasn't guaranteed if the book wasn't published.

Madison shook her head. "I can't believe you would involve yourself in this. While I think you have the softest heart ever, and the best of intentions, I'm not sure it's your place."

Frustrated, Lauren whispered, a bit too harshly, "Of course, it isn't, but I can't stand by and do nothing. You wouldn't, either, so don't try to convince me otherwise.

"If you can contact James and give him my cell number, I'll speak with him. I know this isn't . . . I know it's not my place, but Charlotte and Lee have no one. I couldn't sleep a wink if I didn't try to help them."

Madison's eyes pooled with tears. "And that's what I love about you. You're the kindest woman I know. And to answer your question, yes, I will call James, give him a heads-up and your number, then it's up to you."

"That's all I'm asking. I knew I could count on you," Lauren said. "I've got to get back to the store. I'll keep you posted." She gave her friend a quick hug and left the room, not bothering to stop in the office as she would have under different circumstances.

She was pulling into the parking lot behind the store when her cell phone rang. "Hello," she said, not bothering to get out of her car. She didn't want the girls to hear this conversation.

"It's been a while, Lauren. What gives? Madison said it was a matter of life and death that I call you."

Flooded with relief, she quickly explained Lee's story. "I just felt that I had to do something."

"I understand. I'm not sure what I can do, but I may be able to pull a few strings, keep her there a few more days. As far as costs, there are so many factors that go into this, I can't give you an exact figure, but I do know most hospitals have what they call an indigent fund. It's not spoken of, but it is there for situations such as this. Let me make a couple of phone calls, and I'll get back to you as soon as I have a definite answer."

"Thank you so much, James. I truly appreciate this, and I know Lee will, too," Laura said, before hanging up.

She grabbed her purse and keys, unlocked the door, and went inside. Dropping her things on the desk inside her office, she stepped into the store. The three girls were gathered around the fireplace warming their hands. It was bitterly cold inside.

"I'm back," she said with a huge smile on her face.

"We didn't have any customers, except for a couple of ladies who stopped to admire the window display," Lacey said. "It's really nice, too."

"Thanks. I enjoyed setting it up; it's my favorite chore here, if you can even call it one." She didn't want to tell Charlotte what might happen, but she had to explain why she'd run out of the store. "A friend of mine is checking into your mother's situation. I hope we can convince her doctor to keep her a bit longer."

Charlotte looked at Lauren. "Why?"

Lauren leaned against the fireplace mantel. She was chilled to the bone. "She needs to stay there at least until she's . . . maybe she'll get to have the bone-marrow transplant, after all. I'm not saying this is going to happen, but I wouldn't give up on your mom. I'm guessing she's a survivor and will fight as long as she's able."

Darn! That didn't come out right. "I mean she needs to have the strength to get better, and if she's released too early, I don't know much about her disease, but I do know her immune system isn't functioning as it should, so it would be harmful to release her just now." She felt so ignorant.

"But the hospital says her insurance won't allow her to stay," Charlotte explained. "I don't understand why they would change their minds."

Again, Lauren wasn't sure if she should give the girl false hope. Yes, James would put a word in, but until she was one hundred percent sure, she would have to keep this information to herself. Not wanting to lie, yet knowing these girls were smart enough to suspect she knew more than she was saying, she said, "There could be extenuating circumstances that could change her current situation."

"I hope whatever you did will make a difference," Lacey said. "We know you did something, and it's okay for you not to tell us now."

Lauren gave a half-hearted smile. "We'll have to wait and see."

"Whatever you did on my mom's behalf, I appreciate the effort, no matter how it turns out," Charlotte said. "No one has ever reached out and tried to help her."

Lauren could have cried at hearing the young girl's words, but she had to keep it together. The girls came to her, and she would remain the adult in control. She could cry another time.

Deciding they deserved to know a few details of what she'd been doing, she said, "A friend of mine knows a doctor who may be able to convince your mom's doctor and the hospital to keep her there for a few more days. No promises, but we can certainly hope." She realized that she sounded like her mother, and instead of cringing as she would have done as a teen, she was proud of the sense of right and wrong her mom and dad had instilled in her.

"I really can't thank you enough," Charlotte said. "I hope Mom can stay, too. Not that I like her being in the hospital, but it's the best way right now. Does Mom know?"

Lauren expected this question and had her answer. "I spoke with her, but that's it. I didn't have anything to tell her then, and I still don't, but we can cross our fingers and send up a prayer that this friend of my friend can help out." Lauren knew she was sounding like a broken record, yet she couldn't give false hope to Charlotte, or Lee.

She knew in her heart that James would most likely come through, and that thought alone warmed her. There were good people in the world, despite all the negativity one heard on the news and read in the papers.

"If you hear from your friend, can you call my mom if it's good news?" Charlotte asked.

"Of course." Lauren jotted down her cell phone and her home phone number, and gave them to the girls. "You can call me anytime, too. You've been great advocates for Lee. I'm sure she's proud of all three of you."

She walked the girls to the front door, promising to call the minute she had any news.

Back in her office, Lauren made a note to get a new coat for Charlotte. With the temps expected in the low teens, the thin jacket she was wearing would do little to keep her warm.

She turned her thoughts to Angela's call and what she'd agreed to do. If, and that now was another very big *if*, John Gerard Giampalo still wanted her as his biographer, she'd agree to whatever terms he wanted. She needed the money more than ever. There was much more at stake. Lee's life. If she had to eat a bit of crow, then she would do so, happily.

Chapter 7

Her cell phone rang. Angela.

"He's agreed," she said, as usual not bothering with niceties.

Lauren breathed a sigh of relief. She'd felt sure he'd tell her to go eat rocks. "And the conditions are the same?" she asked.

"Pretty much. How soon can you leave for Seattle?" Angela asked her.

Lauren mentally checked all that a trip to Seattle would entail and just how quickly she could put her mental list into action. Knowing what was at stake, she said, "I can catch the first flight out."

"That's my girl," Angela said, a new zing to her voice. "Of course, Mr. G will take care of your flight and accommodations. Let me call him, tell him you're a go for tomorrow, if we can get a flight out, though I'm sure that won't be a problem. I'll call you back with the details."

"I'll be waiting," Lauren said, then hung up. Now all she had to do was find someone to fill in at the store for a few days.

Maggie, her mother's best friend. She quickly dialed her number, using the store's phone. In case Angela called back on her cell, she didn't want to tie up the line, even though she knew she could put Maggie on hold.

Quickly dialing the number, she heard Maggie answer on the second ring. "Hello, Lauren. Is everything okay with your dad? And Ilene?"

Since his diagnosis, this was always the first question anyone close to them asked when she called. "They're fine, at least they were when I left the house this morning. Mom would call if something drastic happened. Listen," she paused, trying to gather her thoughts, "I need a huge favor. As in gigantic."

Maggie's laughter trilled across the phone line. "I'm open. What's this 'huge' and 'gigantic' favor?"

"Hear me out. This has all happened so fast, I haven't even had a chance to tell Mom or Dad, so you'll have to keep it to yourself if you choose to do what I'm about to ask. Then, of course, I'll call Mom and Dad and tell them."

Lauren explained the details of her new contract and why she had to act immediately.

"Lauren Montgomery, I can't believe you would even think I'd have to consider this. Of course, I'll fill in for you. I know that place like the back of my hand. I still have a set of keys."

Lauren knew that, as Maggie had worked with her parents many times when an extra employee was needed, but she wasn't one to assume that, just because Maggie was like family, she would be able to work on demand.

"Thank you so much. I can't tell you what this means to me. Now I'm going to call Mom. If all goes according to plan, just show up at the store tomorrow, and I'll stay in touch."

"I'm going to cancel a few craft sessions," Maggie said. "I can't wait."

Lauren had no more than ended the call when her cell lit up.

She answered immediately. "Details," Lauren said, using Angela's briskness.

"Dang, you're sounding more like me with every call," Angela said.

"Time is passing. Tell me the details. I've got a boatload of things to do before I leave."

Angela explained the travel arrangements and all that Lauren needed to know for her trip to Seattle tomorrow afternoon, promising to e-mail the flight information.

"Okay, then. I'll keep you posted from my end," Lauren said. "Talk soon."

There were a zillion and one things to do before she left, but first, she needed to call her parents and tell them before Maggie decided to break the news. Not that Lauren expected her to, but she was known for sharing good news a bit too soon, as she excited quite easily.

She dialed her parents' landline, the same number they'd had since she was born. Her mother answered. "Hello."

"It's just me, Mom," Lauren said. "How's Dad feeling?"

She heard her mother's intake of breath, which could mean anything. "Oh, he's in a mood today."

Lauren smiled. At least it wasn't his health. Her mother's "in a mood" meant they were out of her father's favorite breakfast cereal, which ruined his day. Lauren didn't want to hazard a guess as to why.

"I'll stop at the grocery on my way home."

"Thanks, honey. Your dad is a total grouch if he doesn't have his favorite brand of rice puffs. He acts like a two-year-old, but don't tell him I said that."

"My lips are sealed. Listen, I have a reason for calling." Not that checking on her father's health wasn't a good reason; she checked on him daily, but this was something her mother needed to know right away.

"Angela called me this morning."

"Oh, dear. Remind me who Angela is."

Lauren chuckled. "She's my literary agent. From New York."

"Of course. Old age is creeping up on me. So, how is she these days?" her mother asked, even though she had never met her.

"I'm going to venture a guess and say today is probably one of the best days she's had in a very long time." She knew what was coming next.

"That's wonderful, dear."

Yup, Lauren thought. Mom's typical answer. She thought anything and everything was wonderful. The thing was, she truly believed it. Lauren thought she was the most positive person on the planet. Truly a pure soul.

"I suppose you want to know exactly *why* her day is so extraordinary?"

"Of course, I do," her mother replied.

"She just landed one of the biggest contracts of her career." Lauren paused a few seconds, giving her mom time to articulate what this meant.

"That's wonderful, Lauren."

"Mom, you're not catching on, are you?"

"To what?"

"To what I'm hinting at. Angela's big contract." Lauren knew she shouldn't drag the news out like this, but she couldn't help herself.

"No, I don't believe I am," Ilene said in her sweetest voice. "But you are going to tell me, right?"

More laughter. "Mom, Angela's big contract is for me."

Silence.

"Mom?"

"I'm here."

"John Giampalo wants *me* to write his biography." There, let that sink in for a minute or two.

"Lauren, I'm sorry, you know I am not current on anything Hollywood. Would I know of his movies?"

"Mother, he isn't an actor. He's the CEO of Global goods.com, the largest online retailer in the world."

Lauren could envision the look on her mother's face when she recognized the web address, as it had been discussed at great length during many dinners since her return to Fallen Springs.

More silence.

"Mom?" Lauren prodded.

"Yes, I'm listening."

She heard the instant change in the tone of her voice, and Lauren knew her mother didn't need any further explanation.

"Go ahead," Lauren said, "tell me this is a bad idea."

A couple of seconds passed before her mother replied. "Honestly, I can't say that it is. However, your father might have a thing or two to say, even though it's none of his business. You know where he stands on anything"—she paused—"modern."

Lauren knew her mother's use of the word "modern" meant anything technical. This included the Internet, too. Taking a deep breath, she answered, "Yep, I know."

Again, more silence.

"You've accepted this assignment then?" her mother asked.

Not technically. But it was just a matter of signing on the dotted line.

"It's a contract, Mom, not an assignment." Forever the teacher, Lauren thought, as she corrected her mother.

"Have you told your father?"

"No. Not yet."

There. The elephant in the room. Dad and the modern age, as her mother would say.

"Would you like me to tell him for you?"

"No, no. I'll tell him. Tonight. At dinner."

Lauren had so many things to check off her to-do list and only a matter of hours in which to do them. Explaining her decision would take time, and right now, she didn't have a lot to spare.

"Are you sure? Maybe you could tell him after the holidays," her mother suggested. "Might be easier on you too, dear."

She glanced at her watch. "Actually, I need to tell him tonight. I have to"—she was going to say "leave" but decided she'd tell her parents face-to-face at dinner tonight. "I need to make a couple of pit stops before I head home, so I'll be a little late."

"Of course, dear, and don't forget your dad's cereal," her mother added, resuming her cheerful tone. "I'll hold off serving dinner until you're home."

"Thanks," Lauren said, and ended the call.

Where to begin, she thought, as she glanced around the store. Though it wasn't quite closing time, Lauren decided to close early, given the errands she had to take care of before heading home. An hour wouldn't matter one way or the other. She seriously doubted they'd have an onslaught of customers this late in the day. Hurrying to the entrance before she could change her mind, she flipped the sign over, letting possible customers know they were closed for the day. She checked the shelves of shirts, smoothed a bright red one on top of the pile, tucked a few stray branches back in place on the artificial tree in the window, then shut off the gas fireplace. She'd make sure to leave a note for Maggie, telling her she could bump the thermostat up as high as she needed to keep warm. Lauren kept the temperatures as low as she could, using the gas fireplace to make up the difference, plus she always dressed in several layers to stay warm. Maggie was doing her a huge favor. No way would she ask her to play miser in regard to the store's enormous electric bills. The building was old, and the insulation all but gone. Someday, she would make the necessary repairs to the building, but for now, she'd live with tossing an extra bit of cash toward the utilities.

In her office, she recorded a new message for the answering machine, tidied the desk, and wrote another note for Maggie, reminding her they didn't have Internet service at the store, and if she needed to go online, she could use the pharmacy's next door, explaining she had Wilbur's permission to do this and leaving the password—which reminded her, she had to stop off at the cable company for the boxes she'd ordered. While she wouldn't have time to install the service here, she would do so at home. After she told her dad about her new contract.

Glancing around to make sure she hadn't forgotten anything, she grabbed her purse and keys, and, locking the door behind her, she stepped out into the brisk afternoon air. In her car, she shivered as she waited for the engine to warm up so she could switch the heat on. Maybe it was time for a new car. It took this old Honda forever to warm up, even after Jimmy's tune-up. "Maybe later," she said, shifting into reverse and heading to Threads, a locally owned clothing shop she liked to frequent. The prices were fair and the styles up to date. Lauren found an empty parking spot in front of the store and reached for her purse, checking inside to make sure she had her debit card. Last time she'd been to Threads, she'd had to ask Claire Conroy, the owner, to hold her purchase as she'd hoofed it back to the shop, where she had carelessly tossed her card on her desk. Inside, she was greeted by Bing Crosby's "It's Beginning to Look a Lot Like Christmas."

"Be right there," Claire called from the back of the store, her Irish accent music to Lauren's ears.

"It's just me," Lauren called out as she eyed a rack of puffer jackets.

She heard a tinkle of laughter. "Have a look about, lass."

Lauren grinned. Claire called everyone "lass" or "lad," no matter their age. Cracked her up, as Claire was around her age and had lived in Fallen Springs since she was a teenager.

"Will do," Lauren called out as she perused the jackets. She wasn't sure of Charlotte's size, so she'd have to wing it, which should be easy enough since they were similar in build. She removed a charcoal-gray jacket from its hanger. Hanging her purse on the end of the rack, she took off her heavy sweater, then slipped the puffer jacket on. It fit her perfectly, loose enough to allow for layers, if needed, yet warm enough to wear with a T-shirt, and according to the label, the jacket would sustain one in temperatures twenty degrees below freezing.

This would be perfect for Charlotte, though she thought the color pretty bland. Then she saw another of the same size in a deep purple. She remembered that Charlotte wore a purple sweater that first day they'd visited the store. Didn't all teenage girls like purple? If not, she'd make sure Claire was okay with an exchange, just in case. Lauren figured she might as well purchase a set of gloves, along with a matching hat and scarf, because Charlotte would certainly need those, too. Choosing the same purple shade as the jacket but with a mixture of pink and lavender swirls, she thought Charlotte would like them.

Claire appeared from the back of the store. "Looks like you found my newest shipment of outerwear."

"Yep. Is this something a fifteen-year-old would wear?" she asked as she placed the items on the counter.

"Absolutely. Those puffer jackets never go out of style. Purple is all the rage this season."

"You would think red or green, but I guess those colors are too bold," Lauren said.

"For some teens, I suppose so. Is this a gift? I can wrap it if you want."

"Yes, it's a gift, sort of, but it doesn't need to be wrapped. I've got a new friend in need of a warmer coat."

"I can cut the tags off," Claire added.

"Better leave them, just in case there's a problem. I'm

sure the fit is fine, but not one hundred percent on the color."

"No worries." Claire scanned the bar codes, then carefully wrapped each item in white tissue paper. Lauren inserted her debit card in the machine, punched in her PIN, then removed the card as instructed.

"If you might need to exchange this, just keep the receipt," Claire told Lauren as she handed her a large brown bag with hefty plastic handles.

"Thanks, Claire. I'm sure the recipient won't have any issues—well, other than possibly the color, and that's doubtful. She's in need of a coat that'll keep these unusually chilly temperatures at bay. I'll see you at the next chamber of commerce meeting?" she asked.

"Count on it, lass."

Back in the car, Lauren cranked the ignition over, grateful that the car's engine hadn't had time to cool. Wickedly cold, she would swear the temperature had dropped at least ten degrees in the fifteen minutes she was inside.

Her next stop, Appalachian Cable, was out of her way if she were going straight home, but close to her preferred grocery store, Harris Teeter, where she would pick up her dad's cereal and a few other items they would need while she was gone. Again, she located a parking place close to the entrance, though this time, she left the engine running, knowing it was risky, even though Fallen Springs was a relatively safe city. She wasn't sure how long she'd be, as the weather was deteriorating by the minute. If this winter storm continued, odds were her flight to Seattle would be canceled. In her rush to leave the store, she hadn't bothered listening to an updated weather report, and her car radio had conked out last summer.

Hurrying inside, she was greeted by a young man wearing khaki slacks, a blue chambray shirt with a navy vest displaying the Appalachian Cable logo, a beige-colored stitching of their namesake's mountains, along with a name tag that read BRAD. He looked like a Brad. His light brown hair was combed into the latest style, which appeared to require a gallon of hair gel to hold in place. His smile was as white as an actor's in a toothpaste commercial. "May I help you?" he asked, flashing his blindingly white teeth.

"I'm Lauren Montgomery. I called earlier. I'm picking up cable and Internet boxes."

"Of course, I spoke with you. Follow me."

He stepped behind a counter, removed four small white boxes, and placed them in a plastic bag. "Now if you'll just sign here, I can go over the installation process." Lauren skimmed the agreement and signed the required papers. She was in a rush and was sure she wasn't going to be ripped off. She'd had cable service and Internet when she lived in Florida, though she hadn't installed them herself. Lauren guessed all services were relatively equal. Ten minutes later, she was back inside her warm car with printed instructions on how to install the boxes. With luck, she'd have Internet service before bedtime.

Lauren was distracted as she pulled into the grocery's parking lot. The place was jam-packed, which was unusual at this time of day. Must be having a sale. She grabbed the reusable bags she kept in the back seat and rushed inside, where she was greeted by the smell of burnt coffee and freshly baked bread. Lauren grabbed a shopping cart, noticing that there were only a few left, and pushed her way to the front of the store to find out why they were so crowded at this hour. Voices buzzed throughout the front of the store. She was able to discern that folks were concerned about the weather, hence the need to stock up on supplies. Not having heard an updated forecast since the morning, she was somewhat surprised, especially when she spied Scott Murphy pushing a cart down aisle seven. "Hey," she said when she caught up with him, "what's the latest weather report? I've been out of touch this afternoon."

Scott Murphy, Madison's husband, seemed surprised to see her. "Lauren Montgomery, long time no see." He moved his shopping cart to the side and gave her a quick hug.

"Sorry, it's good to see you, too. I stopped by the school today and saw Madison," she said after she placed a friendly kiss on his cheek. Scott was the brother she had never had.

"She told me." He motioned for her to follow him. "Let's get out of their way." Two elderly women with carts overflowing tried to pass through the narrow space between their two carts.

In the back of the store, near the produce section, Lauren positioned her cart next to Scott's. "I take it the weather report isn't what we're used to around here."

"A rare winter storm," Scott said. "Ice."

"No wonder," she said, glancing at the crowd. Concerned her flight would get canceled, she'd call the airline just to make sure. And if the flight was canceled? Surely John Giampalo wouldn't fault her if she were unable to travel due to weather.

"Madison called with a list." He indicated the supplies in his shopping cart. "I'm betting this storm won't produce much, but it's good to be prepared."

Lauren eyed the items he referred to. "Looks like the healthy stuff is all sold out?" She grinned.

"Yep. Just in case the weatherman's right," Scott said. "I'll tell Madison I ran into you. She'll ask if I invited you over, so if you're brave, pop over later. We'll have plenty of munchies, and we could have a glass or two of wine."

"Thanks, but I'd best get what I came for and go home. Tell Madison I'll try to call her later." She gave him another hug, then maneuvered her way to the front of the store.

The shelves were emptying quickly. She spied the cereal she had come for, took four boxes of her father's favorite brand, plus a large container of oats. She grabbed an extra two gallons of milk, three loaves of wheat bread, a giant jar of Peter Pan peanut butter, and a jar of Welch's grape jelly, even though she was sure her mother had plenty of homemade jellies stored in the pantry. Remembering her time in Florida during hurricane season, she also picked up a case of bottled water, three packs of various-sized batteries, and two cigarette lighters. They would be easier to use if they ran out of matches. Actually, she had no clue if her parents had matches in the house. Mom didn't like candles burning as she had a massive fear of leaving them unattended and starting a fire. This never made a lot of sense to her since they always used the wood fireplaces throughout the large house. Finally, as she made her way to the long lines at the front of the store, her cell phone rang.

"Yes, hello?" she said.

"It's James. I told you I'd call if there was news about your friend."

Lauren smiled. "Thanks so much. So how did it go?"

"I convinced the chief of staff to have another look at her medical files; he contacted her oncologist, and they've agreed to keep her a few more days. And there's a chance I can get those indigent funds applied toward her bone-marrow transplant. Of course, your friend has to agree to this, but all in all, good news."

"That's *wonderful* news. I can't thank you enough." She paused, unsure if she should tell him of her plan to finance Lee's transplant. If this book deal failed, she wouldn't be able to pay for the entire procedure, but in the state Lee was in, could she hold off telling the doctors to plan for the transplant? Madison was right. She'd overstepped her boundaries, but she couldn't help herself. "James, if there's a way to fund this transplant, do you think it would be possible to keep her in the hospital until then?" She pushed her shopping cart forward a few inches as the line slowly moved. If checkout continued at this rate, she'd be holed up in this grocery store for the duration of the storm.

"Yes, those funds can go toward whatever her insurance doesn't cover. I hope this helped," James added.

"I'm guessing this is going to be a very merry Christmas for Lee and Charlotte if all goes according to what you've told me. Again, thanks, and I'll be in touch." Lauren ended the call, unsure if she should call Lee or keep to the sidelines. Which reminded her, she had to deliver Charlotte's jacket before the storm. Unsure where she was staying, Lauren pulled from her bag the slip of paper on which Lacey had written her phone number and Kiley's—just in case, Lacey had said as she slipped the paper into Lauren's hand. The girl was way more mature than her age, Lauren decided as she punched in her number. A woman answered on the first ring. "Hi, this is Lauren Montgomery. Is this—"

"Lauren, Lacey said you might call. I'm Beth."

She sounded cheerful, friendly. "Yes, Beth, I was wondering if Charlotte is staying with you tonight. The girls came into the store and told me about Lee. I wanted to let her know my friend has arranged for Lee to stay in the hospital a few more days."

"That's wonderful! Char will be thrilled. Hang on a second."

Lauren heard muffled voices, then Charlotte took the phone. "Hey, Lauren. Beth says you have good news."

"I think I do. My friend was able to pull a few strings, and he says they'll keep your mom in the hospital."

"Awesome! Did she say she'd do the transplant thing? I'm ready to do my part, just so she knows," Charlotte added.

"I don't have all the details just yet. It might be a good idea to call your mom, check up on her, see how she feels about this new . . . development. I'm pretty sure she hasn't been told yet."

"Sure, I'll call her now. Mom hasn't been feeling like celebrating Christmas this year, but I think this news might just change her mind. I really, really appreciate this." Charlotte paused. "I could help out at your store, you know, to, like, repay you. Sort of."

Her heart lurched. "Oh, sweetie, that's so kind of you." She was going to add she didn't need extra help, but wondered if Maggie would appreciate an extra hand? "I might have to leave town for a few days, a business trip. I'm having a family friend working at the store. She might need a hand. Is it all right if I give her your phone number? Just in case. Her name is Maggie, and she's a close friend of my family." This was all contingent on the weather. Lauren could very well be working at the store herself if her flight was canceled.

"Yes, please tell her we all can help. We're kinda like our own version of the three musketeers."

Lauren couldn't help but laugh. "I'll tell Maggie. I'll let you go now so you can call your mom, share the news, and maybe convince her this is what you want, too."

"Okay, I will. And Lauren, thanks so much. No one has really helped mom this past year, at least not like this."

"It's fine, Charlotte. This is what the season is all about, helping others. Now go ahead and call your mom. Wait!" She almost forgot about the jacket. "Listen, I stopped at Threads and saw a really cute jacket. On a whim, I thought you might like it. Would it be okay if I dropped this off on my way home?"

"Cool! Sure, I don't think Beth would mind," Charlotte answered, excitement lifting her voice a few octaves. "You know the blue house on the corner of Westbury and Skyline?"

Lauren laughed. "Of course I do. I'll see you shortly," she said, then disconnected.

She had not wanted to embarrass the girl with her offer and was very glad that Charlotte hadn't seemed the least bit offended when she mentioned the jacket. *A good kid*, she thought as she inched her way through the shrinking line.

When it was her turn at the checkout, a tall, blue-eyed, blond-haired young girl, probably no more than eighteen, scanned and totaled her items quickly. An elderly man, whom she'd seen at church but whose name escaped her, quickly filled the bags she provided. "Tell your dad that Neil said it's time to get his flu shot."

"Okay," she said, having no clue why he would know that.

"He comes in every year with your mom. They get their shots here at the store. I haven't seen him this year."

"Yes, I'll make sure to tell him. Thanks."

"Most welcome, ma'am," he said, placing the last of her bags in the cart.

Outside, a piercing, blustery wind lifted the ends of her scarf, momentarily blocking her vision. Pulling her scarf away from her face, she blinked, the cold so bitter her eyes teared up. Lauren felt confident she would not be flying to Seattle tomorrow. Though Scott said he doubted the predicted forecast would amount to much, she wasn't so sure. She hurriedly put the bags in the back seat, not worried about spoilage, as the cold temps would prevent that.

She wound her way through the parking lot, the rear tires sliding on the slick surface. "That's not good." She didn't have a lot of experience driving in hazardous conditions, as Fallen Springs rarely got any snow, but she knew enough to know that it was time to finish her errands and call it a day. She glanced at the clock on the dash. After 7:00. By the time she dropped off Charlotte's jacket, it would be close to 8:00 before she made it home. Debating whether to call her mother in order to let her know she might be later than she thought, she decided it could wait; she'd be home soon enough. If her mother became concerned, she knew she would call her. Lauren guessed her mother might need the extra time alone with her dad before she came home with her news.

This all sounded so juvenile, though living with her father, one expected to exist in a continuous time warp.

Chapter 8

Lauren saw the blue house she'd passed hundreds of times without having any idea who lived there. She parked her old Honda in the long driveway, took the bag with the jacket, and stepped out into the bitter-cold evening air. Lauren swore the temperature had dropped again during the ten-minute drive.

The dark blue house was a large two-story, with a wraparound deck and, downstairs, floor-to-ceiling windows, through which anyone inside could peer around the edges of the main entrance for a view of visitors. She was about to ring the bell when it opened.

"Hey, Lauren," Charlotte said. "That was, like, superfast. Come on in."

"Thanks." Lauren stepped inside and was greeted by sumptuous cooking smells, the scent of a wood-burning fire, and a few giggles. She directed her gaze upward. A giant loft overlooked the large entry. Kiley and Lacey gave a short wave, then disappeared for a few seconds.

"We could see you from the street," Lacey explained. "Hope you don't think we're, like, weirdos or anything."

She shook her head. "Not at all. If I had a view like that, I'd be up there, too."

"Girls?" A stunning woman around her own age appeared. She wore dark skinny jeans and a black cashmere sweater. Her jet-black hair was twisted on top of her head in an artfully arranged topknot. Diamond studs sparkled from her ears, and a matching diamond necklace rested just below her clavicle. Silver bracelets dangled from her slender wrists. She had unique, silver-gray eyes, and Lauren couldn't help but stare. She felt dowdy in comparison. "You must be Lauren. I'm Beth, Lacey's mom. We're baking cookies, or rather some of us are baking cookies. Would you like a cup of tea and a cookie? Frankly, my feet could use a break."

Why not? she thought. "Uh, sure, that would be great. It's freezing out there. Do you mind if I use my cell? I need to let my mother know I'm here."

Beth gave her an odd look. "Sure, no worries."

Lauren clarified, "They're expecting me for dinner."

"I'm that obvious, huh? Sorry. Make your call, and I'll put on the kettle. Girls, come help me in the kitchen, please," she called to the girls while she filled a kettle with water. The three teens busied themselves getting cups and plates out of the cupboard.

Appreciative of Beth's allowing her a moment of privacy, Lauren made her call. "Mom, I'm going to be later than expected. Don't hold dinner for me." Her mother assured her it was not a problem since all she had made was homemade vegetable soup and cornbread, which were easy to reheat. She and her father had eaten without her. "I'll see you after a while."

Lauren entered the kitchen, still carrying the shopping bag from Threads.

"Here, let me take that," Beth said, reaching for the bag. "I'm not much of a hostess these days."

"Thanks. I hope I wasn't overstepping my boundaries." Lauren handed over the bag.

"No, not at all. Lee asked me last week if one of the girls had an extra jacket. I told her I'd get her a new one, so really, you just saved me a trip. Thanks," she said. "Char, go on, let's see your new jacket," Beth encouraged.

"Okay." Charlotte took the purple jacket from the bag, then the scarf, gloves, and matching beanie. "Wow, this is so awesome! I love it all." She slipped the jacket on, and it fit perfectly. She twirled around. "It's so sweet of you. Thanks so much."

"You're welcome. I'm just glad I found the right size, though I have to admit, I tried it on just to make sure. We look to be about the same size."

"We said that, right?" Charlotte looked to her friends for confirmation. "That you're smallish."

Kiley and Lacey both agreed.

Lauren laughed. "That I am."

The trio of teenage girls gathered around the table, waiting for her before digging into the plates of sumptuous treats. "We've made five different kinds of cookies. Gingerbread, and rum balls, and they really have rum in them; they're Dad's favorite," Lacey added. "Of course, I had to have mom's chocolate-chip crunchies, and Char likes the candy-cane snowball cookies. So, what do you want?"

Lauren laughed. "Well, if I said one of each, I don't think I'd be able to keep the top button of my jeans fastened, so how about a gingerbread cookie? They're one of my favorites."

Beth placed a tray with five cups of tea in the center of the table. Cream, sugar, lemon, plus a pot of honey, along with a few types of artificial sweeteners. "This smells incredible," Lauren said, nodding at the display of cookies and tea. "Definitely worth missing dinner for."

"Mom would never let me have dessert before dinner," Lacey said.

"True, most of the time," Beth said.

Over tea and cookies, the girls asked her many questions, some about the store, including why didn't they have the Internet, and Kiley asked why she still lived with her parents. Lacey was very interested in the fact that she wasn't married.

Lauren chuckled. "I guess I haven't found the right guy. Sometimes it takes a while, and I'm in no hurry."

"So you can't go to the library and get on one of those online dating sites to look for a date?" Lacey asked.

"Lacey Anne! Stop being so nosy," Beth said, smiling.

The teenager was a miniature of her mother. In a few years, her parents would have to keep a close eye on this budding beauty. "Sorry, I was just curious. I mean she *is* thirty-five, and you're thirty-seven, not much older."

Lauren couldn't hold back her laughter, almost choking on her gingerbread cookie.

"Lacey, that's very rude," Beth admonished in a firm tone.

"Sorry," Lacey replied. "Lauren, I don't mean to be nibby."

Lauren cleared the remaining cookie crumbs from her throat, then took a small sip of tea. "It's fine. Really. I don't think I'd do very well with a dating service. I'd rather go the old-fashioned route," she said in what she hoped was a humorous way.

She changed the topic before poor Lacey got into any more trouble. "Charlotte, how is your mom? Is she willing to stay in the hospital a few more days?"

"She was kinda tired-sounding, but I could tell she was relieved. I think she'll do the transplant. I told her it would be the best Christmas present in the world."

"It certainly would. I am going to do everything in my power to help out, so just stay positive." Lauren finished her tea and took her cup and plate to the sink. "I really need to get home." She looked at the girls still seated around the table. "I used to have a condo on the beach in Florida, but my dad became ill, and I moved in with my parents so I could help care for him." She winked at Beth. "Maybe the four of us—no, five, including your mother when she's well—can all have a girls' spa day or something like that." She looked to Beth.

"It's a plan, as soon as Lee is able. I say we do the town."

Lauren said her good-byes, then Beth walked her to the door. "It's beyond kind, what you're doing for Char and Lee. I haven't seen her this happy in months, and I know it's because she has hope now."

"I'm happy to do what I can. I'm glad we've met, Beth. I'll definitely stay in touch with you and Charlotte. I may be out of town for a few days, but she and Lee have my cell number."

"Good," Beth said. "We'll talk again."

Lauren stepped out into the now-freezing night air, praying that the weather wouldn't get any worse. As soon as she was home, she would call the airlines to check on tomorrow's flight.

Chapter 9

Shivering, with arms full of bags, Lauren used her elbow to ring the doorbell. "It's just me, Mom," she said. Her mother never opened the door without taking a look through the peephole.

The heavy doors opened, and Lauren dropped several bags in the entryway.

"Looks like you bought more than a couple of boxes of cereal," her mother said as she took some of the bags from her.

"Just a few extras. I thought we might need them with this storm they're predicting."

Lauren felt the tension in the air and knew she'd caused it by accepting John Giampalo's offer. "Mom, is everything good? With Dad?"

In the kitchen, Lauren placed her bags on the counter alongside those her mother carried.

"I haven't spoken of your new . . . job just yet. He's in a bit of a tizzy with this storm brewing. He's been glued to the television most of the day, listening for updates. I thought I should wait."

A zillion scenarios ran through her mind. "I'll tell him, Mom. It's fine. Actually, I need to run upstairs and make a couple of phone calls. You okay putting this stuff away?"

"Of course," her mother said. "I'm perfectly capable, dear."

"I know you are." She leaned in to give her mother a hug. "I'll be right down."

Lauren hustled out of the kitchen with the bag from the cable company in hand. Her mother hadn't noticed, and that was fine. Once inside her room, she read through the printed instructions that Brad with the white teeth had given her. First, Lauren booted up her laptop, installed the router and modem, connected this to the cable outlet, then plugged both into the electrical socket, launched the software, and boom, the Montgomerys had Internet access. Lauren almost felt a little guilty for going behind her dad's back, but, she reminded herself, she was a grown woman, with every right to do this. When she had returned to Fallen Springs three years ago, she had, in a sense, given up a modicum of freedom, though her parents had assured her they would never interfere with her private life, and they hadn't, at least not enough that it mattered. The nature of her relationship with Brent Ludmore was a touchy subject, one she tolerated now and then because they'd been friends forever. She'd told her parents on more than one occasion she wasn't interested in him in a romantic way, but her mom always said they crossed their fingers and hoped for the best. She smiled at this memory. Her mother wanted grandchildren, she knew, and someday, if the right guy came along before her childbearing years were over, she hoped to grant her that wish. Being thirty-five years old didn't give her a lot of wiggle room.

She clicked a few keys on her keyboard, and poof, she was Wi-Fi-enabled. "Yes!" she said, punching a fist in the air. First things first. She checked her e-mail for the flight information Angela had sent, then she logged onto the airline's website, checking tomorrow's flight.

Canceled.

Knowing Angela, she was probably on Facebook, so she logged on, saw the green dot, and clicked on her name to send an instant message.

Lauren: FLIGHT HAS BEEN CANCELED!

Angela: SHIT!

Lauren: ;c NOT WHAT I NEED!

Angela: I'LL CALL MR. G, BRB.

Lauren: OKAY . . .

While Angela did her thing, Lauren changed into sweatpants and a baggy T-shirt.

Glancing at the screen, she saw the gray dots bouncing.

Angela: WE'RE GOOD! DELAY APPROVED UNTIL WEATHER CLEARS!

Lauren: PERFECT. THANKS!

Angela: I'LL CALL YOU TOMORROW.

Lauren: OKAY!

She clicked out of the app and googled John Giampalo. While looking forward to this particular endeavor, not to mention the enormous payday that came along with it, she was relieved that she now had a few more days to digest what she'd signed on for. More time to research the man who'd become a household name across the globe. The files Angela had sent earlier were just the tip of the iceberg. She was planning on using this extra time to dig deep into his life and prepare herself for this once-in-a-lifetime opportunity. Hundreds of blue links appeared on her computer screen, and she clicked on the first one. Just the basic information, nothing she didn't know. Later, when she wasn't rushed, she'd refine her search and read as much as she could before meeting him. Lauren liked to be prepared. She logged off the Internet, dreading what she had to tell her dad. Part of her was miffed that she was in this position; the other part of her knew that even though her father was set in his ways, he would be just fine.

She pulled her hair into a ponytail, slipped her Uggs on, and headed downstairs. She wanted to be as comfortable as humanly possible, given the discomfort she was about to cause her father.

Her parents were seated at the table in the kitchen, and as was the norm, they were having coffee and dessert, though tonight, somewhat later than usual.

"Smells delicious," she said as she helped herself to a slice of pecan pie. "I'm sure the calories are off the chart."

"Of course they are, but it's the beginning of the holiday season. It's only natural that we gain a few extra pounds here and there," her mother teased, patting her slim hips. "I try to cut out the cream and sugar in my coffee to make up the difference."

"Neither of you two girls need to watch your weight. If anything, it wouldn't hurt if you gained a few pounds."

"Thanks, Dad. I love to hear that, even though it's not true." Lauren could gain a few pounds, and no one would notice except her waistline. The same for her mother, as they were built alike.

Lauren filled a mug with coffee and sat down opposite her father. "Dad, I need to talk to you about something that's happened, and before you say anything, I need you to hear me out."

"I'm listening," he said.

Lauren glanced at her mother, then back at her father. "I've accepted a contract to write another biography."

His eyes lit up. "Lauren, that's wonderful news. Who's the lucky one?"

This was the part she'd been dreading. Lauren knew her dad was proud of her work, often bragged about it, but since the biography was of this particular person, she was certain that he'd raise the roof the minute she spoke his name. "John Giampalo."

He appeared puzzled. "Never heard of the guy."

She looked at her mom. Of course, he knew who he was. They'd discussed him on more than one occasion. Lauren would swear that he'd totally lost his memory, or that he knew exactly who she referred to and wasn't letting on that he did.

"Dad, are you sure?" she asked a second time. Maybe there *was* something to his forgetfulness?

"I'm sure. Who is he?" he asked.

"Dad, we've talked about Globalgoods.com before. I distinctly remember our conversations. You know, the Internet? Online sales?"

She saw a slight change in his facial expression. His mouth turned down at the corners, and his eyes squinted ever so slightly.

"Nope, I don't know the guy," he persisted.

"Mother? Do you remember us talking about this?" She turned to her because Lauren knew for a fact her mother knew exactly who John Giampalo was. Earlier, they'd discussed how much her dad disliked what Global goods.com represented.

"I do," she answered.

"That's it?" Lauren asked, aggravated at both her parents. "You and I discussed this, you said you would wait and let me tell Dad."

"Yes, I did," her mother agreed.

"And we talked about Dad's lack of enthusiasm on the topic, or did I imagine that?"

"We did, and no, you did not imagine anything."

"Dad? Would you please speak for yourself?" Lauren huffed. "This is beyond childish."

"I think your mother is doing a fine job speaking for me."

Lauren gave her mom the evil eye. "Mother, what is going on? Or isn't?"

"I don't know what you're talking about, dear. We're having coffee and dessert." She lifted her cup in front of her lips.

"I can see that." Lauren knew she'd have to take control of the conversation; otherwise, the three of them could banter back and forth all night.

"Dad, you know the World Wide Web? The Internet? Online shopping? You are aware of what this is, right?" She shot out the questions with more force than normal.

"Of course, I do. I'm not senile," he answered.

Lauren questioned that at this very moment but went on. "The guy who started online shopping, John Giampalo, he wants *me* to write his biography. And I said yes."

He stared at her but didn't say a word.

He knew exactly who she was referring to. This was the stubborn side of her father showing, and thankfully, he didn't let it appear too often.

But she was as stubborn as he was, and she could return the stare as long as he dared, knowing now that this was a battle of wills. "I know you know who he is. And for the record, I think you're acting ridiculous. You too, Mother. If you don't want to discuss it, fine. I'm going to bed. Someone has to run Razzle Dazzle, despite the dwindling sales. If you two will excuse me, I'm calling it a night." Lauren dumped her half-eaten slice of pie into the garbage disposal, rinsed the plate off, and put it in the dishwasher. She felt their stares but was not going to give in. Her parents were dolls, but sometimes they acted like dolts. It was one of those times.

"Good night," she called as she left the kitchen.

Upstairs, in the privacy of her own room, she mentally chastised herself for losing patience with her father, and her mother too, but at the same time, she felt justified. They were treating her like a child, and in doing so, they themselves were acting so childish.

"Heck with it," she said, grabbing her laptop and plopping down on the bed. Feeling like a sulking teenager who had been sent to her room, Lauren logged on to the Internet and continued to research John Giampalo. She read several more articles and decided she liked the man already. He was quite the philanthropist, donating to dozens of charities, not to mention numerous social and humanitarian causes. A supporter of art, culture, and education, John Giampalo had certainly shared his wealth, and it appeared that he truly tried to make a difference in the lives of so many. She read through at least a dozen more items, and all were positive. It seemed no one had a negative word to say about him. Lauren knew this was apt to change. He sounded like a decent guy, certainly intelligent enough to seize the moment when the World Wide Web was in its infancy. Lauren read yet another article and was surprised to discover John Giampalo was a University of Florida alumnus. Why she didn't know that was beyond her, but in her opinion, it only added to his likability factor.

Lauren bookmarked several web pages to peruse later when she wasn't so dog tired. She still had to contact the newspapers in the surrounding towns and place the ads she'd discussed with Brent. Having the ability to do this at home—using the Internet was so easy—she completed the task in minutes. If she'd called, as her father would have done, she would have been on the phone forever making sure the ads were correct. And she could not have done it until the morning. Why he couldn't bring his life and her mother's into this century continued to baffle her. Lauren would try to convince him this truly was the way of the future, but not now. She was completely wiped out. Slipping into a pair of flannel pajamas, she slid beneath the covers and was asleep within minutes.

Chapter 10

Lauren couldn't believe what a good night's sleep could do for one's disposition. She'd gone to bed a bit ticked at her father's stubbornness and her mother's willingness to play along.

But it was a new day, and she decided that she would keep the details of her newly acquired contract to herself. Angela had sent her a copy of the book contract late last night, and she'd read through it this morning while she lingered in bed. Though it was so common in most households, she decided against revealing she had access to the Internet at home. That old saying "What you don't know, won't hurt you" could be applied in this case.

Lauren closed her laptop and quickly made up the bed. Twenty minutes later, she was showered, dressed, and sipping a cup of tea in the kitchen. Her parents were still sleeping. She enjoyed the early-morning quiet, the privacy, and was having second thoughts about continuing to live in the house. She could stay in the guest cottage, though it would require a few repairs; she would mention it to her mother later, when they decided to act like grown-ups instead of ten-year-olds. Or not. But then she'd be acting like a kid herself. That would be silly, and she laughed at the pure childishness of her thoughts.

"Somebody's in a good mood," her mother said, entering the kitchen.

"Mom, you're up early," Lauren commented. "Dad okay?"

"I let him sleep in; he needs his rest."

Lauren placed a pod of her mother's favorite Dunkin' Donuts coffee in the Keurig—the sole twenty-first-century item to be found in the house, only tolerated because Lauren had insisted on having one when she had come home three years ago—then clicked the BREW button. As soon as the cup finished, she held the cup out to her mother. "No cream or sugar, right?"

"Watching my waistline, dear. Thank you." Her mother was wearing the same yellow chenille robe she'd had since Lauren was a little girl. The bend in the elbows had thinned, and the belt she wrapped around her waist was not much more than a few strands of material struggling to stay together.

Definitely time for a new robe. Lauren would order her one for Christmas. And she'd use the Internet. A flash of humor crossed her face.

"What are you smiling about?" her mother asked. "You didn't seem too happy last night."

Lauren sat in the chair across from her mother. "And you know why, too. What I don't understand is why you didn't back me up, at least tell Dad to listen to what I had to say. I felt a little blindsided, if you want to know the truth." She took a sip of her tea.

"No, that was not my intention. I'm sorry. Your father was so hyped up over the weather, I just didn't want to upset him more than necessary. He's been so touchy lately."

"Mother, you're just putting off the inevitable by treating him like an invalid. First of all, he's not mentally encumbered in any way, at least none that I know of. He can either accept what I'm going to do for John Giampalo or not. It's his choice. And while we're speaking of choices, I think it's time I told you that the sales on Black Friday weekend weren't that good. I placed a few ads in the papers last night, but I'm not sure if they'll help at this point." Lauren took another drink of tea. Now was the time to tell her mother the cold, hard facts. Before her father joined them. "Yesterday, I called my financial adviser. I asked him to deposit enough money in Razzle Dazzle's account to keep us going for a couple of months. If Dad doesn't make the leap into the twenty-first century, there isn't going to be a lot of hope for the store's future."

"But I thought you said the sales were decent."

"We sold all of Jenny Farrow's pieces to one couple. Had it not been for that, we would've barely covered the commissions on a couple of your crafters' sales." She knew it was not what her mother wanted to hear, but she didn't see much point in putting off telling her the truth any longer. She was bound to see the bank statements; most likely, they'd arrive in today's mail.

Lauren's heart saddened at the expression on her mother's face, hating that she'd had to be so real, so blunt with her. This living in the past had to stop, and new attitudes might as well start immediately, with her new writing contract. They couldn't remain in the dark forever.

"All you have to do is take a close look at the bank statements, Mom. While we're not in debt, thank goodness, we aren't making much profit in the store. Again, if you and Dad would consider adding a website for Razzle Dazzle, I wouldn't be surprised if sales for the month of December would carry us throughout the year. You both have to open your eyes and see what's really happening in the world today." Lauren went to the sink, rinsed her mug out, and placed it in the dishwasher.

"I can see exactly what is happening," her father said, entering the kitchen. He was fully showered, shaved, and dressed. The scent of Prell shampoo clung to his damp hair, and the faintest odor of a new cologne wafted off him.

"Dad," Lauren said.

"Lauren," he returned, his voice matter-of-fact.

Her mother hurried to make a cup of coffee for her husband. "Al, sit down. Lauren wants to talk to you. I'm not going to play referee, either."

"Good morning to you too, Ilene," her father said, in what Lauren thought of as his king-of-the-castle tone of voice. He sat in his usual place, and Lauren saw no sign that his movements were a struggle. Maybe today was going to be one of his better days.

Her mother placed the coffee in front of him. "I'm going upstairs to shower. You two can help yourselves to cereal or whatever you want."

Lauren couldn't help but laugh. This was her mother's way of telling her dad to "deal with it or else," without actually saying the words. There had been a few episodes like this when she was a teenager. Times changed. She was not going to play along with their childlike games.

"I'm not having breakfast," Lauren said. "You need help with yours?" This was the least she could do. He was, after all, on many days unable to do much of anything other than sit down.

"I am perfectly capable of making my own bowl of cereal, Lauren," he said. "I'll eat in a bit." He sipped at his coffee, his gaze appearing to be a million miles away.

"Look, Dad, I know you're upset with me. About the book. But I can't pass up this opportunity. It would be foolish of me. And of you to think I shouldn't take it."

"I haven't said anything about this to you, so why do you assume that I'm against it?" He directed his gaze to hers.

"Last night. You didn't acknowledge what we both know you're trying to avoid. You let Mom make a fool of herself, and I think you'd at least be a little bit remorseful about that."

"I suppose I deserve that," he said. "I didn't want to discuss this man last night, and frankly, it isn't something I want to talk about now. Lauren, you do what you must, and that's all I'll say. Now, if you'll grab me that carton of milk, I'm going to fix myself a bowl of cereal."

Stunned, it took her a minute to absorb what he had said. "As you said, you're 'perfectly capable of making *your* own bowl of cereal.' I won't stand in your way," Lauren stated before sailing out of the kitchen and heading upstairs. She didn't ever recall a time, at least since she'd returned to Fallen Springs as an adult, when she'd had any major disagreement with her parents. Or at least one that was so divisive, pitting her against them. Or her against her father. Both of them would have to learn to live with the decisions she made for herself. And if they didn't climb out of the past, they were going to lose a lot more than an argument with her. They'd lose a family legacy when Razzle Dazzle Décor fell headlong into bankruptcy. Even though she would do whatever she had to in order to prevent that from happening.

Chapter 11

Lauren was glad she'd caught Maggie on her way out. She'd been so irked earlier this morning, she had forgotten to call her to tell her she wouldn't have to work at the shop today. She was thankful that she had remembered as soon as she'd unlocked the back door. With her flight canceled, there was no reason for Lauren to stay at home while someone else worked. Now that she could set up a Wi-Fi connection to use at the store, she could just as easily do her research between customers. If they were lucky enough to have any.

In her office, settled in, Lauren had read through dozens of articles on John Giampalo when her stomach reminded her of the time.

She'd been in such a rush this morning, she hadn't bothered to bring anything for lunch, so she called over to Ruby's Diner and placed an order. She hadn't eaten dinner last night, only that gingerbread cookie at Beth's and half a slice of pecan pie, and she was famished. Glancing at the clock, Lauren hurried to the front of the store, placed her OUT TO LUNCH sign in the window, exited through the front door, and raced down King Street, covering the two blocks to Ruby's in record time. The midmorning air cut right through the heavy wool sweater she wore. As she picked up her pace, she felt silly for not taking an extra minute to put on her jacket. The sharp icy air stung her cheeks, and the gusty wind sent her long, blond hair dancing around her shoulders. She managed to gather a handful, smoothing it down as she stepped inside Ruby's. Lauren smelled the famous yeast rolls and smiled. She'd ordered the lunch special, no clue what Tuesday's was, but she knew that whatever it was, it would include those soft, buttery yeast rolls that practically melted in her mouth. She found a seat at the counter while she waited for her order.

"I thought you wanted this to go," Ruby called out from the kitchen. At almost noon, the place was practically empty, but Lauren knew that in ten minutes, the place would be packed with diners from many of the local businesses.

"I'll eat it here today," she said, suddenly changing her mind. She hadn't had a single customer all morning, and she needed a change of scenery.

"Gotcha," Ruby called to her. "Two minutes."

"No hurry," she replied.

Ruby came bursting out through the kitchen's double doors, a plate in each hand. She placed them on the counter. "Tuesday's special. You let me know what you think," Ruby said before returning to her kitchen.

Macaroni and cheese, with chunks of ham, a large portion of green beans, a freshly made salad, and, of course, three yeast rolls. Lauren wouldn't be able to zip her jeans if she ate all the food, but she was hungry and was going to give it her best.

Each bite tasted divine, and each warm, buttered roll practically slid down her throat. Eating at Ruby's was heavenly. It was a good thing she didn't eat here often or she'd be in big trouble. A couple of times a week was more than enough. "Ruby, you're the best. I don't think I've ever tasted mac and cheese like yours."

"Nope, you haven't. It's an old family recipe, and Louise and me are takin' it to our graves," she called out from behind the counter. "Glad you approve. You want to take some home for your mom and dad? I've made enough to feed the entire town."

"No, thanks, I think they're starting to watch what they eat for the next few weeks, just so they can consume all the goodies Mom will bake, but I'll tell her you offered. Gotta run. I'll see you later," Lauren said. She left a ten-dollar bill under her plate and left just in time to see the lunch crowd gathering outside the diner. She hurried the two blocks to Razzle Dazzle, crossing her fingers that she'd have a few customers this afternoon. Entering through the back door, Lauren walked to the front of the store, removed her OUT TO LUNCH sign, and unlocked the door.

When she'd left for lunch earlier, a big gust of wind had blown in, causing some of the ornaments on the tree in the window to get tossed around. She made a few adjustments to a delicate glass star and a handblown, tree-shaped ornament before returning to the office to continue her research on Globalgoods.com. As far as she could tell, this man who'd changed the way most of the world shopped was truly a generous, kind man, though she would wait until she met him in person before she made up her mind. Anyone can look good on paper. Lauren had good instincts, and she trusted them. Rarely had they been wrong.

The little bell she'd hung at the entrance chimed, letting her know she finally had a customer. She hurried out of the office to greet her lone visitor.

"Madison, what in the world are you doing here? Aren't you supposed to be teaching great things to all those little minds?" Lauren gave her a hug.

"Today was a half day. Yesterday, the high school and middle school had their turn, so here I am. I thought I'd check on you, see if you learned anything more from James, plus Scott told me he saw you at the store last night. Said you looked 'distressed,' though I'm not sure in what context. Things okay with your parents?"

Lauren sighed. "Let's go in the office. I'll make us a cup of tea and fill you in."

"Sounds good," Madison said.

Lauren put her glass kettle in the microwave and took two clean mugs, dropping a black tea bag in each. "Dad's fine physically, Mom's good, but I swear I had the craziest falling-out of sorts with them last night, and it continued this morning." She filled the cups with boiling water, added sugar for Madison, and handed her the tea.

"How so?" Madison asked, seating herself on the sagging sofa.

Lauren sat beside her. "How long do you have?" She laughed. "Seriously, the past twenty-four hours have been crazy. I was going to tell you, but I haven't had a chance. I got an e-mail from Angela yesterday—you know, my agent?"

"The one from New York."

"The one and only." She blew on her tea to cool it off. "She has a new contract, another biography, and you will never guess who the subject is."

"Okay, so you want me to drag it out of you? That means it's a goodie. Okay, first guess: Brad Pitt?"

"Not even close," Lauren said.

"Okay, Chris Hemsworth?"

"I wish, but nope. Way too cold."

"Let's see. Hmm, George Clooney? No, he's too old, never mind. I think Brad Pitt is old, too. A little bit."

"I don't write bios of movie stars."

"Hey, a girl can hope, right?"

"I suppose. I'll give you one more guess, and that's it."

"Has to be someone in the business world." Madison drummed her perfectly shaped nails against her mug. "I give up. I can't think of anyone worthy enough," she said.

"I was shocked myself, so I know you will be, too. John Gerard Giampalo."

Lauren observed her best friend, curious how she'd respond.

Madison set her cup on the side table. "You're joking? Isn't he one of the richest men in the world, or America, or something like that?"

"Yep, the one and only. He's the head of Global goods.com and the king of online commerce." Lauren smiled, and for the first time since she'd learned of this opportunity, she was extremely excited.

"Oh, Lauren, that is the best news ever. Give me all the dirty details. You know what I mean," she added.

"Actually, I don't think I've comprehended this myself until now. The timing is off, and Dad—well, you know how he feels about online anything, so it wasn't pretty when I told him. Actually, he was ticked off last night *and* this morning when I broached the subject."

"I know your dad; he's not real hip on the web. He'll warm up, I'm sure, once he realizes what a huge opportunity this is for you."

"I'm not going to hold my breath on that. He's so determined to keep this family-lineage thing, if you will, as it was in his day and Grandpa's, that part of me feels like this is a lost cause. Mom, she'll be okay with it. I think she'd enjoy using the Internet, too, but she stands beside her man and all that jazz." Lauren sipped her tea.

"That's just her generation," Madison added. "Though your parents aren't that old."

"No, they're not, but I think they enjoy their fifties-style marriage, though I have to say Mom is very independent. She did have her own career."

"Well, I'm sure you'll work this out. So, how are you going to manage to run the store *and* write a book?"

Lauren shook her head. "Shouldn't be too hard considering we're not all that busy this year—Black Friday was awful—so I'm using that as my baseline for what the rest of the season will be like. I can work here just as easily as I can anyplace else. I went to the cable company yesterday, and I now have access to the Internet at home and here, so that part will be easy. I was supposed to fly out to Seattle this afternoon. Of course, with this storm, my flight was canceled, so here I am."

Madison drained the last of her tea, placing her cup on the small table beside the old sofa. "Are you heading north after this storm, or do you know?"

"Yes, and I'll let you in on the details as soon as I have them. Speaking of details, I can't tell you how much I appreciate your making that call to James. He's given hope to a family, and right now, it seems that's about all they have."

"You're talking about Lee and her daughter?" Madison asked.

Lauren nodded. "I bought a jacket for Charlotte, and took it to Beth Keener's house, that's where she's staying until her mom is . . . better."

"You mean Beth Simms, the knockout?"

"Said one knockout. You know her?"

Madison rolled her eyes. She was not the least bit vain. "Yes, she was a couple of years ahead of us in high school. Homecoming queen, cheerleader, and I'm pretty sure she was a runner-up in the Miss North Carolina Pageant back in the day. I always thought she'd move up north and become a famous fashion model or an actress."

"That explains it. She's stunning, and so is her daughter, Lacey. She's super nice; I had tea and cookies with her and the girls. Apparently, Charlotte and her daughter have been BFFs since they were babies, plus there's another girl, Kiley. They refer to themselves as the Three Musketeers. No matter, Beth is acting as a stand-in parent while Lee's in the hospital."

"Then I'm thrilled to have helped out, even in a small way." Madison got up and put the teakettle back in the microwave. "I have an idea."

Lauren held out her mug. "Dare I ask what it is?"

"I'm thinking. I know Lee—rather, I used to. She married some guy right out of high school; it didn't last, as you know, but get this," Madison said, filling their cups with hot water and fresh tea bags. "She would be perfect for Brent Ludmore."

Lauren reached for her mug and stopped. "She's sick, Maddy, like not-sure-if-she'll-make-it sick!"

"Let's not think that way. We have to be positive. You, of all people, should know this. Let's say she beats this disease. She's beautiful, at least when I last saw her she was; she's kind, and we know her. I think she and Brent would make a perfect couple. Yes, we'll have a few hurdles to jump, but promise me you'll think about it."

Lauren laughed. "I can do that, but first, we have to make sure she's well. As in forever. I wouldn't want"—she was going to say she didn't want to strap Brent down with a dying woman, but that was too crude—"to pressure either one. But if she gets through this, I'll do my part in steering Brent in her direction, or vice versa."

"Tell me what you know about her illness," Madison said, returning to the old sofa.

"Not much more than I told you yesterday. She has leukemia, that's all I know. Oh, and her daughter, Charlotte, is a bone-marrow match. Lee needs a transplant, as in yesterday. She was going to be released last evening, and that's why I asked James to step in, see if he could pull a few strings, keep her there a while longer. She's doomed if she gets a cold, or any kind of infection. Frankly, that's all I know about the disease. I probably have overstepped some boundary here, but she needed help."

"And it's genetically programmed in your DNA to help," Madison said, though she was smiling. "Same as Brent's."

"Apparently," Lauren agreed.

"Why do I feel like you're not telling me everything? Remember, I know you."

Madison knew her well. Lauren wanted to keep the financial end quiet, but if she was going to involve herself in Lee's health, Madison was her best friend. Lauren wanted her to know what she'd committed to, even if it was only to herself.

"Yep, there's more."

"I'm listening."

"This book contract is financially life-changing, though, of course, it depends on whether I can write it and it finds a home with a publisher." She took a deep breath. "That aside, I was going to help fund Lee's hospital bills."

There. The cat was out of the bag.

Madison stared at her.

"Tell me if it's not my business, but exactly how much is life-changing?"

They didn't have secrets. Though they never discussed their financial situations in detail, Lauren knew Madison's salary, knew Scott made a hefty wage, and Madison knew she was financially stable.

"Three-point-five million dollars' worth."

Madison's lips formed a circle, but no sound came from her mouth.

"I know. I'm still in shock. Of course, Angela has her fees, taxes, you know how it is, but it's more than enough to cover Lee's medical costs. James told me there's a thing called an indigent fund at the hospital. Says most hospitals have them, but they don't advertise it. He was pretty sure that Lee's treatment would qualify her."

Madison shook her head, her raven-colored hair swinging from side to side, her blue eyes sparkling. "Amazing. Doesn't she have insurance from her job at the post office?"

"Apparently, it's catastrophic. Although I don't know how much more catastrophic one can get. So, long story short, I'm going to try to help out, set up an account for them. It'll be my good deed for the month."

"Month? You mean the year, the century."

"Now you're all caught up on my life. Your turn," Lauren said.

The bell on the customer entrance jingled.

"You are literally saved by that bell I hung up earlier. Don't move."

A young couple, probably in their mid-twenties, said hello and walked up and down the aisles, then thanked her and left. "Sure," Lauren said to the door, then hurried back to the office to resume her conversation.

"Okay, it's still your turn."

"Don't you have customers?"

"No, they were browsers."

"I do kind of have something to tell you, but you have to keep it a secret."

"Always."

"This is a really *big* secret, Lauren. As in humongous. Probably the biggest secret I'll ever tell you."

"Stop it! Just spit it out and tell me."

"I'm pregnant!"

"Holy moly! Are you serious?"

"Would I joke about something we've been trying for since forever? Yes, Scott and I are going to be parents! Isn't that the most exciting news you've ever heard?"

Lauren reached across the old shabby sofa, hugged her best friend, and immediately looked at her stomach.

"I'm not showing yet, if that's what you're looking for. It's too soon. I'm only eight weeks, and I can't tell you how much I wanted to tell you yesterday, but I had to wait until we had some girl time."

Tears filled Lauren's eyes because she knew how much Madison and Scott wanted a family. "That's the best news I've heard in a very long time. That explains all that junk food in Scott's shopping cart when I ran into him at the grocery last night. You little sneak, you!" Lauren hugged her again. "Wow, this is big."

"Here's the not-so-fun part. Other than Scott, I haven't told anyone else. I wanted to wait until I was through my first trimester. You okay keeping this to yourself for a few more weeks?"

"No, but since I don't have a choice, yes, I will keep it to myself. Though Mom would be on cloud nine if she knew this. Dad too."

"We haven't even told our parents, so yours, they'll just have to wait. I know it's asking a lot to keep this quiet. I just couldn't keep this to myself any longer. Scott said you commented on the junk food in his shopping cart. I thought you might figure it out, so I wanted to tell you face-to-face, hence the real reason I stopped by."

"I'm beyond happy for you two. So, boy or girl?"

"I don't know yet, and won't for several more weeks."

"I get that. I meant what are you and Scott hoping for?"

"I don't care, either will be absolutely perfect. A baby! Oh, Lauren, I am so over the moon, I don't know if I can wait seven more months to meet this little bean. That's the size. Can you believe it? A bean or, the doctor said, a raspberry. Just so itty-bitty!"

Lauren chuckled. "You'll be a great mom, Scott a great dad. This changes a lot. Right?"

"Yes and no. I'll have a bump, which I can't wait for, and no, I'll continue life as usual. I'll probably take some time off work once the baby is here, but I don't foresee any huge changes."

They burst out laughing.

"That's bull, and I know it. My entire life will change,

but Lauren, it'll be in such a good way. Listen, I need to get out of here, let you do your work." She paused, a dazed look on her face. "Did I just blow the wind out of your book sails, pun intended?"

"Never! I don't think my news compares." She walked Madison to the front of the store. She saw her bright red Corvette parked outside. "You might have to consider another vehicle, though."

"I don't like that car anyway. I'll be getting an SUV or a minivan. Something family-like. Oh, Lauren, let me hug you one more time, then I'll get out of your hair."

Lauren gave her a hug, promised to keep her updated on Lee's health, and congratulated her once again.

Inside the store, she couldn't help but smile, despite herself. Madison's was the best news she'd heard all day.

Chapter 12

Lauren left the shop, shocked at how the temperature had dropped; it was a mere ten degrees, according to the gauge on the dash. Hundreds of tiny white snowflakes flurried from the inky sky and were wiped away by the windshield wipers as fast as they fell. She drove slowly down the sleeted highway, the Honda's wheels struggling to get a firm grip on the icy road. The heater did little to keep up with the bitter cold. Lauren couldn't wait to get home, take a hot shower, and continue to work on her research.

She was surprised when she saw that the house was dark, with no warm light reflecting in the windows. That was unusual. She hurried out of the car and jiggled with her keys. Inside, the house was dark and too cold. She went to the kitchen and flipped on the lights. On the center of the table was a note in her mother's perfect cursive handwriting.

Lauren, dear,
We've gone to visit Grandpa. Will be home late. There's soup in the fridge if you're hungry.
XOXO,
Mom.

"In this weather, Mom? Really," Lauren said to an empty room. She adjusted the thermostat in the living room, then returned to the kitchen. She wasn't hungry after the lunch she'd had at Ruby's, but a cup of tea would warm her up. Using her mother's old-fashioned cast-iron teakettle, she clicked the stovetop on and waited. She chose an orange-spice tea, knowing it had a kick. Lauren needed a kick just then. She was tired, and knowing her parents had to drive back from the Upside in Pine City, the luxury assisted-living facility her grandfather called home, she would be lucky to accomplish any work until they were home safely.

She rolled her eyes. She was worse than her mother. Still, this kind of wicked cold was not normal for the area, and Lauren wasn't sure her mother or dad could handle the roads. She'd crawled home at fifteen miles an hour, fearing she'd slide off the slick surfaces. Neither of her parents had a cell phone, so calling them was out of the question. Just one more twenty-first century convenience her father dismissed as frivolous and unnecessary.

Lauren took her tea upstairs to her room and took a warm shower. She slipped into leggings, a sweatshirt, and warm socks, then sat on the bed with her laptop, ready to research her new subject. She read article after article on

Giampalo, finding nothing too negative. When she glanced at the bedside clock, it was after ten. Her parents should have been home already. Worried, she peered out her window at the winding drive leading up to the house. Her heartbeat steadied when she saw the lights of their old Chevy station wagon coming up the drive.

She put away her laptop and headed downstairs. She really did want to hear about their visit. She hadn't seen her grandfather in a couple of months, and now with her new book contract, she wasn't sure when she'd have time to make the hour-long drive to Pine City. Lauren did talk with him on the telephone weekly, but she knew that was no substitute for an actual visit. Again, if he would step into the new age, they could FaceTime, but just like her father, he refused to acknowledge what most of the world now thought of as normal.

She put the kettle on for a second time, knowing they'd appreciate a hot drink. Lauren heard them bustling through the front door, keys dropping into the dish, coats being hung in the closet. She smiled. If you wanted routine and predictability, her parents were the textbook definition.

"Hey, Mom. Dad," Lauren greeted them as they entered the kitchen. She felt the cold emanating from them. "I've made tea," she said, and placed two large mugs on the table.

"You should be in bed," her mother commented, "though I appreciate this. I don't remember it ever being this cold in Fallen Springs. The weather forecast was certainly accurate." Her mother was wearing black slacks and a heavy, dark green wool sweater. Her cheeks were flushed from the cold, her hair alive with static from her sweater and the lack of moisture in the bitter night air. She slid into her usual seat across from her husband.

"This is nice, Lauren. Thank you," her father said, his speech stilted and void of his usual cheerfulness. Obviously, he was still upset with her.

"No problem. So, how was Grandpa?" she asked, wanting to change the subject. "I miss him."

"Al is doing fantastic at the Upside. He's made so many friends and is involved in all they have to offer, which is one of the reasons we're so late. They have a Christmas play every year, and we watched them rehearse. They're quite exceptional. I told Al we would try to make it to opening day, provided this weather isn't a factor. It was a treacherous drive home."

"I was concerned when I came home and saw you two weren't here," Lauren said, though she was smiling when she said this to let them know she wasn't upset with them. And why should she be? They were entitled to get out of the house. She had to stop thinking of them as older than their chronological ages. Maybe if they weren't so stuck in the past, she could.

"Lauren, thank you for the tea. I'm going to call it a night. I'll see you two ladies in the morning," her father said as he took his cup and placed it in the sink. Her mother quickly followed behind him, rinsing his cup and placing it in the dishwasher. In the past, Lauren hadn't paid that much attention to these minute details, but now she did.

"Night," she called out, but she was more concerned with her mother's actions. As soon as he was out of earshot, she spoke. "Can't he put his own cup in the dishwasher anymore? He's moving easily enough tonight."

"Lauren, why in the world would you say that? I always take care of these silly things."

"I know, Mom, but he's capable, too. I know this

rheumatoid arthritis is tough on him, but I think he needs to stop expecting you to wait on him hand and foot when he does have good days. He's ticked at me, but that doesn't mean I'm going to follow him around as though he's a two-year-old, catering to his every wish." Lauren drained the last of her tea. "He needs as much independence as his health allows."

"Actually, his doctors have had him on a new medication for a couple of weeks. It's in pill form, so he won't have to have those injections. He's terrified of needles, so this news has lifted his spirits tremendously."

Lauren squinted. "What? Dad doesn't like needles? Since when?"

"Since forever. He's actually quite embarrassed about it. That's why he refuses when you offer to go to Dr. Keller's office with him. To be honest"—her mother looked toward the door, probably making sure her husband wasn't listening—"it's stressful on me, though I've never told him this. It's bad enough he has this debilitating arthritis."

"I know it is, but he's always been so . . . well, a bit controlling. In a nice way," she added, so her mother wouldn't take offense.

"I don't mind doing extra chores for your dad. I enjoy taking care of my family. You too," she added.

Lauren felt silly and childish for her remarks. There was no point in arguing with her mother, if that's what you could call what she was doing. Her mother was as stuck in her wifely ways as her father was in refusing to step into the modern world everyone outside this house lived in.

"Just forget I said anything. It's been a long day, Mom. I'm going up to bed. Is there anything you need before I go upstairs?" She always asked this, and rarely did her mother or father ask much of her.

"How were sales today?" her mother asked.

Not usually so blunt, Lauren took a deep breath, preparing to exaggerate the number of customers. But it was wrong to do that, and she knew she had to stop. She would start now. No time like the present. "They were terrible, Mom as in, none. *Nada.* We had a couple of people come in to browse, and that was it. Madison stopped by for tea, we had a nice chat, caught up with each other's lives. That pretty much sums up my day." She hadn't told her about Lee Hessinger—she would eventually, but only when the time was right.

"I don't understand why. Razzle Dazzle has prospered for decades. This isn't normal, Lauren. I remember a time when I could barely keep the shelves stocked," her mother said, clearly disappointed in Lauren's answer.

Here we go again, Lauren thought. *But no, I am not getting into this with her now.* She'd already tired of the discussion, which had been going on for the past three years. Eventually, they would understand. If not, that was the end of the line for Razzle Dazzle Décor. And while she felt that it was her duty to fund the shop for a couple of months, after that, her parents would have to come to terms with the new reality, and she prayed they would join the rest of the civilized world in the twenty-first century.

"Mom, we've had this discussion so many times that, honestly, I'm too bushed to get into it all over again right now. You know where I stand, and so does Dad. It might help if you'd convince him to think of expanding." She walked over to where her mother sat, gave her a hug, and kissed the top of her head. "Night, Mom."

Upstairs in her room, Lauren slipped on her flannel pajamas and slid beneath the heavy covers. Her mind went over the events of the day. She smiled when she thought of Madison's news. She and Scott had been trying for years to get pregnant, and now it was their new reality. She couldn't wait until this new little being was introduced to the world. She often thought of her own biological clock, her dreams to one day have a family of her own. It might not happen for her. She thought she was good with that, but now, hearing Madison, seeing the joy, the excitement of what lay ahead of her, she couldn't help but feel a tad bit envious. Some women weren't meant to have children, and maybe she was one of those women. Career-oriented. Driven. A cat lady.

"Geez," she said in the darkness, but in that darkness an idea formed, just a seed, but still, it was something she could pursue on her own and would bring her so much joy. The more she thought about it, the more determined she was to set her plan into motion.

Yes, she would be busy with this book, if all worked as Angela seemed to think it would. And yes, she had to help her parents with the family store and all the issues that came along with that, but this was something she could do for herself, and in doing so, she'd be providing a home for an animal in need.

Lauren was going to adopt a cat. With that in mind, she went to sleep, at peace with the world.

Chapter 13

Lauren was out of the house before her parents were up. She had plenty of time to do what she'd planned before she had to open Razzle Dazzle.

It took fifteen minutes for the heater in her car to warm up. If the gauge on her dash was correct, it was a mere eight degrees, well below freezing. She hadn't lowered the thermostat in the shop, so hopefully it wouldn't be too cold. But first, she had to make a stop at the local animal shelter.

Waking up at 4:00 A.M., she hadn't been able to get back to sleep. Having the Internet at her fingertips, she was able to learn what she needed to do to adopt an animal from the local shelter. She was fairly certain she met the requirements, but still, one never knew. They opened their doors at 7:30, and she planned to be there. She'd often thought of getting a pet when she'd lived in Florida but could never commit because of her lifestyle. She was footloose and fancy-free, and at the time, it would have been unfair to have an animal, then leave it all alone. Now her life was different. She was settled now and knew the responsibilities associated with having an animal. In addition, Lauren felt confident that her parents would welcome another pet. They'd always had a dog or a cat when she was growing up, and their last cat, Buzz, named for his short coat of fur, had lived to the ripe old age of twenty-two before giving up the ghost. When she'd moved to Florida, any thought of another pet was put aside.

She parked the car, bundled up with her coat from two seasons ago, plus two extra layers for added warmth, and was still shivering when she stepped out into the early-morning chill. The skies were gray, and dark clouds hung low over the Blue Ridge Mountains. Yet jewel-toned evidence of autumn still clung to branches that would soon be barren. The wind bit into her exposed skin, and she secured her scarf so only her eyes were exposed to the elements.

As soon as she stepped inside the shelter, she heard dozens of cats meowing, dogs growling, barking, and producing a few mournful howls. A parrot resting on a man-made branch screeched, "Good morning. Please have a seat."

"That's Beau, our receptionist. At least he thinks he is," said a young girl. "Are you here to adopt or volunteer?"

Lauren paused for a second, "I'd love to do both, but today I'd like to adopt. A cat. For now." The more barking and meows she heard, the more she wanted to adopt every single pet in the shelter, but she knew that was unreasonable. However, she had another thought. Didn't shelters need donors, *financial* donors? Of course they did. She added them to her mental checklist.

"Then follow me, and I'll introduce you to our family."

Lauren trailed behind her, then went through a set of steel doors. The animals were all lined up on either side of the walls in cages, which broke her heart, but the cages were huge, and most of the dogs were together. Some lay side by side, others jumped up on their hind legs, paws on the mesh, as though they were saying, "Pick me, pick me." Tears filled her eyes. She wanted all the animals. Dogs, cats, birds. They all tugged at her heartstrings, but again, she knew she had to be reasonable.

"We've got a momma cat, she just had two kitties, and they're as sweet as sugar." The young girl took her to an area away from the rest of the animals. Inside another fenced-in area was a big fluffy tabby cat and two tiny matches snuggled against their mother. "They need a home."

"No way am I taking kittens from their mother, or vice versa."

"Of course not. We don't allow that here, anyway. However, we do allow one to adopt these little felines, but only as a family."

"Oh," was all Lauren could say.

Rooted to the floor, she stooped and stuck two fingers through the mesh. The mother cat meowed, then edged herself and her babies up to the mesh. Momma cat rubbed her nose against Lauren's fingers, giving off a soft meow. "I can take all three?" she asked, but her mind had already been made up the second Momma cat rubbed her soft little nose against her fingers.

"That would be awesome, but we ask that you keep them together. It's one of our conditions."

"I'll promise you they'll stay together." Lauren quickly signed the required adoption papers and agreed to allow Dr. Melloh, a veterinarian who volunteered his services at the shelter, to come to her house and inspect it. While she didn't know they'd go to such an extreme, she was glad they did. Sending an animal into a new home was a very big deal. Of course, it should be investigated.

"Dr. Melloh will be there tomorrow, but I'll have to call you with an exact time, if that's okay?" the young girl asked while Lauren signed the papers and stacked them into a neat pile. "We've named the kittens, but, of course, you're free to change the names if you want."

"What are you calling them?" Lauren asked.

"Momma is Daisy, the female is Evie, and the male, well, since it's Christmas time, we called him Yule."

Lauren burst out laughing. "I love it! Would Evie, *Eve*, refer to Christmas *Eve*?"

"You're a quick study. Though Daisy was named by her original owner. She's four. Sadly, she lost her mom right before she had the kittens. She was brought here by a neighbor who'd wanted to keep her but couldn't because of an allergy. So she's been queen of the house, and we hope these two little buggers will be a prince and princess."

Lauren's heart filled with instant love for her new furry family. She'd make sure they were treated like royalty. Now all she had to do was let her mom and dad in on her decision. "Oh, they're gonna be well loved and cared for. I can promise that."

"I can see that. Now, as soon as Dr. Melloh makes his

house call, we'll contact you, and if all goes well, and I'm sure it will, you can take these little kitties to their new home. We have a few basic supplies we can give you, but if you're able to purchase beds, litter boxes, bowls, we'd appreciate it. We are in constant need of supplies so the animals that stay with us have what they need until we find them a forever home."

"I'll purchase whatever they need. Keep your supplies, please."

"Thanks, we appreciate it since they're getting more and more expensive, and lots of people want animals but forget that they need their own beds, bowls, things of that nature."

"Exactly how many dogs and cats can you house here?" Lauren asked, another brilliant idea forming.

"We keep as many as fifty, and as few as five. Though as long as I've been here, we've always had at least thirty, both dogs and cats. We do get a few wild animals, but we do what we can, then try to return them to their natural habitat, if at all possible. It's a lot of work, but all of us volunteers love it."

"So you just volunteer here?" Lauren asked, more impressed than ever.

"This is my third year, and I'll do it as long as I'm able."

Lauren didn't want to be nosy and ask about her finances, so she said good-bye, telling her she'd look forward to Dr. Melloh's visit and that she couldn't wait to introduce her new family to their new home.

Outside, it was still bitter cold, and snow was falling in big flakes, sticking wherever it landed. Maybe they'd have a white Christmas. Somehow, she doubted this cold spell would last over the next three and a half weeks, though one could always hope.

A million thoughts ran through her head as she drove to the store. The first, and most important—would the store have any customers today? She'd funded the place, but any additional monies Razzle Dazzle earned would be a bonus, at this point.

Not liking to start the holiday season with a negative attitude, she forced herself to set aside the negativity and count her blessings. She had so many. Her family, her friends, her health, and she was in a good place financially. Now she had three little cats to care for. And a ginormous book contract that would enable her to do so much good, not just by adding a few more zeroes to her bank account but by giving to those who were truly in need. Lee Hessinger. Charlotte. The shelter. She could go on, but for now, she was going to focus her attention on the positive, just as Madison had said. Just thinking of her best friend and what lay ahead for her and Scott brought a smile to Lauren's face. Yes, she was blessed in so many ways, and she had to remember that.

She parked her old Honda in its usual spot behind the store, unlocked the back door, and went to her office. She'd brought her laptop with her, as there was still a great deal of research to do on Mr. Giampalo. Plus, she needed to call Angela and preferred to make the call away from her parents, as she knew it would upset them. That was the last thing she wanted to do. She'd been a bit of an ass when she responded to them yesterday and was feeling incredibly guilty. She would do her best to try to be more understanding from now on.

She bumped up the thermostat and used the remote on

her desk to switch on the Christmas lights in the main window. She turned on the gas fireplace and was instantly comforted by the warmth it provided. As usual, she walked up and down the aisles, checking to make sure everything was in its place, stopping to rearrange a new display of wrapping paper she'd received yesterday. Hand-painted, it would garner a hefty price, but anyone who knew this particular artist, Heather Hanson, as many locals did, would not question it, knowing all the love and creativity she put into her work. Lauren tried to recall if she'd ordered this last year or the year before but couldn't. Heather's wrapping paper was in high demand, and rare. She wondered if it was too late to include this new addition in the ads she'd placed in the papers in the region surrounding Fallen Springs.

In the office, she checked her e-mail, saw she'd asked for all of the ads she placed to appear in many of the upcoming Sunday editions. She e-mailed the papers, asking them to please add that Heather's Hanson's unique wrapping paper was available but supplies were limited. This was so easy, since she had the Internet at her fingertips.

Next on her list, she went to Globalgoods.com and ordered everything she would need for her new pets: beds, bowls, litter boxes, litter, several fun toys, plus two cases of the food she'd been told to get. She clicked the PLACE ORDER tab, and a few seconds later learned she would have her shipment tomorrow.

"Wow," she said.

She took the papers from the shelter out of her bag, located the address, then ordered fifty new beds, in all shapes and sizes. Toys and new food dishes. Most important, she ordered one hundred cases of several varieties of dog and cat food. She'd seen this particular brand stocked at the shelter and hoped she hadn't gone overboard. Next, she wrote out a five-figure check from her personal checking account, then went to FedEx's website and placed an order for a pickup, asking for her check to be sent same day to the shelter since it was located in Fallen Springs. She was putting a dent in her personal funds, but she didn't care. If luck remained on her side, she would have a boatload of money to add to her accounts once she finished her biography of Mr. Giampalo. She was getting super-excited when she heard the little bell jingle, letting her know she had a customer.

"Duty calls," she said as she plastered a big smile on her face. She stepped out of the office into the main aisle of the store. What she saw caused her to stop dead in her tracks.

Chapter 14

It took a couple of seconds for her to find her voice. "May I help you?" she asked, suddenly realizing what she must look like. She had on a faded pair of jeans with her old Uggs, which were stained from years of use and definitely should have been replaced years ago. Knowing how cold it would be this morning when she'd dressed, she wore an undershirt, then added a worn but comfortable chambray shirt; on top of that, she wore a thick, red wool sweater. Her braid hadn't lasted throughout the night, and she'd done nothing more than run a brush through her long blond hair. She'd even forgone her usual black mascara, leaving her blond lashes bare. All this came to mind as she stared at her customer, who was so well put together, she wanted to cringe just thinking about what she must look like to him.

He was tall, probably at least six-three, and over two

hundred pounds. And it was all muscle. His thighs strained against dark denim, and the cream-colored sweater he wore was stretched to the max by his broad shoulders. Dusty-blond hair, way too long for her taste, touched his shoulders, but he'd tucked the sides behind his ears. He had the bluest eyes she'd ever seen. Bluer than Madison's, bluer than her own.

Good grief! He was a real-live version of Thor, the Marvel character played by Chris Hemsworth. She'd lost her ability to speak, so she just stood there, dumbfounded by this . . . hunk. What was someone like *him* doing in her store?

"The door was open," he said, breaking the silence, his voice deep and sexy.

"Uh, yes, sorry. I was, uh, working. In the office." She raked her hand through her messy hair. "What can I help you with?" In her wildest imagination, she'd never seen such a stud. She couldn't help it. There was no other word in her broad vocabulary to describe this man.

"Well, I'm not really sure. I was looking for . . . something unusual. A gift. For a friend. Their birthday. It is Christmas."

All hope gone, but of what she had no idea, other than a sick, sort of sinking feeling, but she'd wished for customers, and here he was. "Okay, well, did you have something particular in mind? A unique decoration? A sweatshirt? They are hand-painted, one of a kind."

She watched him watch her. Butterflies danced in her midsection, and she felt dizzy. Before she did or said something she'd regret, she turned away and walked to the back of the store, where she had a display of Christmas music boxes. She felt his presence before turning to face him. "These are exclusive to Razzle Dazzle. We're the only store in North Carolina that sells these, so the chance of your friend having received one as a gift is slim to none. Of course, if you're new to the area, and your friend has friends who might shop here, then, well . . ." *Good grief! What in the name of Pete is wrong with me?* She was sounding like a thirteen-year-old who's just come face-to-face with her first crush. She felt heat rise to her cheeks.

He leaned in to examine each music box. "Exquisite." He actually looked at the price tag located on the bottom. "Exquisite price, too," he added.

Another gush of heat rose to her cheeks. "Yes, but worth every penny," she managed to squeak out.

"Actually, I was thinking they're worth much more than you're selling them for."

Surprised, she was at a loss for words. Lauren couldn't recall any customer she'd had in the past three years telling her their prices weren't high enough.

"Personally, I would double the price," he added as he ran a large, well-manicured hand across the globe of one of the more expensive music boxes. "I'll take all of them. How quick can you have them wrapped?"

"What? You want all of them?" Her heart sank even more; whoever the recipient of this gift was had to be someone super-special. She casually glanced to see if he wore a wedding band, which nowadays didn't mean much, but still, she couldn't help herself. His ring finger was minus any jewelry. "It will take a couple of hours if you want them packed for shipment, but if you just want them in their boxes, gift-wrapped, I can have them ready in about an hour."

"Perfect," he said, whipping out his wallet. "Gift-wrapped will be fine."

Lauren mentally tallied the total and decided that if she didn't make a sale the rest of the month, this alone would match half of what she'd added to Razzle Dazzle's business account.

"Sure. You can pay me when I finish wrapping them," she said. "Did you want to wait?"

Part of her hoped he would, and another part of her wished he would leave, give her a few minutes to calm her rapid heartbeat. Brush her hair. Put on mascara. And lip balm.

"You said an hour?"

"Yes, to gift-wrap them."

"Is there a place a guy can grab breakfast around here? I could use a bite to eat."

Angels were smiling down on her today. "Yes, two blocks west of here, right on King Street, you'll find Ruby's Diner. Best food in Fallen Springs," she added, because it was true.

"Thanks. I'll go have a bite and see you in an hour."

She nodded because her mouth was so dry that her tongue was sticking to the roof of her mouth. Before she did anything stupid, she went to the office, chugged a bottle of water, brushed her hair, took the mascara from her purse, and added three coats to her pale lashes. She searched for lipstick, but all she could find was an old tube of Dr. Pepper lip balm, her favorite since high school. Right now, more than anything, she wished Madison was here with her purse full of high-end makeup.

As soon as she finished, she packed each music box into its original packaging; then she wrapped them, one by one, all in different paper, as Mr. Hunk hadn't specified any particular style of paper. Of course, she had been so flustered that she hadn't shown him her selection, either. She'd hope for the best. She took her time with each box, sad to see them go but thrilled with what their purchases did for Razzle Dazzle's bottom line. Mom would be beside herself when she told her about this huge sale. Dad would be reinforced in his beliefs that the store would continue to hold its own.

Lauren packed each wrapped music box in three of Razzle Dazzle's reusable cloth bags, and then placed in between them a few larger bags, in the hope they wouldn't bang against one another and break. After the amount this was going to cost Mr. Hunk, surely he would be extra careful when he loaded his car with his purchases—though she didn't recall seeing a car parked in front of the store, and this early in the day, she would have noticed. Maybe his friend who has the birthday on Christmas dropped him off. No, that didn't make sense because Lauren would have seen that, too. There was one taxi service in Fallen Springs, and she hadn't seen it either. Maybe he had walked. But from where? The only lodging in Fallen Springs was the Langdon House, a beautiful bed-and-breakfast that rarely had a vacancy, as it only had four rooms.

This was absolutely none of her business, though Lauren knew he was not from Fallen Springs. She would have known had someone like him lived here. He stood out like a giant, and a very handsome one, too. No, he definitely was not local, of that she was sure.

She placed the three bags on the counter next to her old-fashioned cash register and prayed that he would be writing a check, because if he used a credit card, she'd have to use their ancient slide machine. Something about this guy was sharp and contemporary, and he probably didn't have a clue what an old credit-card machine like the store's looked like.

She'd no more had the thought when the bell jingled again, only this time instead of Mr. Hunk, it was Brent Ludmore. Lauren felt her stomach knot and wished to high heaven he'd chosen another time to pop in. "Hey, Brent, what's up?" she forced herself to ask.

"Not much. Just trying to keep the citizens of Water County safe for one more day."

She laughed. "That's pretty easy, I would think." She regretted the words as soon as they came out of her mouth. He'd just told her at dinner the other night that illegal drug use was rampant in Fallen Springs, and the Sheriff's Department was hiring more deputies just to keep up with it. "I didn't mean that the way it came out," she added, hoping to curb any hurt feelings her comment might have caused.

"Granted, it's not the toughest job in the world of law enforcement, but we have our moments. I thought I'd stop by, check on you, see how your dad's doing."

"Dad's just fine. He actually drove to Pine City yesterday to see Grandpa. If you didn't know, you would think he was in perfect health. Yesterday was a good day, though. He's starting a new medication, so I'm hoping he'll have more good days rather than bad ones once he's been on it for a while. I guess time will tell."

Brent walked over to the empty display, where the music boxes had been. "What happened to all the fancy boxes?"

"I sold them," she added, wanting to ask wasn't it obvious, but she kept that thought to herself.

"Nice," he said.

"Actually, I just sold them this morning. To a new customer. I sent the customer to Ruby's so I'd have time to wrap them all."

"A collector?" Brent asked.

"I don't think so. They"—she didn't want to say *he* because Brent would question her even more—"said they were buying them for a birthday gift. Apparently, the lucky person's birthday is Christmas Day."

"Not sure if I'd like that."

"Me either, but it's not like one has a choice," she said, grinning. "It's kind of out of your hands." She thought of Madison's new baby. Not a Christmas birthday but maybe a Fourth of July baby. *That would be a bang*, she thought.

"Pretty much," Brent said.

She nodded.

"So, you have any plans tonight?" he asked.

She knew checking on her dad wasn't the only reason he'd stopped by. She did not have plans, other than working, then realized she hadn't told Brent about her new book contract. And for some odd reason, she didn't want to tell him just yet. Later, after her trip to Seattle, she would, but at the moment, she wanted to keep this to herself. "Actually, I'm doing some research, so I'll be glued to the"—she almost said Internet, but he didn't need to know that either—"books. Just a project I'm interested in."

"Well, I hope that's all it is," he said.

"What's that supposed to mean?"

He shook his head. "That you're not just saying that to keep me away."

"Brent, I don't want to get into this now. You know how I feel." And this was not the time to discuss her lack of romantic interest in him. "I do have some good news to share with you. I'm going to be a mom," she said, but when she saw the look on his face, she realized she'd left out one critical word. "A cat mom."

She saw the relief on his face.

"I went to the shelter this morning, and not only did I adopt a momma cat—her name's Daisy—I also adopted her kittens. Evie and Yule."

He laughed. "For a minute, I thought you were having a baby. Yeah, that's a good thing to do. Animals are a good substitute for kids."

"Brent! That's mean," she said, and she wasn't joking.

"You know what I meant," he said. "Until you settle down and have a family of your own. Pets are almost as good as kids. Unconditional love and all."

Lauren wanted to tell him there weren't a lot of choices in Fallen Springs, but that was a low blow. She wasn't that cruel. "Yes, they do give love in return. The shelter wouldn't allow the kittens to be separated from their mother, and I agreed to take all three. I think Dad will get a kick out of it. You remember how crazy he was over Buzz?"

Brent laughed. "He thought that cat was a dog."

"He did, and Buzz acted like a dog, too. I miss that furry guy."

"Well, as I said, I just wanted to stop in, check on your dad. You tell him I'll stop by for a beer this weekend," Brent said. "And I'll bring pizza from Papa Joe's."

"Sounds good, I'll tell Dad," she said, relieved that he was leaving.

"Saturday or Sunday? Which day is best?" he asked.

The bell jingled on the door, and, of course, Mr. Hunk's timing couldn't have been worse.

"Uh, I'll call Dad and ask. I'll get back to you," she said, feeling the heat of embarrassment rise to her face.

"Do that," Brent said, walking past Mr. Hunk as he exited the store.

She nodded and hoped her face didn't show what she really felt. "So, how was your meal?"

Really, Lauren!

"Excellent. Some of the best biscuits and gravy I've had."

"Good, well, I have your packages ready." She pointed to the three bags sitting on the counter.

"Perfect," he said, reaching for his wallet and pulling out an American Express card.

Lauren almost laughed. Yes, they took credit cards. Yes, the machine was ancient. But no, they did not take American Express. Her father's reasoning—their rates were too high.

He held the card out for her to take. "Sorry, we don't accept American Express." She was embarrassed. Truly red-faced and humiliated.

"Well, try this." He took another card from his wallet.

"Visa," she said. "That we take." She reached under the counter for the machine, and one of the carbon copies she used to get an imprint of the card number.

"Oh, boy," he said. "This is a tap and go."

"A what?" Lauren asked.

"Tap and go. Touch the terminal," he said again.

"This," she said, pointing to the machine on the counter, along with the carbon slip, "is all we have."

Mr. Hunk burst out laughing. "Tell me you're joking." He was shaking his head, but his grin was such a turn-on, Lauren laughed with him.

"Sadly, I'm not joking. This is it."

"Then it's a good thing I always carry a couple of blank checks with me." He put the credit cards back in his wallet and took out a check.

Lauren couldn't wait to see his information on the check. "Checks are fine," she said, smiling. "Just make it payable to Razzle Dazzle Décor."

"How much?" he asked, accepting the pen she held out to him.

Lauren gave him the amount, and he didn't flinch. Not even a little bit. He wrote out the check, and she was about to ask to see his driver's license so she could write the details on the back of the check as her father always did, even if he knew the customer, but she couldn't bring herself to ask this man one more question that would make her appear to be even more of a country bumpkin.

At that moment, she would have gladly strangled her father if he were there. Instead, she pushed the CASH button on the ancient register, the same National Cash Register machine her grandfather had used in his day, pulled the handle, and the drawer opened. She placed his check inside, then closed the drawer.

Mr. Hunk watched her, seemingly fascinated. "Is that original?"

Puzzled, Lauren asked, "This?" She nodded in the direction of the register.

"Yes."

She took a deep breath. "Everything is original here. My grandfather used the same machine in his day." Lauren thought he would laugh, but he appeared intrigued.

"You sure don't see many of these around anymore," he said. "Mind if I have a closer look?"

Her heart rate doubling, and for a minute, she thought maybe this was a newfangled way of committing a robbery and wished Brent would return, but common sense took over. This man was not here to rob her of the ninety-nine dollars and change she kept in the drawer. Though she wished she'd read the name on the check, just in case.

Hesitantly, she said, "Go ahead."

He must have picked up on her nervousness, because he just peered around the counter to look at the keys on the old register. "Very special. I doubt there are more than a handful of these still in service," he said after a minute. "Thanks for your time," he added, taking the three bags and walking toward the exit. "Oh, and Merry Christmas," he called out, grinning and causing her insides to twist in a knot. In a good way.

She waved but didn't return the sentiment. Lauren returned to the office, in a bit of a daze. She'd never had this kind of response to a strange man before. Or any man, if she were honest. Though it'd been more than apparent that he didn't have any sort of reaction to her, other than amusement at the antiquated cash register.

She opened her laptop, intending to see if she had any e-mail, when it occurred to her she hadn't looked at the name on the check. Racing out of the office, she took the check out of the drawer, then read the name:

JAG ENTERPRISES
METLIFE BUILDING
200 PARK AVENUE
NEW YORK, NEW YORK 10166

New York City? She looked at his signature, but it was illegible. "That's lovely," she said out loud, tossing the check on her desk. There wasn't even a phone number. *Odd*, she thought, *because all checks have phone num-*

bers. Or is JAG Enterprises so upscale, they don't feel they need a phone number on their checks?

It didn't matter. The check was drawn on a major international bank, so she'd deposit it on her way home. If it bounced, she would deal with it.

Lauren returned to her e-mail account and saw that she had nine e-mails from Angela. All had been sent two hours earlier. "Doesn't she know how to pick up the phone?"

Lauren took her cell phone out of her bag. No charge. No wonder Angela kept e-mailing. She dialed her office, using the store's phone, and Angela picked up on the first ring. "I swear I couldn't find the number for your little store, and your cell keeps going to voice mail. Listen, things have changed."

"Okay," she said. "Fill me in." She raked a hand through her hair, loosening the tangles.

"I know the weather is still crappy there because I've been watching the Weather Channel."

"Yep, it's snowing."

"It's not a blizzard, right?" Angela asked.

"No."

"Listen, Mr. G wants you to get started on his bio as soon as possible. He knows the weather is not ideal, but get this—he's sending his private jet to Asheville to fly you to Seattle. Is this awesome or what?"

"All flights are canceled, you know that."

"All commercial flights. Private planes can still fly into Asheville, Lauren."

Dumbfounded, it took her a few seconds to reply. "If commercial airlines aren't flying, I am not going to fly in this weather, I don't care what kind of aircraft the man owns. Is he crazy? If he can't wait for this weather to clear, I'm not sure I want to write the bio of some guy who's willing to put me in danger. Besides, I just adopted three cats, and I have to be home tomorrow for an inspection."

Silence.

"I didn't say you have to leave today. I meant in the next couple of days. His secretary called this morning, said he would be happy to send his jet for you when it's clear, Lauren."

"Oh, well, you didn't tell me that."

"Now you know. So are you good with hopping a private jet to Seattle to earn three and a half million dollars?"

She laughed. "I e-signed the contract, so I don't think I have a choice. Though I have to be here when Dr. Melloh comes for the inspection."

"You know, Lauren, we've known one another for a long time. I think we're friends, right?"

"Of course," Lauren said.

"In all this time, not once have you ever mentioned you were a cat lover."

She chuckled. "See, there's more to me than meets the eye."

Angela cackled. "You're good people, but a cat lady? I had no idea."

"I had cats growing up. A couple of dogs, too."

"Just promise me you can be ready on a moment's notice and get yourself to the airport in Asheville so you can meet Mr. G in Seattle."

Lauren rolled her eyes. "I said I would. It's a couple of hours to Asheville in good weather, just so you know."

"I do. Keep your phone charged," Angela instructed. "And give me your shop number and home number."

Lauren gave her the numbers, promising to be on Mr. Giampalo's private jet when the weather let up.

Finally, having a few minutes to herself, Lauren made a cup of tea, her thoughts returning to the mysterious customer who'd spent a small fortune, at least in the store's world, on music boxes. JAG Enterprises. She'd never heard of it. With her new Internet access, all she had to do was type the name in the search engine. Did she really want to? She knew there were those who thrived on this practice, finding out every single crumb they could on the unlucky, or lucky, soul who happened to be the subject of their search. In a way, it seemed sneaky, but in another way, the ability to have whatever you wanted at your fingertips was so tempting that she found herself typing JAG ENTERPRISES into the search bar. She hit the RETURN button and dozens of blue hyperlinks filled her screen.

She clicked on the first link. Nothing there, a food supply company. Next link, still nothing. She tried a few more, then logged off. Why did she even care who he was? Just because he was beyond handsome, and sexy, and just so happened to show up in her store? She needed to get to work on something substantial. The bio would fill her time. Once her initial meeting was over, she could focus on reality. And her new kittens. Smiling, she decided to take an early lunch, go to Ruby's, and just relax. Again, she'd left the house without making a lunch. Lauren put the OUT TO LUNCH sign in the window, then, making sure to put her coat on, she walked the two blocks to her favorite restaurant. If she continued this pattern, she'd be the size of a barn. Inside Ruby's, the smell of the yeast rolls made her mouth water. She sat at the counter because she knew that in less than half an hour the place would be filled with the business-lunch crowd, and she was just one person. She took her coat off and draped it across her lap.

Ruby saw her. "You having lunch again?"

"I couldn't resist," she said. "What's today's special?"

"Meat loaf, mashed potatoes with butter beans, and a salad," Ruby said.

That was a little too heavy for her. "How about a grilled cheese with a cup of your vegetable soup?" Lauren asked. She was a big fan of meat loaf and usually would have jumped at the chance to have it at Ruby's, but not today.

"Coming up," Louise called out. "Anything to drink?"

"Coffee."

"Just made a fresh pot."

"Sounds good; it's freezing out there," Lauren said.

"You want a roll? Just out of the oven," Ruby asked her.

"Sure," Lauren said. She might as well. She'd run around the store and burn off the extra calories.

The door behind her opened, bringing in a gush of cold air.

"It is cold out there," said Mr. Hunk as he sat down on the stool next to her.

"Back again?" Ruby hollered to him. "I thought those biscuits and gravy would tide you over for at least a couple of hours."

"What can I say?" he quipped. "I'm a growing boy." He laughed, and Lauren's stomach did flip-flops.

During their exchange, Lauren hadn't turned to look at him, fearful of her reaction. *What is he doing here? Doesn't he have birthday gifts to deliver or something?* Her pulse quickened when his arm brushed against hers.

"Excuse me," he said to her.

Crap. I can't ignore the guy now. "You're fine."

"Hey, it's the girl from the Christmas store."

She cringed. "Yeah, that would be me," she said, hoping Ruby and Louise didn't notice the blush on her cheeks.

"So, does the girl from the Christmas store have a name?" he asked, not unkindly.

Girl? Please. "Yes, I do."

"I tell you what, if you tell me yours, I'll tell you mine."

Her cheeks burned with embarrassment. "Lauren."

"Lauren, I'm John." He swirled his barstool around so that he faced her.

"Nice to meet you," she said.

Louise chose that moment to slam Lauren's coffee cup on the counter, sending coffee flying through the air and landing smack-dab in the middle of her sweater. "Oh, honey, I'm sorry. You okay?"

Lauren jumped up and used her coat to blot her sweater. "I'm fine, no worries. I piled on a few layers this morning."

"Here, let me," Mr. Hunk, *John*, said, grabbing several napkins from the holder and blotting at her sweater. An inch below her chest.

"No, really, it's fine," she said, feeling all tingly inside. To prove it, she stood up and, with her back to him, pulled the heavy sweater over her head. Her chambray shirt was dry, as was the light T-shirt she was wearing underneath it. "I'm fine." She sat down facing the kitchen window where Ruby placed the orders for Louise to deliver them.

"I'm sorry, kid. I'm just a klutz," Louise repeated.

Lauren needed to get control of herself. "It's fine,

truly. I wasn't hurt. But I would like another cup of coffee." She smiled, doing her best to act like an adult. She wished people would stop calling her "kid." She was small, knew she looked younger than her biological age, but right now, it was embarrassing.

John, though she struggled to think of him as anything other than Mr. Hunk, spoke to her. "Do you come here for lunch every day?"

Plastering a smile on her face, she turned to him. "No. Just when I forget to bring something from home." Her heart beat so fast, she knew that if he looked closely, he would see the pulse pounding in her neck.

Lauren felt another wash of cold air. She looked at the clock. Noon. The lunch rush had begun, and she couldn't recall ever waiting this long for a sandwich. She thought of asking Ruby to pack it to go, but then it might be obvious that the man seated beside her was having an effect on her. At least, she thought it would.

"You're new in town," she said, then took a sip of her coffee.

"I'll be around just for a few days. I'm here on business."

Lauren couldn't possibly imagine what a man from New York City could do as a profession that would bring him to Fallen Springs on a business trip. "That's nice."

"It is somewhat of an inconvenience. I'm here only as a favor to my business partner. I needed a break from the city, though."

"Then you must be staying at the Langdon House." That was the only place to stay in Fallen Springs.

"No, I'm at the Biltmore."

"That's not very convenient." Lauren's words flew out of her mouth. She thought about Brent Ludmore, what he said about drugs, and wondered if this slick, handsome guy was a drug dealer. No way was she going to ask him what type of business he was in. Obviously, from his appearance and the amount of money he'd spent at Razzle Dazzle, he earned a decent salary.

"No, it's not, but I like the place. My driver doesn't seem to mind."

He has a driver?

"That's probably a good thing, then, especially since the roads have been so icy. We don't usually have harsh winters."

"Yes, that's what I've heard. Personally, I like the snow, at least in small amounts. We have plenty of the stuff in the city, but after a day or two, it's nothing but a messy gray slush."

"Here ya go," Louise said, placing her soup and sandwich on the counter.

"Smells good. I'll have what she's having," John said to Louise.

"Ya know, I thought you was just here to stay out of the cold, maybe flirt a little with Lauren. Give me three minutes, and it's on the house."

Lauren prayed for an earthquake, anything to take her away from the utter humiliation she was feeling.

He laughed. "Thanks, and a coffee too, please."

Louise poured him a coffee and also refilled Lauren's cup. Lauren took a bite of her grilled cheese, feeling self-conscious eating with this man beside her. It was how she used to feel in college when she was on a first date.

Three minutes later, Ruby brought John's soup and sandwich to him. "As my sister said, it's on the house." She winked at him, and Lauren laughed. Ruby was a flirt.

"So what kind of night life do they have around here?" John asked her.

She almost choked but managed to force a chunk of bread down her throat. "In Fallen Springs?"

"That's where we are," he said.

We. As in the two of them? It was lunchtime. He must be referring to Christmas-birthday girl.

"There's a movie theater," Lauren struggled to come up with an answer because there wasn't a ton of nightlife here. "O'Brien's usually has a band on the weekends. It's a local bar, mostly where the younger crowd hangs out."

"What about you? What do you do in your free time?"

Take care of my parents, but she wasn't going to tell him that. She'd tell him the partial truth. "I'm an author by profession. I read a lot."

He looked at her as if for the first time.

"Seriously?"

Lauren couldn't help but grin. "Seriously."

"Anything I would know?"

"Depends on what you like to read," she said. Suddenly, she didn't feel so backward, out of place in his presence. After all, she'd written four *New York Times* best sellers, and she was far from a novice in her profession.

"I read everything from thrillers, legal procedurals, biographies, and sometimes, I'll give Stephen King a read."

Not bad, she thought.

"Good variety," she said, then took another bite because she really was hungry. Her soup was cold, but she'd take it back to the store and heat it in the microwave. The last thing she wanted to do was slurp soup in front of this man.

"So you're hoping to publish a book? That's quite the undertaking, but admirable," he stated.

Lauren stopped chewing, slowly turning her stool so that she faced him. Knowing she was being rude, she didn't care. She continued to stare at him, and as expected, he turned his barstool to face her.

He looked at her, the beginning of a smile tipping up the corners of his mouth. "What?"

"You said 'hoping to publish a book.' What makes you think I haven't already?"

"You would've told me," he replied. "Most authors, at least the ones I've met, can't wait to tell you about their work."

Okay, I'll give him that. But he was wrong to assume that just because she didn't toot her own horn, it didn't mean she hadn't published a book or any kind of written word. She could be a poet, for all he knew. Or a horror author. "I keep my professional life to myself."

"I totally understand," he said.

Sure he does, she thought. *Probably has a car full of drugs just waiting to find a club where he can sell the stuff, getting the kids Brent talked about hooked on some deadly concoction.*

Focusing on her food, Lauren took another bite, washing it down with coffee. "Louise, could you pack up my soup? I've got to get back to work." She had to get away from this man, but no one needed to know that.

"Sure thing, kiddo. Gimme a minute." Louise disappeared into the kitchen, returning with a take-away bowl and lid. "Here ya go."

"Thanks," Lauren said, then went through the process of pouring her cup of soup into the plastic bowl. She felt him watching her. Her hands shook. She chewed the sides of her mouth, anything to keep her from doing or saying something she'd regret, like *Could you stop staring at me?* or something to that effect, as his gaze made her insides turn to mush. Doing her best to ignore him, she packed up the soup, took a ten-dollar bill from her pocket, and, as always, tucked it under her empty bowl.

He reached out and took the ten-dollar bill and held it out to her. "My treat?" he asked.

Lauren was getting all kinds of mixed signals from this guy. Most of them she didn't need or want. "I can pay for my own lunch," she said, then tried to take the ten-dollar bill from him. He yanked his arm away, holding it high in the air. The only way she could reach it was to stand on the barstool and rip it out of his hand. No, even Lauren knew what a fool she'd make of herself if she did this, so she said, "Thank you."

"You're welcome, Lauren." He handed her money back to her and placed his ten dollars on the counter.

Before he had an opportunity to speak, she grabbed the take-out dish and rushed out the door. A few local business owners said hello, but she didn't bother responding. She wanted to get back to the store, back to her comfort zone. Mr. Hunk was not part of her comfort zone.

Chapter 15

As soon as she returned to the store, Lauren took down the OUT TO LUNCH sign, bumped the heat up a few degrees, and went to her office. Apparently, Razzle Dazzle wasn't going to be overrun with customers, so she logged onto the Internet, read her e-mails, and saw nothing of great importance. As she prepared to add a few facts to her file on Globalgoods.com, she heard the bell over the door jingle, letting her know she had a customer. Running a hand through her hair, she smoothed her shirt and managed to put a smile on her face.

Surprised to see her mom and dad, Lauren lit up. "What are you two doing out in this nasty weather?"

Her mother wore a heavy coat, with a yellow-and-black-plaid scarf wrapped around her neck. Dad had his usual leather jacket on, with a navy knitted cap and gloves, courtesy of her mother. "We just left the doctor's office and thought we'd take you to lunch," her mother said.

"I just had lunch at Ruby's. I wish I had known you all were coming," she said. "I'll make tea." Heading back to the office, she stopped halfway. Her parents weren't following her, as they normally did. She turned around to find them staring at the shelves, still full of all the extra stock she'd ordered in anticipation of a busy shopping season.

"What's going on?" her father asked, his voice still sharp. "Why is there so much"—he waved his hand at the shelves and racks—"stock?"

"Because we're not selling anything," Lauren explained.

"Oh, dear, it must be this bitter-cold weather. It's very difficult to drive in. I'm sure as soon as this storm passes, we'll have these shelves emptied in no time at all. Right, dear?" She smiled at Lauren.

"Let's have some tea, and we'll talk." She went to the office, hoping they'd follow her. She didn't want or need them staring at what should have been half-empty shelves waiting to be restocked. Maybe seeing this for themselves would give them second thoughts about having the store set up a web page. *One thing at a time*, she thought.

Her parents sat on the sofa while she made them tea. First, she needed to tell them about her visit this morning and try to get them in a good mood. "I have a surprise; it's kind of a Christmas gift to myself and you two." She paused. They stared at her. They could be odd at times, but she adored them. Here goes nothing. "I went to the animal shelter this morning. I adopted a cat."

"That's fantastic, dear. We need an animal in the

house. I so miss old Buzz," her mother said. "I don't know why I haven't done this myself."

"Dad, you're good with this?" she asked him, hoping to break through the wall he'd erected between them.

"Your mother and I adore animals, so to answer your question, I think it's grand."

She breathed a sigh of relief. "Actually, the cat I adopted, she's four. Daisy is her name, but she just had kittens. Two. A boy and a girl. Evie and Yule. The shelter wouldn't let me adopt Daisy unless I agreed to take her kittens, too."

The twinkle that had been gone from her father's eyes returned like a ray of sunshine that had been hidden behind a dark cloud. He actually began to laugh. Lauren looked at her mother, raising her brows in question.

"So, one for each of us," he declared. "That's a good deed, hon. Of course, we'll help with their care if we have time. I miss having an animal, too."

Like a kid at Christmas, Lauren clasped her hands together. "Here's the deal. The shelter has a veterinarian come to the house first, kind of an inspection, to make sure the animals are going to a good home. They're going to call with an arrival time, but said it would be sometime tomorrow. I'm glad you guys are okay with this. I ordered—" She'd best stop while she was ahead. They didn't need to know she'd purchased their necessities from the Internet. "I bought beds, bowls, litter boxes for them," she finished.

"We can set them up in one of the spare rooms. They'll have a bedroom to themselves, like Buzz had," her mother said. "This is a wonderful gift, Lauren, for all of us. We need a bit of action in the house. It's so empty when you're not there."

Lauren could forget moving into the guest house. At least until after the holidays. Maybe she'd use it as a temporary office while she worked on this new bio when she wasn't at the store. She'd need the uninterrupted time. "It's a big house, that's for sure." Lauren had often wanted to approach her parents with the idea of turning the place into a bed-and-breakfast, give the Langdon House a bit of competition, but the timing was never right. Now wasn't either, but maybe someday she would. For now, she wanted her dad to step into the future, and that could take years. By that time, neither of her parents would be young enough to run a bed-and-breakfast. Just thoughts.

"Why don't you tell me about all that extra merchandise out there?" her father asked, reverting back to his stern-dad voice.

Lauren was truly tired of this. At that moment, she wished she had the courage to tell her parents the store belonged to them, not to her. She had her own career, which she'd cast aside to run the store. This was getting way too old for her. "Honestly, Dad, are you sure you really want to know?"

Her mother pursed her lips and gave a slight shake of the head as if to indicate now was not the time.

Tough, Lauren thought. *The truth is needed here*. "Dad, Razzle Dazzle is old and outdated. No one shops here anymore except for a few like-minded locals. We get an occasional straggler from out of town if we're lucky. The stock is awesome, but we're not putting it out there for the public beyond these walls. And I'm not referring to the people here in Fallen Springs. Our artisans' work is unique, so extraordinary, it's a shame they're not getting the exposure they deserve from us. It's almost like we're doing them a disservice." Lauren was surprised they were still able to carry some of their work, though she knew that many of them had their own websites to display and sell their pieces. Several continued to sell to Razzle Dazzle because it was an institution in Fallen Springs.

"I disagree. I hate to say this, but it must be said. Lauren, your mother and I believe you're mismanaging the store. We've talked about this at great length, and we're coming back to work. Maggie has agreed to return part-time if needed. This should give you time to devote to your own work. My rheumatologist believes I'll be able to return to most of my normal activities with this new medication. I haven't felt this alive since I was diagnosed. So, starting tomorrow, you can stay home, get things situated for the cats. You can use one of the spare bedrooms as an office if you choose to."

She was so shocked by her father's words, she had nothing to say in objection. She sat there with the mug of tea in her hand, dazed and bewildered. "Dad, Mom." She put the mug on her desk. "Are you serious? Do both of you really think I can't operate this place"—she tossed her hands out—"properly?"

"Dear, it's not that," her mother said.

"Mother, don't placate me. I am not a child."

"Ilene." Her father placed an arm on her mother's shoulder. At any other time, she would have thought the display of affection sweet, but now she thought of it as controlling, as though he were preventing her from saying more. "I know this must be hard for you, Lauren. You're a modern girl, hip. What you don't understand is this is a business, and it's been a very successful one for decades. I know you've tried your best these past few years, but as I said, I feel more like myself now, and duty calls. I'll return this afternoon, after your mother and I get something to eat. With your mother, of course, and you know how good she is at persuading the customers to make that one extra purchase. This way, starting this afternoon, you'll have all the time you need to write."

She let his words soak in. Modern and hip. A girl. As much as she wanted to tell him he was off his rocker, she didn't. Legally, it was still his business. Grateful he'd begun to feel more like himself, but stunned at his sudden decision, Lauren could play his game. It wouldn't take long before he reached the same conclusion. She'd added enough funding to cover the place until February; anything beyond that—she couldn't think that far ahead now. Let her parents figure things out on their own. She'd had no clue that either believed Razzle Dazzle's failing sales were due to her lack of managerial skills. Let them learn the hard way. Seems like she'd heard this a few times from them when she was a kid.

Taking a deep breath, she plastered a smile on her face. "You're probably right, Dad. I don't have any experience *managing* this place. I do have that book contract, and now I won't have to worry about the store." She'd play along. "I'll be going to Seattle in a few days, and now I won't have to worry about asking Maggie to step in. And I'll see to it that the cats are looked after. It'll be too much for both of you, on top of all this." She held her hands out to indicate the expanse of the storefront.

"Don't be upset, dear," her mother said. "This happened at the perfect time, don't you think? You can write your little story, and we'll all be as we were before."

Another deep breath. Lauren felt like screaming, and she hadn't felt this way since Larry Oxford tied her shoelaces to the legs of her desk in fifth grade. When she stood—or rather, as she'd tried to stand up—she'd fallen, landing on the floor beside her desk, the entire classroom laughing at her. She was an adult now, even though her parents didn't seem to realize it, so she would not scream. Lauren stood up, closed her laptop, stuffed it in the oversized bag she carried, then took the router and the ethernet cable she'd connected, and stuffed those in one of the cloth bags reserved for customers.

"What is that contraption?" he asked.

"It's nothing, Dad," she answered. *Poor guy.* She would have felt sorry for him had she not been so aggravated with him.

"Lauren, you seem upset," her mother said.

"No, just getting my writing toys ready to take home, that's all." She wished this ice storm would move on because she needed to get away for a few days, and the trip to Seattle would be a perfect reason for doing so, given what she'd just been told.

"Don't leave those lights on in the window display when you leave. Runs up costs. And lower the thermostat as well, another unnecessary expense. Before we're hit head-on with the usual Christmas craze, let's make a note to take cash and checks only. No more credit cards; they're too expensive to use. Personally, I think anyone using them is foolish. If you can't afford to pay for something, then you don't need it in the first place. Learned that from my granddad," he said. "Ilene, let's grab lunch at Ruby's since Lauren's already had hers. Lauren, we'll come back after we've had some lunch. You can leave anytime you want. I know this isn't what you wanted to hear, but it can't be helped," he said. "I'll see you tonight."

Lauren looked at her mother. She just smiled, as usual.

"I'll take care of dinner tonight, dear," she said, then followed her husband out through the back entrance.

If she didn't know better, she would swear two strangers were inhabiting the bodies of her parents. Were they both becoming senile? Or was it just her father, and as was the norm, hadn't her mother just agreed with anything he said? Or did they really think her lack of skills, whatever you wanted to call it, had created this slump? Whatever, she'd do as they asked. Lauren sincerely believed that once they returned, saw how sad sales were, they'd have a change of heart. Until then, she'd focus on her career.

As soon as they were gone, Lauren turned the window lights off with the remote. She turned off the gas fireplace, adjusted the thermostat to a low sixty degrees, as she knew this is what her father deemed acceptable. Part of her felt it was childish to just agree to his terms, and another part felt justified, as she was sure that, given time, he would draw the same conclusion she had: Razzle Dazzle's days were numbered if they didn't step into the twenty-first century. As she looked around the office for anything she'd missed, an item that might be important, she saw there were none. Tears blurred her vision, and her nose felt stuffy when she left through the back door for the last time. Or maybe the last time as a so-called employee, and if she believed her father, not a very good one at that.

She unlocked her Honda, tossed in her bag and the store bag with its Wi-Fi system that she no longer needed, and shivered. It was very cold, and it took the Honda forever to warm up. Before going home, she'd stop at the animal shelter, to explain her change of circumstances, and hoped it wouldn't matter. "The cats couldn't care less," she said aloud, puffs of cold air coming from her mouth. She hadn't heard of any updated travel arrangements from Angela other than to be ready when Mr. Giampalo's plane arrived. She'd have no trouble doing so now since her parents had practically kicked her out of the store. No, more like they'd fired her. If it weren't so pathetic, she'd laugh. It was sad because one way or another, her parents were bound to figure out that the lack of sales wasn't due to her lack of experience. *It is what it is*, she thought as she made the turn onto Oak Street. The shelter was virtually on her way home, so she'd stop by, see her little feline family, then go home.

The second she entered the shelter, she was greeted by Beau, the friendly parrot, and the young girl, whose name she didn't know. "Back so soon?" she asked, grinning.

Lauren nodded. "Just wanted to check on the fur babies since I was on my way home."

"Awesome. They'll love seeing their momma," she said. "Follow me."

Lauren followed her to a different room, which contained only a handful of animals. She spied Daisy in the corner, all comfy on her bed, with Yule and Evie nestled closely beside her.

The girl opened a gate and stood aside. "Stay as long as you want. These lucky creatures are waiting to join their new families; we separate them once they're adopted."

That explained the move. "I'll just be a couple of minutes." Lauren lowered herself to the floor next to the kitties. "I'm going to be the best friend you've ever had," she said as she stroked their tiny heads. "And you too, Momma cat," she said, running her fingertips across the top of Daisy's head and receiving a lengthy purr as a thank-you.

Her cell phone buzzed in her pocket. "Hello," she said as she took turns stroking the kittens' soft fur.

"I just heard from Mr. G," said Angela in her usual no-nonsense manner.

"Hang on." Lauren gave her new family one last pet, then returned to the front office, where she briefly explained her situation to the young girl, asking her if it was possible to change the vet's visitation for later today. While she checked their schedule, Lauren spoke to Angela. "So, what's new?" Lauren asked while she waited.

"Mr. G said he's sending his plane for you tomorrow. Apparently his pilot and copilot have some special knowledge of the latest aviation weather report, and you should be ready to travel with no weather concerns."

Tomorrow?

She hadn't even packed, nor had she mentally prepared herself for a flight. It wasn't her favorite mode of travel, but it beat driving any day. "Did he give a specific time?"

"His office will call me half an hour before they land, so that should give you plenty of time to get to the airport."

"Are you serious? Asheville is over two hours from here, longer in this weather."

"Don't get your undies in a wad. They're flying into Fallen Springs. I think it's called Mountain Aviation, a small airport there. According to the map on my phone, you're twenty minutes away. With traffic and bad weather. Ten on a good day. I tried each scenario on Google Maps, just so you know."

Lauren hadn't even considered the local airport. She thought it was for small planes. "Are you sure?" she asked.

"I wouldn't be calling you if I weren't," Angela quipped. "Make sure you dress like a professional. You might make more of an impression if you try to look your age."

Lauren laughed. "I'm not sure if that's a compliment or an insult."

"It's a compliment," Angela said.

The young girl at the reception desk cleared her throat.

"Hang on again," Lauren said, then directed her attention to the girl.

"Dr. Melloh will be in your neighborhood in forty-five minutes tops, he said. Will that work?"

"That's perfect. So I can take the cats home tomorrow, then?"

"If the inspection goes well, sure," said the girl.

Lauren asked, "What's your name?"

"I'm Brandy," she said.

"Then I thank you, Brandy, for rearranging his schedule for me."

"Hey, it's all good. Now I'm guessing I'll see you sometime tomorrow?"

"Count on it," Lauren said, then dashed outside to her car. The engine cranked over right away, and the heated air from the vents soon warmed her.

"You still there?" Lauren asked, putting Angela on speaker. She needed both hands on the wheel.

"I'm here."

Lauren drove carefully down Oak Street. Even though it wasn't snowing, she felt the Honda's tires straining to keep traction. "So, you trust this guy? The weather and all?" Lauren asked, inching down the street at ten miles per hour. "I don't like to fly as it is."

"You won't even know you're in an airplane. From

what I hear, Mr. G's plane is luxury at its finest. We're not talking puddle jumper here. We're talking a 777, probably more decked out than Air Force One. I've heard it holds a Rolls Royce, too."

"I'd have to see that to believe it," Lauren said. "I can't see the point of such extravagance."

"Remember who you're dealing with. Think of the Biltmore Estate. Mr. G's playroom, according to what I've learned, is larger. So, having a Rolls Royce at your disposal would be normal for him."

"I could never get used to living that way."

"Whatever you do, don't say that when you interview him. He's totally self-made, so I'm going to go out on a limb and say there's some pride in all he's accomplished. Just keep that in mind when you start the interview."

"Sure, but I need to hang up because I'm driving home, and the vet is stopping by to scope out the house. You're sure this is a done deal?" Lauren suddenly felt as though she were about to be duped, as in ha-ha, the joke's on you. Why in the world would a man so wealthy choose her as his biographer?

"You need to show some self-confidence, Lauren. You've got a stellar reputation, so yes, I'm sure this is a done deal. Remember, I brokered this myself, and you trust me, right?"

"Of course I do; it's just this e-signature thing. Somehow, it lessens the, I don't know, excitement, the thrill of signing on the dotted line, so to speak. I guess I'm old-fashioned in that way."

"Lauren, do you hear what you're saying?"

"Yes," she replied. "Why?"

"Think about it for a minute," Angela encouraged.

"I'm missing whatever it is you're trying to tell me," she said as she drove down the long drive to the house.

"Your dad."

"Oh, crap! I get it." She parked by the guest house. "Yeah, I sound just like him. Okay. You made your point. I'm good with the e-signing; it's just different."

"Good, then do whatever you need to do, and I'll stay in touch."

"Yep, talk soon," she said, then hung up. She glanced at the fancy Rolex on her wrist. She had half an hour to kill before the veterinarian arrived. Inside, the house was warm and cozy, the aroma of her parents' morning coffee lingering in the air. She went to the kitchen, poured herself an orange juice, and sat down at the table. It seemed strange not having her dad waiting for her when she arrived home. That'd been their routine since she returned. She liked routine and all, but change was good, too. While she was still in a state of semi-shock over her dad's decision, and the reason he'd made it, she was truly thrilled that he could go back to work, feel useful again. The sad part was he'd have firsthand knowledge of what she'd been trying to tell him for years. Razzle Dazzle had lost its appeal.

She finished her juice and rinsed her glass, placing it on the drain board. Peering out the kitchen window, she saw a white van pulling into the driveway. "The vet," she said, glancing around the house as she headed for the front door. Nothing out of place. Perfection, her mother's claim to household fame. The doorbell rang, and she promptly opened the door.

"Hello, I'm Lauren, and I'm going to guess you're Dr. Melloh." She held out her hand.

"Yes, ma'am, the one and only," he said.

"Please, come in." She stood aside to allow him to enter. He was a big guy, as in well over six feet tall, though he was slim. Lauren would bet he'd been a basketball player in his day. He was probably in his midfifties. He wore wire-rimmed glasses, and his balding head was shiny, like a new penny. He wore jeans and a gray-flannel shirt.

"So, you're the one that took the new mom and her kittens?"

"I couldn't resist. They're so adorable, and I've been wanting another pet for ages. We always had a cat or a dog when I was growing up."

"So you're experienced with animals. Good." He smiled at her. "Where are you going to keep the pets?"

"Our old guy, Buzz, stayed all over the house. Mom thought it might be a good idea to let them have a room to themselves at first. We'll put their beds in a guest room, and if it turns out they want to hang out elsewhere—well, as you can see, we have plenty of room."

"That's excellent. And someone will be here with them daily? Feed them, change the litter box? See to it they're vaccinated as needed?"

"Sure. As a matter of fact, I'm going to be here all day. I'm going to work from home while my parents take care of Razzle Dazzle."

He brightened. "You're the writer! I've read all the biographies you've written. And I know your father. We used to sit on the board at the chamber of commerce back in the day."

"Good. I'd taken over for him. He was ill for a while, but he's back at the shop now, so you might want to stop in, tell him hi sometime. He'd like that."

"And I would as well. I'm pretty sure those little kittens are going to be living large, so I'll sign off on the paperwork as soon as I get back to the shelter. You can pick them up anytime tomorrow."

"Thank you, Dr. Melloh. I'm a cat lover, and my parents are too. They'll be much loved," she said, following him to the door. "Thanks for changing your schedule to speed up the adoption. I really appreciate it."

He chuckled. "All in a day's work. Take care."

"Thanks," Lauren said. "You too." She closed the door, relieved to have the "inspection," if one could even call it that, over with. Not that she had expected anything else in particular; she just wasn't familiar with the process. It'd been a while.

Once again, her cell phone buzzed, and she took it from her back pocket. "Hello, this is Lauren."

"Hey, Lauren, it's me. Charlotte."

Taken by surprise, it took Lauren a second to shift gears. "Hey, there, what's up?"

"I went to the store; some man said you didn't work there anymore. Is that true? I thought you, like, owned it or something."

Lauren couldn't help but smile. "Actually, it's my parents who own the store. It's been in my family for decades. My father's health has improved"—she almost hated saying this, given Lee's diagnosis—"and he decided he wants to work again."

"Darn, but can I still call you, will that be okay?"

"Anytime you want," Lauren promised. "How is your mother?" She was almost afraid to hear the answer.

"Well, that's why I stopped by the store. Mom's agreed to do the bone-marrow transplant. I wanted to thank you for making it happen."

Tears came to Lauren's eyes. "That's the best news ever. I'm so happy for you and Lee."

"I have to, like, go into the hospital soon. Mom says I need to be isolated for a few days while they do some tests, but I don't care. If it helps her live, I'll do whatever she wants. Though it'll be in Chapel Hill, at the cancer center. Mom says it's kind of a specialized place, with special pressure filters, so all the air is clean, no germs. It was kinda complicated, but we'll get to hang together once I get, like, majorly checked up."

Amazed at the girl's maturity level, Lauren felt a wash of pride, almost maternal, when Charlotte spoke of her willingness to do whatever it took in order to save her mother's life.

"I am so very proud, and if I'm being honest, in awe of you, your bravery. I don't think I could have done this when I was fifteen."

Charlotte laughed. "Yeah, but you gave up a beach house and boyfriends to take care of your dad."

She laughed. "Then I guess we do have something in common, though in all honesty, Charlotte, your mother's diagnosis is much more serious than my father's was. Actually, he's decided to return to the store because he's on a brand-new medication and says he feels like his old self." She paused. "But I think he's being a little ornery, if you ask me." A thought occurred to her. "Charlotte, I'm curious. What time did you stop by?"

"About three, right after school. The store was open even though the lights were off in the window display, and I went in and saw . . . I guess it was your family in the store and thought you were still there in your office or something."

"My parents said they were going to return after they

had lunch. They were all over town today," she said, more to herself than to Charlotte.

"You're not upset with me for stopping in?"

"No, of course not! You can stop in whenever you want, though I won't be there for a while." She'd probably be there to help close the place down for good when the time came, but Charlotte didn't need to know that. "I'm going to Seattle tomorrow for a few days, so I won't be around, but if you need to call me, you can."

"Wow, Seattle, that's where they throw the fish around, right?" Charlotte asked.

Lauren grinned. "You're referring to the Pike Place Fish Market, and yes, they do throw fish around, after you buy whatever kind you choose. At least I think that's how it works." Charlotte's naïveté was refreshing to Lauren.

"So why are you going there?" Charlotte asked.

"I am going to interview a man and write about his life; that's what my real job is."

"You're a writer? That's the most awesome job ever! Do you know J. K. Rowling?"

"No, I don't. Are you a fan?"

"The biggest in the world—well, Kiley and Lacey are, too. Lacey's mom buys the books, and we share them. But I still think it's super-awesome that you're a writer."

"Thank you, I enjoy what I do—most of the time," she said.

"So, like who are you gonna interview? Like a famous person or something?"

"Yes, he is very famous. Actually he's probably a household name by now. He's the founder and CEO of Globalgoods.com."

"We used to shop online sometimes, when Mom felt

better and was working. Is it okay if I tell her? She loves books and will want to read it when you finish."

"I'll deliver a signed copy to her myself," Lauren promised. She couldn't help but wonder if Lee would be around when the book hit the stands. She'd never say this to Charlotte, but she knew it was possible that she wouldn't be if the transplant did not work.

"I'll tell her tonight when I call her. I just wanted to thank you again for getting Mom some extra help. I know this might sound corny or whatever, but your stepping in is probably gonna save her life."

More tears; Lauren blotted her eyes with the hem of her chambray shirt. "No, I think that honor goes to you."

"Whatever, but we're grateful, and Mom said to make sure to use that word."

"I'll see you and your mom when I return. Do you have an e-mail account? If you're quarantined, I could e-mail you."

Charlotte recited both her and Lee's e-mail addresses. Lauren gave the young girl hers, too.

"Remember, you can call me anytime. Even if you just want to talk about nothing. Okay?"

"Thanks, I might. I'll probably talk with you soon, so bye for now," Charlotte said, ending the call.

Lauren could probably have sat for hours thinking about how amazing a kid Charlotte was, but she had a million and one things to do, so she'd best get packing. Literally.

Chapter 16

Lauren was up at 5:00. She hadn't slept well, too occupied with thoughts of the day ahead. She wasn't a great flyer and had spent half the night psyching herself up with all the usual platitudes. *Flying is safer than driving. Flying is faster. Flying is convenient.* All her usual thoughts. She'd never flown in a private plane and didn't know what to expect. She felt sure that when Angela said Mr. G's plane was nicer than Air Force One, she'd been exaggerating. She'd watched a special once where a crew of photographers had full access to the president's plane. It had been out of this world. She supposed a president deserved to fly in style. And then there were all the safety measures that had to be taken before the president himself was allowed to board. She felt sure her plane ride would be nothing out of the ordinary.

It was too early to call Angela, so she went downstairs

and made herself a cup of coffee. Normally, she was a tea drinker, but she needed a little more caffeine if she were to get through the day. There was a three-hour time difference, and she'd factored that in. She'd probably drink a gallon of coffee. *Isn't that what people do when they visit Seattle?* She rolled her eyes at her harebrained thoughts.

She sat down in the kitchen, still wearing her flannel pajamas, her mind wandering from one topic to another. Madison's pregnancy. Charlotte and Lee. Daisy, Evie, and Yule. Lots of exciting things to come. Her new book. Her father's seemingly miraculous recovery. And *him*.

Try as she might, she could not get Mr. Hunk—aka John, or so he said—out of her mind. Devilishly handsome, sexy, he was a total hunk. Grateful no one could read her mind, she wondered if Mr. Hunk had delivered the music boxes to Christmas-birthday girl. Or was he the kind who could keep a secret? When she and Eric Porter had dated, his inability to keep surprises to himself irritated her. Took the fun out of gift-giving, no matter the occasion. She liked a guy who could keep things exciting. She'd bet the bank Mr. Hunk couldn't wait to show Christmas-birthday girl the music boxes, and he'd probably tell her exactly what he'd spent. Lauren always removed the price tags when she wrapped a gift for customers and placed them in an envelope, along with the gift receipts. She did not like showy, braggart men.

Eric was that and more. Briefly, she wondered where he was in life now. Had he married? Had children? Somehow she doubted it, as he was too much of a control freak. It would take an evenly matched woman for him to settle down. Not that she cared one way or the other. Her thoughts were all over the place.

She'd called Brent last night. A bit of last-minute planning on her part, she'd asked if he would mind bringing the kitties to the house tonight since she had this quick business trip to make. He'd been way too agreeable, but that was Brent. She truly cared for him, but only as a friend, and he was always good for last-minute favors. Maybe Mom would invite him to stay for dinner.

"Morning, dear," said her mother. "You look like you're on planet Mars." She popped a Keurig pod into the machine.

Lauren gave her a weak smile. "I didn't sleep much last night. You know how I feel about flying."

"I do, and I understand. I remember the first time I flew on a commercial airline. I was so excited. Mother, Dad, and I went to Disneyland in California. I recall it being a late-night flight. Of course, I was just a little thing, seven or eight. Mother let me sit in the window seat. I was so fascinated and felt sure we were in outer space. Of course, once we arrived, and I saw Disneyland, the flight and the mystery of it was temporarily forgotten, as there was nothing that compared to all the rides, the shows, Mickey Mouse; the whole atmosphere was like a giant birthday party. It was my first real adventure. We were there for a week or so, but despite all I'd seen in Disneyland, all I could think about was telling Maggie I'd been in outer space. Of course, she knew it wasn't true, but it was fun pretending. My junior year of college, a group of us traveled to Europe—I've told you this before—and I was so excited, I didn't care that the flight was ten hours long." She removed her mug, blew on it, then took a sip. "I'm long-winded, I know, but my point is try thinking about the end result of your trip. Lauren, you're doing something everyday people only dream about. And I don't mean a trip to Seattle, though that is exciting. I mean why you're going."

Lauren motioned for her mother to sit.

"For the interview?" she asked.

"That, and the historic significance of what your book will mean. The first man, at least that I know of, who created a new and convenient way for people to buy anything from anywhere in the world. You've got this once-in-a-lifetime opportunity to provide generation after generation a glimpse into what this powerful man accomplished, and he chose you to tell his story." She took a sip of coffee. "I am so very, very proud of you."

Tears filled Lauren's eyes. "Mom, stop; you're going to make me cry." But she was smiling as she said this.

"Don't you dare, you'll get all puffy before the flight."

"True," Lauren said as she blew her nose into her paper napkin. "Though I still don't know exactly what time I'm leaving. That makes me even more anxious. Brent is going to bring the kitties by this evening. I hope you don't mind. I wasn't thinking straight when I adopted them." Lauren shook her head. "That didn't come out right. Of course I want them; I just hadn't planned on"—*Dad booting me out of the store and having a private jet pick me up two days after I decided to adopt*—"leaving so suddenly. Maybe you could ask Brent to stay for dinner? Or not."

"I'll invite him over when it's a decent hour for making phone calls," her mother said. "You want another cup?"

"Sure, why not?" She gave her mug to her mother. Something was up.

As soon as their coffees were finished, Lauren knew she needed to clear the air, kick the elephant out of the room. “Mom, tell me about Dad. What’s really going on with him?” She lowered her voice. Her father’s hearing was not impaired in any way.

“It’s almost a miracle, isn’t it?”

“Almost,” Lauren said.

“He started this new medication two weeks ago. We didn’t want to tell you until your father experienced results, if at all. As you’ve seen, the past few days he’s been more energetic than he has in years. When we were at the doctor’s office yesterday, Dr. Keller was amazed at his improvement. But there are side effects. We knew that going in but figured the odds were good that he’d be fine, and he is, so don’t think I’m about to deliver bad news. I’m not. However, with the improvement there was a risk of mood changes. Some are minor; some people experience severe depression, anxiety, and four people that they know of—all of this is from Dr. Keller—had to be taken off the medication because they became suicidal. That is the worst side effect. So when your dad stepped out of the room for his blood work, I explained how moody he’d been. Dr. Keller wanted to take him off the drug, but your dad, being the stubborn old fool that he is, said absolutely not.”

“I don’t get it,” Lauren said.

“Today he started taking an antidepressant. He’s angry. He feels like he’s traded his mental health for his physical health. It will take a few weeks, but the doctor assured us that when the antidepressant kicks in, he’ll be as good as new.”

“That explains a lot. I just wish you had told me. I was wondering if he was in the beginning stages of Alzheimer’s or plain old senility. Brent noticed it, too.”

“Oh, dear, your father would be horrified if he knew

that. I'll tell Brent myself. He deserves to know. He's practically family as it is."

"He's a good guy, no doubt about that," Lauren said, and meant it.

"And handsome, too," her mother added. "Surely, you must have some kind of feelings for him? In my day, the girls would have given their high-priced heels to have a man that good-looking say hello. Are you, uh, my old-fashioned ways won't allow me to say certain things, but you do like men, right?"

Lauren had just taken a sip of her coffee when the words came out of her mother's mouth. Stunned, she choked, the coffee spewing out of her mouth like a geyser. "Mother! I can't believe you of all people would even think that." She took her mother's napkin, wiped her face and her pajama bottoms. Then she burst out laughing at the absurdity of the question.

"Never in my lifetime did I think you and I would have this conversation, but to answer your question, yes, I like men. In the romantic way, as in getting married and having babies someday. I haven't found anyone special that I'd want to commit to for the rest of my life. I can't believe you asked me that. That's one's personal business, but you can stop worrying. If and when I fall in love, I promise you'll know." She smiled. "Does Dad think I'm gay?"

"I don't believe so," her mother said, her cheeks a bright pink.

"It's okay to say the word, Mom. The world is different now. It's changed in my lifetime in ways I never thought possible. I'm hopeful that there's someone out there for everyone, myself included."

Her mother sighed. "I'm so glad we had this talk. We've been concerned, your age and all."

For the second time in a few short minutes, Lauren cackled with laughter. "Mom, women are having babies in their forties, and a few in their fifties. You and Dad are just old-fashioned, and I respect that. If I ever meet someone and fall in love, I want him to knock my socks off, blow me away. You think that's asking for too much?" Immediately, she was reminded of Mr. Hunk. John.

"Too much what?" Her father's presence filled the room when he entered the kitchen. He wasn't limping; he wasn't stooped. He was Dad again, with a touch of something that affected his mood, and that was all right. He would get better.

"Morning, Pops." She hadn't called him that in forever.

He smiled. "Right back at ya, Buttercup."

Her childhood nickname because her hair was so blond.

"Lauren is waiting for the right *man* to knock her socks off and blow her away before settling down."

She heard her overemphasizing the word *man* and sharing a look with her husband.

"Now that we have my love life in context, how about I make blueberry pancakes? I'm going to be out of town for a few days, and who knows if I'll remember to eat." Lauren got up and went to the pantry, returning with the makings for pancakes. "Mom, you have blueberries in the freezer, right?"

"I do. Though it might take a bit for them to thaw."

"If you would let me give you a microwave, it would only take a few seconds. We'll use canned ones then."

She went back to the pantry, returning with a can of blueberries.

For the next ten minutes, she whipped, poured, and flipped pancakes, filling three plates high. "Here you go." She placed their plates on the table. "Don't wait; eat them while they're hot," she said as she poured the last of the batter into the pan to cook seconds for anyone who wanted them. When she finished, she carried her plate to the table.

"These are excellent, Buttercup. You're good in the kitchen, just like your mother."

"One more thing. I ordered the supplies for the cats; they should be in today's mail, several large boxes, I'm guessing. I bought a bit of everything."

"How in the world?" her mother asked.

Lauren might as well spit it out. "I ordered them off the Internet. That's how fast it is." She waited for her father to rip her apart, but he didn't say a word. But when he did, it was more than obvious he wasn't pleased.

"That's that man you're going out to interview. The global thing."

"Yes, it is. It's called Globalgoods.com, with most deliveries next day. You just can't beat it, Dad. I know how you feel, but this is the future. The future of your grandchildren, if I have any. This will be a way of life for them. It is now, for me, at least in a sense. I do all of my work via Internet, e-mail, you know that."

He nodded.

"Mom?"

"Dear, you know how your father feels."

"Ilene, I can speak for myself. Lauren, I don't like it, and I can't change who I am. I grew up in the retail business. I saw my father and grandfather working long and hard, and you know they were both—rather, Dad is still—financially sound. I just don't get how people can buy something they can't see, touch, or smell. I'm sorry, Lauren. I've got a lot of work to do. Someone didn't dust and polish the shelves like I asked them to. Ilene, I'm going in early. Lauren, can you drop your mother off?" Back to his moody self again.

"Sure," she said. "Pops, wait."

He stopped, turned to look at her. "Let's just agree to disagree on this topic. Deal?" She held out her hand to shake on it, something they used to do but hadn't done in years.

Slowly, he reached out, took her hand in his, and gave it a good squeeze and shake.

"Deal, Buttercup."

Chapter 17

Lauren dropped her mother off at Razzle Dazzle, then returned home. She still had a few things to prepare before leaving. She checked her luggage three times, making sure she had packed her most professional, high-end clothes. She'd washed her hair, dried it, then used a flat iron to smooth it. It hung to her waist, but she decided to take Angela's advice and do her best to look all grown-up. She styled her hair in a French twist, using a diamond-studded barrette to secure it. Diamond earrings, and, of course, she wore her Rolex. She added two platinum necklaces, each dotted with more diamonds.

She chose to wear a sleek, figure-flattering, black Chanel suit she'd spent her first book advance on, and a pair of glossy black Christian Louboutin stiletto heels, nearly vertical to add height; the iconic red sole popped beneath the shoes' graceful curves. She'd taken time with her makeup, and when she looked at herself in the mirror, she was confident she looked like an adult.

Her luggage was packed, her laptop was in the black Chloé Vick leather tote that had cost a small fortune, and she had taken out her favorite Chloé red-leather handbag, which had also put a huge dent in her checking account when she bought it. All in all, she guessed that her outfit and accessories were close to the $25,000 mark. Her mother would croak, but this was the best of her best. She wasn't one for trendy pieces. She spent her hard-earned money on quality, timeless pieces that would last a lifetime.

She glanced at the time, hoping she would get the call soon, as she was afraid to sit. She did not want to appear less than perfect when she boarded Mr. Giampalo's private jet. She'd even arranged for the local taxi to drive her to the airport. Her old Honda did not match her outfit, but it had been a classic in its day.

Glancing in the mirror, she barely recognized herself. She'd gone to great lengths with her makeup. Soft brown shadow in the crease, winged black eyeliner, and, of course, her usual deep black mascara. She'd lightly contoured, added a sheer touch of highlight to her cheekbones. A creamy blush gave her a hint of fresh pink color, like she'd been out in the cold. She completed the look with red lipstick. Not too bad, she thought, for an old "girl." She doubted that Mr. Giampalo would look at her and think of a girl. No, she looked exactly the way she wanted to look. Like a professional businesswoman who knew who she was and where she was going.

Her cell phone buzzed, and she grabbed it from her tote bag. "Hello," she said, sounding out of breath.

"The plane will touch down in twenty-seven minutes. You ready to go?" Angela asked.

"I'm on my way," she said, then hung up. She speed-dialed the taxi and waited inside until she saw the white Lincoln winding its way down the drive. Thankfully, there was no snow; the skies were blue and the temperature bitter-cold, but she didn't care.

She was about to write the biography of the richest man in the country.

"How's that?" she asked her reflection in the mirror, then stepped outside, allowing the driver to take her luggage and stow it in the trunk.

Seattle, here I come.

Chapter 18

Lauren expected Mr. G's private plane to be one giant advertisement for his company. It was not. She waited inside the small airport while they loaded her single piece of luggage onto the enormous aircraft. It was all white and sleek, like a giant swan that had swooped down to earth. She saw nothing gaudy or outrageous about the plane. If one could be discreet with an aircraft this size, Mr. Giampalo had accomplished it, hands down. Though she had to wait a few minutes before they took her to board, she couldn't wait to see the interior. She was still nervous about the flight, though, to her credit, Angela was right. No puddle jumper here. She took a deep breath, then slowly let it out, hoping to stay as calm as possible when she met Mr. Giampalo. Though Angela hadn't said he'd be on the flight. *Of course he wouldn't. How juvenile of me to think otherwise.*

"Ms. Montgomery?"

"Yes?"

"We're ready to board," said a nondescript gentleman dressed in perfectly creased navy slacks, a crisp white shirt, and a matching blazer. "If you'll allow me?" He reached for her black bag.

"Thank you," she said.

Feeling awkward and a bit stiff with the unexpected formalities, she supposed this was required of them. Just one small aspect of the man whose life story she'd learn in a matter of days. Lauren took it all in, knowing that when she sat down to write, details that seemed unimportant now would matter to those who spent their hard-earned money to read about a multibillionaire. A self-made one, too. She owed it to them to soak up as much as she could and do her very best to re-create what she had observed firsthand.

As soon as she stepped outside, another man in a spiffed-up golf cart drove her to the plane. Her pal, who still had her bag, sat behind her. This was rich. Truly. She'd file this bit of information away. Lauren had a code she followed when writing a biography: no gossipy tidbits. If an employee, a friend, or a family member revealed a personal habit, anything she didn't deem valuable, it would not go into her biography. Of course, she always gave the first draft to the recipient. So far, she hadn't had any complaints.

They stopped when they reached the aircraft, the chilly wind whipping the tails of her coat around her legs. She was very glad for the silk stockings she'd added at the last minute; otherwise, her legs would be frozen.

"Ms. Montgomery," said the driver. He got out of the driver's seat, then assisted her.

"Thank you," she said, grateful to him, as it wasn't easy to stay balanced in her heels, especially since the wind had kicked up. She should have worn different shoes. Too late now; she'd just have to manage.

Sensing her imbalance, he steadied her with his hand on her elbow, leading her up the red-carpeted stairs. Lauren managed to walk with some dignity to the top, where she was met at the cabin by a beautiful woman, probably close to her age, who was wearing a white blouse and a navy pencil skirt with a matching blazer. Her dark hair was pulled away from her face, her lips shaded the same red as the carpets. "Good afternoon, Ms. Montgomery. I'm Felicia, your personal flight attendant. Anything you need, just ask, and I'll do my best to make your flight pleasant." She helped Lauren remove her coat, folding it across her arm.

For a second, Lauren was speechless, then her manners kicked in. "Thank you, Felicia."

"If you'll follow me. Mr. G said you were to be seated in the executive suite."

"Yes, of course," she said. Angela was proving her wrong once again. This airplane was elegant; the décor, at least what she'd observed so far, was tasteful without being overdone. Four creamy leather seats surrounded wood-grain tables, and each area had a flat-screen television. Felicia headed to the rear of the plane, and Lauren followed her. Obviously, she wasn't going to sit in those first-class seats with a table and a TV, but she was fine with that. She was just an employee of sorts. Of course she wouldn't be seated in first class. Maybe executive suite was another way of saying business class.

Felicia led her past several private pods, with what appeared to be reclining chairs. Built into the arm of the recliners were power sockets and USB ports. "Wow." She couldn't help herself. "This is amazing." Any fear of flying was forgotten as she continued to trail behind Felicia.

"Isn't this the bomb?" Felicia said. "I came out of retirement for this job."

What?

Lauren didn't know what to say, so she said nothing.

"Here you are," Felicia said, opening a door, allowing her inside. "This is the executive suite. Mr. G's personal accommodations. He said to make yourself at home."

She felt like Dorothy in the Land of Oz. Lauren had seen a few pictures of luxurious airplanes, but she'd never seen anything quite like this one. This space was the size of an apartment. Uncaring that she stared, she wanted to soak this in, every last detail.

"Amazing, huh?" Felicia asked.

"I've never seen anything quite like it."

There were plush recliners with built-in notebooks, reading lights, and red-and-white duvets with the famous red G embroidered on them placed on each one. "I was a flight attendant for twenty years, and I retired two years ago. When I learned that Globalgoods.com was searching for a senior flight attendant to assist Mr. G and his staff, I immediately came out of retirement and applied for the job. I have to say, it's not really work. It's exciting every day. I've met fabulous people, famous people, and what I like to call regular people. A dream job, for sure."

Lauren felt a kinship with Felicia at once. She smiled and reluctantly told her she had a terrible fear of flying.

"Ms. Montgomery—"

"Lauren, please," she said,

"Lauren, you won't even know you're flying once this girl is airborne. It's the ultimate experience. Have a look at this," she said, leading her across the large expanse to a door she hadn't noticed.

Inside was a bedroom, as large as her own, with a king-sized bed in the center. Curved walls surrounded the bed, yet there was plenty of room for one to walk around.

"And there's this." Felicia pushed a button. The curved walls opened, revealing a giant flat-screen TV, bookshelves, and a minibar. "And take a look at this," she said, then pushed another button, which opened a door to a giant bathroom.

"This is the best part," Felicia said. "A shower, a tub, and all of this." She motioned to a variety of luxury toiletries, perfumes, colognes. Lauren couldn't imagine anyone having this aircraft at their disposal.

"I'm starstruck, for lack of a better word," she said. "Are you sure I'm supposed to be in here? It's so, I don't know, out of this world."

Felicia smiled. "I feel the same way every time I bring a new guest aboard. Mr. G is an awesome employer. He lets his employees use this plane for our personal vacations. We're entitled to one week per year, and needless to say, it's booked, though Mr. G's travel plans come first. If we have to cancel a trip owing to his change of plans, he gives us an extra three days added on to our vacation. Personally, I think flying in this beauty is the best part of any vacation."

"He really is a generous man," Lauren said. Intrigued, she couldn't wait to meet him and learn his life story, and hoped she would do him justice when she began writing.

"He is, and as down-to-earth as dirt," Felicia said, with a big grin. "We are going to be delayed a few minutes as our copilot is running late."

"I can't see how that would be a problem for me," Lauren said.

"It's never a problem for anyone. We all love Mr. G, plus this aircraft is easy to hang in, delay or not."

That was one of the highest compliments an employee could give their employer. "Does everyone call him Mr. G?"

"He insists on it. Says his Italian name is a tongue twister, and that he has trouble with it, too. Though most people know he's a jokester."

"It certainly is going to be a pleasure to get to know him," Lauren said.

"Wait until you meet his son. You will think you've died and gone to heaven. He's as nice as his father, but oh boy. I'll let you form your own opinion when you meet him."

Lauren laughed. "I'll do that."

"We're serving lunch in half an hour." Felicia opened a drawer and handed her a leather-bound menu.

"Wow again," Lauren said.

"We have a full kitchen. Staff, too."

Lauren could not wait to share this experience with Madison. She'd flip out.

"What's your recommendation?"

"The flight's around five and a half hours, so I would choose something to tide you over until dinner. Of course, you can have snacks, desserts, espresso, ice cream. We have almost any snack you can imagine. Also, there is this." She took another smaller, leather-bound menu and gave it to Lauren. "These are the movie selections if you decide you want to watch a movie."

Lauren skimmed through the list, all movies that were currently in theaters. "I'll see. I planned on reviewing my notes, but who knows? Thanks so much." She returned the movie menu to Felicia.

"I'll try the captain's course," Lauren said. "I like the aviation references."

"I know; that's a great choice. You'll get a taste of everything Seattle."

"It looks like it," she said. "I adore salmon and oysters, so this is a real treat for me."

"Then I'll leave you to get settled, and if you need anything, just press this." She handed her an iPhone. "There's an app for everything you need here. Lights, movies, and, of course, online shopping." Felicia gave her a quick tutorial on the apps, then excused herself.

Lauren sat down on one of the leather swivel chairs. Feeling giddy, she used her high-heeled shoe to take a short spin in the chair and felt like a kid at Christmas. Felicia was right. She couldn't imagine anyone being afraid to fly in such luxury. A virtual home in the sky. She almost wished the flight was longer so she could sleep in the giant bed and have a shower. *Unreal*, she thought.

A tap on her door startled her.

"It's me," said Felicia.

"Come in."

"Marcus said you might need this." Her bag.

"I felt like something was missing. I think I had too much caffeine this morning," she said. "Tell Marcus thank you."

"I'll do that. You get settled in, and I'll bring you a drink. What would you like? We have a full bar."

"Is there anything you don't have?" she asked, grinning.

Felicia laughed. "Probably. There's always that one

little item we miss, but as a rule, Mr. G likes to leave no stone unturned."

"Thank you again. This is a dream," she said. "I think my fear of flying is a thing of the past."

"You'll be as comfortable as we can possibly make you. We're still waiting for the copilot to arrive. He's going to be delayed longer than expected, so just relax, and I'll bring you whatever drink you'd like."

"Oh, sorry. Just a ginger ale. I'm not much of a drinker," Lauren said.

"One ginger ale coming right up," Felicia said. "Now, relax. Enjoy the trip." She flashed a beaming smile. "That's an order."

Who couldn't relax when traveling in an aircraft fit for a king?

She took her laptop out of her bag and opened the file containing her notes on Mr. Giampalo. She would have to remind herself to use his full name when they met; she didn't want to assume it would be okay to call him Mr. G. Not yet, though if he was the man she'd researched, she felt sure he'd invite her to call him Mr. G, too.

She hadn't given much thought to his son, though she knew he had one. Apparently, Mr. G had kept his son out of the business, but she planned to ask about him. She typed several questions that came to mind. Another tap on the door.

Felicia said, "It's just me, with your ginger ale."

"Thank you."

Lauren took the glass from the tray Felicia was carrying. Real crystal, clear ice. Perfect. She took a sip.

"I needed that. Nerves," she said. "I always get a dry mouth when I'm nervous."

"Are you sure you don't want a drink, something a bit stronger, a glass of wine?"

"No, really. I'm nervous, but in a good way."

"All right, but don't hesitate to give me a call if you need anything more," Felicia said. "I'm going to see to your lunch now."

Lauren almost felt guilty, being waited on hand and foot. It wouldn't be hard to get used to this kind of lifestyle. She planned to ask Mr. Giampalo if adjusting to life as a billionaire had challenges. Experiencing how he traveled, she couldn't imagine this ever being an issue. Though having a fortune at one's fingertips didn't necessarily constitute a perfect life. She knew this from the previous biographies she'd written. Money didn't guarantee happiness.

Lauren heard a soft chime from the iPhone Felicia had given her. In text message format, she was told to buckle up as they were preparing to taxi. She didn't hear the engines start up, not a single sound. Maybe these walls were soundproof. She located her seat belt in the swivel chair, clicked it in place, and a second chime from the phone gave a detailed map with instructions on how one must exit the plane in case of an emergency.

"Amazing," she said to herself. She'd bet the bank her dad would get a kick out of this, regardless of how he felt about the World Wide Web.

Surprisingly relaxed, Lauren kicked off her heels and tucked her feet beneath her. This was how she liked to travel. Maybe it wasn't the actual flying part that had always frightened her but the closeness, the feeling of being cramped. Stuck. In here she could get up, walk around, nap, take a bath, watch a movie. The choices were endless, though she'd stay seated until they reached altitude. She assumed this rule applied to private aircraft as well. Comfortable, and totally without fear, she relaxed so much that she drifted off. A tap on the door startled her awake.

"Lunchtime," Felicia announced, pushing a rolling cart into the lounge area of the suite. "You doing okay? Nervous?"

"Actually, I dozed off for a few minutes. No nerves whatsoever."

"Perfect, now let's get you fed, then go from there. I have the dining room all set up." She pushed another button, revealing a dining room that seated at least twelve people.

"You're kidding," Lauren said, stunned by the sheer opulence.

"No, it's the real deal. Mr. G hosted his family Thanksgiving dinner here last year."

Lauren asked, "Where do I sit?"

"Your choice, as you're the only passenger," Felicia said, then started to remove plates from the cart.

Lauren sat at the head of the table, as it made sense. "This smells divine." She was hungry even after consuming that large stack of pancakes at breakfast.

"I'll make sure to tell Jean Simone Laurent. He's our head chef, from France, and he's the best. He'll introduce himself when it's time for dessert."

A French chef, too?

She didn't have a reply because who would question having a French chef preparing their lunch on a flight to Seattle?

Lauren relished the chilled briny oysters. It had been forever since she'd had any. It was not something on the menu at Ruby's Diner. Next was poached salmon, cooled and served with tender greens, fresh tomato, hard-boiled egg, and capers. The food literally melted in her mouth. "I don't think I've ever had salmon prepared this way. It's delicious."

"I'll tell Jean Simone Laurent, and he'll give you his recipe, if you ask."

"Not sure I could re-create this, but I would love to try his recipe at home," Lauren said between bites. She felt a bit intimidated, as Felicia stayed with her while she ate, but if this was the way Mr. G operated, then so be it.

As soon as she finished, Felicia removed her plate and refreshed her ice water. "We have red velvet cake for dessert. I had a taste earlier. It's to die for, like most everything Jean prepares."

"I don't think I could eat another bite, but maybe later. With coffee?" she asked, knowing her wish would be granted. Lauren didn't think it would be too much trouble getting used to fancy meals like the one she'd just consumed.

"Then I'll leave you to roam the aircraft, have a look around, or take a nap. I'm just a touch away," Felicia said.

"Thank you so much. I'm going to roam, see if I can walk off a calorie or two."

"Like you need to," Felicia teased. "I, on the other hand, could afford to lose weight. Three babies almost back-to-back takes a toll on a girl's figure."

"Really? I mean three babies? I don't mean that in a bad way, you just look"—Lauren paused—"so polished, and well put together."

"Trust me, when I'm home, the hairdo and makeup disappear, but I do love those little ones," Felicia said, clearing away the last dish. "Eight, ten, and twelve. All boys."

Lauren laughed. "Well, I think you're lucky. I adore kids. I've always wanted children." She rarely voiced that and surprised herself when the words came out of her mouth.

"You're young; you have plenty of time."

"Not so much. I'm thirty-five."

"No way! You definitely don't look it," Felicia said.

"Thank you. I think." She laughed. "I get a lot of that because of my size. Up close, the wrinkles are there, trust me."

"Well, regardless, you're a beautiful woman, and I'm sure you're going to have beautiful babies when the time is right. Now, I'll get out of your hair and let you enjoy your trip."

Lauren thanked her again, then stood and stretched. She'd put her heels back on. She would have liked to walk around the plane without them but didn't because it wasn't very professional, plus it gave her four extra inches in height.

She went down the aisle toward the front of the plane, stopping to admire each area with all its high-tech gadgetry, amazed that one could virtually do anything here that one could do on the ground. Feeling better, she returned to the suite. Lauren booted up her laptop and was able to use the Wi-Fi to check her e-mail.

She had an e-mail from Madison, with an attachment. She downloaded the file, opened it, and gasped. It was an ultrasound picture of the baby. She replied, telling her she was so excited and couldn't wait to meet him or her. Lauren gave her a few details about the plane and told her she'd call her when she was home. With not much else to do, she picked up the iPhone to turn the television on. It had all the networks she had at home, and she found a program on the Garden Network, settled into one of the big lounge chairs, and kicked off her shoes. She totally relaxed, dozing off and on.

Startled when a male voice came across the intercom system, it took her a minute to remember where she was. Mr. Giampalo's plane. The voice was just an update on the weather in Seattle, the usual spiel the captain gave to update the passengers. A little odd, she thought, since she was the only passenger.

There was a knock on the door, and she tucked a few stray hairs into place and slipped her heels on. "Come in," she said, knowing Felicia would have most likely returned, bearing cake and coffee.

But Felicia was nowhere in sight.

Chapter 19

She had no words. *Am I dreaming?* She blinked several times. This was not a dream.

"It's you."

"No, it's *you*," said a very familiar, sexy voice. "The girl from the Christmas store."

Lauren couldn't find words. All she could do was stare at Mr. Hunk. John. With the girlfriend whose birthday was on Christmas.

"I'm confused," she said, and she was. "Very," she added.

"You look different," said Mr. Hunk.

"You're the pilot?" she asked, seeing his uniform.

"Copilot."

"Oh."

"Yep."

"You were late," Lauren announced. As if it mattered.

"I was," he agreed.

"Why are you here?"

"I fly the plane."

"Oh."

"Yep."

"No, I meant, why are you here in this room?"

"Uh, you don't know?"

"No."

"I was going to take a nap."

Lauren didn't know where this conversation was heading. Something was not right.

"I'm sorry. I was told the executive suite was mine for the duration of the flight."

"Obviously. Look," Mr. Hunk said, "I don't know what's going on here, and from the look on your face, you don't either. Let's say we start over. Properly."

She nodded. "Okay."

"Hello, Lauren, the girl from the Christmas shop. I'm John Giampalo, the guy who collects music boxes."

"What?" She raised her voice several octaves. "Who?"

Another knock at the door.

They both said, "Come in," at the same time.

The door opened. "Oh, boy. I think we have a problem," Felicia said.

"Looks that way," John Giampalo agreed.

"I'm clueless," Lauren informed them.

"I think you two could use a drink. I'll be right back." Felicia turned to exit the room.

"Not so fast," John said. "We have a mix-up, and someone has a bit of explaining to do. Felicia? Are you in on this?"

"John Anthony Giampalo, I swear I'm going to tell your father what a . . . I don't know, a shit you are!"

Lauren laughed. *This is beyond crazy.*

JAG Enterprises. John Anthony Giampalo.

"Have a seat, Felicia. Lauren, please remain in my, *your* seat." He grinned when he said it. Her heart melted like ice in fire.

"I can move," she offered.

"I'm teasing," he said, and winked at her.

Lauren felt a warm glow spread throughout her body.

"Dave Grill, he's our regular copilot. He was late."

"I thought you were the copilot," Lauren said.

"I am. Today."

"What about tomorrow?" she asked, realizing how silly she sounded the instant the words were out of her mouth.

"Both of you, listen up, and don't say a word until I'm finished."

They nodded and directed their attention to Felicia. "Lauren Montgomery is going to write your father's biography. He sent the plane to bring her to Seattle. Bad weather in North Carolina. You were . . . I don't know what you were doing there, but Lauren, Dave Grill, the regular copilot, had to have an emergency appendectomy. John, I am going to assume your father contacted you? Asked you to fill in for Dave?"

"I think that about sums it up," he said.

Lauren was confused. "Then why were you in Fallen Springs?"

"Coincidence?"

"I don't believe in coincidences," Lauren said.

"Me either, but you can't blame a guy for trying."

"Trying what?" she asked.

"Felicia, can we have a minute? Alone?"

Lauren stood up. "No, stay," Felicia said, rising from her seat.

"Felicia, could you bring us a Coke or something? I'd like a few minutes alone with Lauren."

Lauren sat down, relieved for some odd reason.

"Of course. I'll be right back." She whirled out of the room.

"Felicia is awesome," he said.

"She's been very kind to me," Lauren acknowledged.

He raked a hand through his blond hair. She was totally mesmerized.

"I went to Fallen Springs to check you out," he admitted. "Dad has hired a couple of authors in the past, who, well, let's just say they weren't on the up-and-up. He's desperate to get his life story on paper. I had to make sure you were who he thought you were."

Silence.

Lauren took a minute to absorb his words. "Why did you buy all of the music boxes?" That was the first thought she had, and the words flew out of her mouth before she could stop them.

"I collect them."

"Oh."

"Yep."

"You're really a pilot?"

"I am. Copilot today. Not my normal job, but I was where I needed to be."

"Coincidence?" Lauren said, grinning.

"I don't believe in coincidence. I think you just said that."

"Me, either."

"Then what do you think we should call this?" he asked her, all traces of humor gone. "Me. You. Here."

A vague, yet sensuous tension passed between them. She knew he felt it from the tender look in his eyes.

"Luck?" she suggested.

He nodded. "I think it's more than that. I thought so when I saw you in the store, and then again, when I saw you eating that grilled cheese sandwich at the diner. And now, if this is luck, it's the luckiest day of my life."

"Mine too," Lauren agreed.

"How old are you?" he asked out of the blue.

Her mouth formed an O. "Didn't your mother tell you never ask a lady her age?"

"No. She died before I was old enough to need that kind of advice."

Lauren closed her eyes. She'd read that Mr. G had lost his wife when his son was very young.

"I knew that. I'm so sorry."

"It's fine."

"No, I should think before I speak. And to answer your question—wait a second, why do you want to know my age?"

"I don't know. You're so young."

"Like how young do you think?" she asked in a teasing tone.

"Twenty-eight?"

"I'll take that," she said.

"Okay, well, it's a bit young."

"So you say. What about you?"

"I'm thirty-nine."

"Perfect, because I'm really thirty-five. Is that too old?"

"It's perfect, Lauren." He stood, closing the distance between them. He reached for her hand, gently pulling her out of the chair. He lowered his head and touched his lips to hers.

At a knock on the door, Lauren fell back into the chair, a wicked grin on her face. "Felicia?"

"Probably," he said, returning her wicked grin with a wicked and sexy one of his own.

"Come in," he said.

Felicia entered, carrying a tray with three glasses filled with ice and three cans of Coke. "Am I interrupting something?"

"Yes, we were discussing Dad's life," he said, taking a can of Coke and a glass of ice from the tray. He popped the tab, filled the glass, and gave it to Lauren.

"Well, I can assure you, he is one of the nicest men you'll ever meet," Felicia said as she poured a soda for John, then one for herself.

"I'm excited to meet him," Lauren said. She was feeling so many different emotions. This morning, she'd told her mother that when she met a guy who knocked her socks off, blew her away, she'd tell her. Lauren was pretty darn sure she'd just met that guy, and even better, she knew he felt the same. Actually, she'd known that she had met him the second he'd entered Razzle Dazzle.

"He's a piece of work, that's all I'm saying," John said, a grin on his face. "Speaking of which, I better get back to the cockpit and get this biographer to Seattle safely because something tells me we're going to be seeing a lot of one another in the future." He looked at her, and once again, she turned to mush.

"Yes, and I'd best let Lauren rest," Felicia said. "We'll be landing soon." She hurried out of the room with the tray and empty soda cans.

"Thanks for the Coke," Lauren called out to her.

"So, you're good with this?" John asked.

"This what?"

"Us," he said.

Lauren knew that he felt whatever it was she was feeling. This was a knock-your-socks-off moment, or love at first sight. Whatever one called it, she would meet it head-on. "Yes. I'm good with us," she said, knowing these words were about to change her life forever.

"Then let's seal the deal," he said, and once again pulled her into his arms, touched his lips to hers, and sealed the deal of a lifetime.

Chapter 20

Lauren spent the night at a luxurious penthouse apartment owned by Mr. Giampalo. She'd slept like a baby and was wide-awake at 3:00 A.M. With the time difference, she'd expected to awaken at the crack of dawn.

A limousine would take her to Giampalo's office at 9:00. When she'd left Fallen Springs yesterday, no way would she have guessed how her evening would end. She and John went to dinner at Bisato. He was the perfect gentleman. She, on the other hand, wanted to devour him. He was so handsome, so sexy, it hurt to look at him. She was a little disappointed when he declined her offer to have coffee in his father's penthouse.

This wasn't her usual mode. She couldn't help herself. This man, this kind, sexy man who collected music boxes adored her as much as she adored him. She was hesitant to use the L word, but who was she kidding? She knew she was falling madly, deeply in love with this man. She was not a naïve young girl. She'd been in serious relationships before. But nothing had ever come close to how she was feeling about him.

She twirled around the room, her long blond hair hanging loose and touching her waist. She wanted to call her mother, or Madison, to tell them about this man, but they'd think she was crazy. No one falls in love so quickly. At least no one she knew. And could she write this biography without bias? She had no answers. Clearly, she would have to focus on her original goals. John would have to take a back seat to his father.

This was indeed going to be one of the best holiday seasons she'd had in a very long time. If only Razzle Dazzle could recover from its sales slump, it would make the holidays even better. However, she knew as well as anyone that unless her parents moved forward, joined the contemporary world, Razzle Dazzle would fade, sadly, into nothing more than a memory for the residents of Fallen Springs.

The penthouse was equipped with every kind of electronic gadget available and a couple she'd never heard of. Prototypes, she guessed. The espresso machine took her a few minutes to get the hang of, but once she did, it was too easy. She carried the tiny cup into the bathroom. Beyond lux, it too was a techie's dream. Flat-screen TV above a huge soaker tub, a spa area with lotions and potions, and all sorts of contraptions for one's hair. She just wanted a shower. She put her espresso aside, stripped off the nightshirt she'd slept in, punched a few buttons on a panel, and sprays of warm water from all directions drenched her body. "I can't believe this place," she said to herself. A mechanical, though distinctly female, voice said, "I will tell Mr. G." Lauren looked around the shower, then saw where the sound had come from. A Siri-like application was placed behind a glass panel above the main showerhead.

Lauren felt a bit creeped out. While she liked the high-tech everything in the penthouse, she didn't want whatever she said to be questioned or heard by anyone or any*thing* in this place. She quickly finished her shower, used the plush robe provided, and, pulling her long hair into a bun, secured it with an unused toothbrush.

She glanced at the time—there were clocks all over the place. She wasn't sure she liked that, either. John told her this place had been turned into a home of the future, though all the kinks hadn't been ironed out yet. She was okay with some of it, but she liked her privacy. Which brought to mind her father, of all things. She had a slight understanding of his aversion to all the technological changes in the world. If she were honest, she didn't like that female voice in the shower. While she'd used the Siri app on her cell phone and on her laptop, that was useful. Getting a response after talking out loud in the shower? She didn't like that at all.

Seeing the time and knowing that her mother would be awake making breakfast or at least coffee, she took her cup of espresso and cell phone to the living area. She used a remote to open the shades. She had a perfect view of Seattle's Space Needle and the city lights. *All is calm, all is bright*, she thought, thinking of one of her favorite Christmas carols.

She dialed her home number, knowing that her mother would have that little moment of wonder, a question of who was calling at such an early hour because they did not have caller ID, even though that technology was old hat by this point.

"Hello," came her mother's cheery voice.

"Morning, Mom," Lauren said. "Just wanted to call and check in." She didn't really, but that was all she could come up with at this hour.

"Lauren, you're up with the chickens. Are you feeling all right?"

"Yes, this time difference is messing with me, but I'm fine. I just wanted to call, check on the kitties. Did Brent manage to get them home without any trouble?"

"Yes, and they're as snug as a bug in a rug right now. I've put their beds in the den; they're loving the warmth of the fireplace, though we're being very careful. Your dad is tickled pink. That was a good move." Her mother seemed extra chirpy this morning.

Lauren knew that her furry family would bring joy to the house. "I think so too. I don't know why I didn't think of it sooner. I'm glad you all are there; I'm not sure how long I'll be in Seattle." Especially given the complete about-face that was now her life.

"Do your job, and don't worry about anything here. We'll take care of everything."

"Thanks, Mom," Lauren said, ending the call. She'd so wanted to tell her about John Giampalo, but it was too soon. Even though her socks were long gone, she needed time to get used to the idea that she'd actually fallen quickly, madly, and deeply in love. She'd never believed in love at first sight, thought it was a gross exaggeration when people spoke about it. But now she knew better. It had happened to her.

Lauren spent the next hour writing notes and preparing questions for her first interview. It would be a process, and she knew there was no way she'd learn about Giampalo's entire life story in their first meeting, but first impressions set the tone for her writing style, so she wanted to be as prepared as possible.

After a while, she couldn't come up with any more questions to ask, but she knew she'd have many more after she met him. For the time being, she wanted to take Angela's advice and dress the part of the successful author. She wished she'd saved her Chanel suit for today, yet she knew she'd packed wisely, and her black Escada sheath dress would do just fine. She'd wear her low-heeled Stuart Weitzman pumps.

She did her makeup the same way as yesterday, minus the winged eyeliner. Her hand wasn't that steady this morning. She did the same with her hair, twisting and tucking, using the same diamond barrette as before. She still wore the same diamond earrings and necklaces; they were staples and could be worn with just about anything. Though she felt pretty sure Mr. Giampalo wouldn't care one way or another.

At 8:40, Lauren grabbed her bag, put her laptop inside, then took the private elevator to the main lobby, where a car would drive her to the Global Goods corporate office in downtown Seattle.

She was greeted by a middle-aged man wearing a Seattle Seahawks cap, denim jeans, and a polo shirt with the company's G logo on the pocket. "You're Ms. Montgomery?" he asked, and held out his hand. "I'm Derek, Mr. G's personal driver. He asked me to take you to headquarters."

Surprised at his casual attire, she hoped she wasn't overdressed. "I'm Lauren Montgomery; nice to meet you," She shook his hand, liking him instantly. His warm brown eyes sparkled, and his wide grin reached his eyes. *A genuine soul*, she thought.

Lauren expected a limousine, a Rolls Royce, but the tiny electric car, a Chevy of some kind, was not in the same league as the company airplane.

"Thanks," she said. He held the passenger door open, and she managed to squash herself and her bag inside.

"Mr. G would croak if he knew I was using my own personal car to bring you downtown. The company car is being serviced this morning. You okay riding in this little gal?"

She laughed. "It's fine, really. I have a ten-year-old Honda." And she didn't mind, though there was much to be said for vehicles with a bit of extra leg room, even for someone as short as her.

"This your first time in Seattle?"

"Yes," she said. "I hear the traffic is formidable."

"It is, but I've got this route down pat. I zip through a few side streets, and I'll have you at Mr. G's in record time."

When he said zip, he wasn't kidding. She felt like she was on a carnival ride. Stop. Go. Slam on the brakes, swerve around corners. She held onto the armrest and closed her eyes. She and her mother had a terrible problem with car sickness. Lauren sent up a silent request to the powers that be that she wouldn't get sick in this tiny little car. On her clothes. Or, even worse, when she met Mr. Giampalo. She wanted to ask Derek to slow down, take it easy on the corners, but feared if she even opened her mouth, that would be the end of her self-control. The next ten minutes was the worst time she'd ever spent in a vehicle trying not to lose her cookies. She rolled down the window, allowing the cold air to hit her face. It was the only thing she could do.

A squeal, and another hard slam on the brakes.

"Told you I'd get you here on time."

Lauren couldn't speak. Struggling to hold back the waves of nausea, she took as deep a breath as possible, then eased herself out of the car. She had no idea where they were or if this was even the main office. At this point, she didn't care. All she wanted to do was sit down and be still. No movement, because all it would take for her to lose it was one more unexpected jar.

"You okay?"

She couldn't even shake her head. She stood beside the car, her bag at her feet.

"Ms. Montgomery?" he asked again.

Lauren swallowed back the bitter espresso she'd had earlier. "No," she managed to say in a whisper through clenched teeth.

"You carsick?" he asked her.

She didn't dare move her head to respond, so once again she spoke through clenched teeth. "Yes."

Derek shook his head. "Dang, I guess that ride was a bit rough, huh?"

She didn't dare answer. Lauren wanted to sit down somewhere cool and quiet and motionless. She managed to point to the entrance. The building was at least ten stories high, and she could only hope the office was on the ground floor.

"Ah, got it. Let's go inside." Derek took her bag and plowed ahead of her.

Managing to reach deep within herself, Lauren inched her way inside the building. One. Step. At. A. Time.

The blast of warm air hit her the second the automatic doors opened. Lauren then proceeded to empty the contents of her stomach on the marble floors at the corporate headquarters of Global Goods.

Chapter 21

Her black Stuart Weitzman pumps, along with her stockings and the white-marble floor, were covered in the contents of what had been in her stomach.

Lauren wanted to die when another gush forced her once again to empty whatever remained in her stomach. She was mortified beyond words, and so sick she truly didn't know what to do.

"Derek," came a male voice.

"Yes, sir?"

"Take care of this. Now."

Lauren felt dizzy, her head was throbbing, and the back of her throat felt like it was on fire. Ever so slightly, she moved her head to see the man who stood a few feet away from her and the pool of regurgitated espresso.

"You must be Lauren Montgomery. I'm Lucas, Mr.

G's personal assistant. It seems Derek has taken you on one of his infamous shortcuts," he said.

Lauren thanked the powers above that this wasn't Mr. Giampalo. At this point, though, would it matter? Whatever first impression she'd hoped to make was ruined. Right now, she wished she was at home with her old-fashioned family. Anywhere but here would be a bonus.

"Lauren, I hope you don't mind me using your first name; we're not very formal here," Lucas said. "If you will allow me, I'll have Sandra Marie show you where you can clean up and change out of your clothes."

All Lauren could manage to think of was that she didn't have a change of clothes with her. And who was Sandra Marie? Lucas must have read her thoughts. "Sandra is my assistant. Now, if you'll allow me." He took her arm and gently guided her to the elevator.

"I don't think," was all she managed to say before another bout of nausea overtook her, and though her stomach was completely empty, she still felt sick.

"Hang on," Lucas said.

Before she could protest, the elevator stopped, the doors swished open. "Sandra, Ms. Montgomery has been on a joyride with Derek."

"You poor thing." Sandra Marie was not what Lauren expected, though she could have been Mrs. Claus for all she cared. She was older than her mother, with white hair, and she had a glow about her.

Clearing her throat, Lauren managed to say, "I'm so sorry."

"No, Derek is the one who should be sorry," Sandra Marie said. "Let's take it slowly, and we'll get you cleaned up."

Lauren nodded, thankful for this woman, more than she could ever express. She followed her to a good-sized bathroom. Inside, it looked like a locker room. "This is for our female staff. Some of us are so busy we stay the night. Let's get you out of that fancy dress and into the shower."

"Oh, I'm so embarrassed," she managed to say.

"Derek is the one who should be embarrassed. You're not the first person he's delivered in this condition. I bet he was in that tiny trap he calls a car."

"Yes, it was a small car," Lauren said. She sat down on a padded bench, kicked off her soiled shoes, and managed to remove her stockings without getting dizzy. "If you could unzip me, I think I'll be okay."

Sandra Marie unzipped her dress, and Lauren stepped out of it, glad she'd worn matching black bra and panties. "If you'll show me the shower," she said, starting to feel slightly human.

"This way," Sandra Marie directed.

Lauren followed her to a room that looked like a spa. It was darker in there, thankfully, and it smelled like aloe or cucumber. It was not unpleasant. The same brand of toiletries that she'd seen in the airplane were here also.

"This shower has a seat," Sandra Marie said. "Just toss your underthings in the plastic bag, and I'll have them cleaned. I'll have something for you to wear before you finish your shower."

Lauren wasn't about to ask how. "Thanks," she said.

"There are towels and washcloths, everything you need in here." She opened another door, revealing a giant, glassed-in shower with a seat.

It was all marble, the fixtures a soft gold; Lauren wondered if they were the real deal. She didn't care as long as they worked.

"I'll be right outside the door if you need me."

Lauren nodded and closed the door. She adjusted the shower and, removing her underclothes, stepped under the warm spray, letting the water wash away the vomit from her body. She used the shampoo to wash her hair, then scrubbed herself with body wash. When she felt she'd removed all traces of her nightmare car ride, she wrapped herself in the same style of robe she'd worn at the penthouse. She wrapped her hair in a towel and returned to the bench to sit down. She was still lightheaded, unsure if she could pull off this interview that day. She certainly wasn't feeling confident and sure of herself. This very well could cause her to lose this contract. Angela would be outraged.

"These should fit just fine," Sandra Marie said.

"You have clothes here?" she asked, stating the obvious.

"We have everything here. I took a guess, brought a size-two dress; it's last year's Calvin Klein. I hope that's okay. Underclothes, stockings, and I guessed a six in a shoe."

"Perfect," she said. "I'll just take a minute to rest, if that's okay." She felt quite weak; she probably should eat something, but right now, that was out of the question.

"Rest all you want. I've got ginger ale, some saltines, and a box of Dramamine if you want them."

"Ginger ale sounds wonderful." She tried to stand but felt a wave of dizziness wash over her.

"Stay right there. I'll bring it to you."

"Thanks," she said, feeling like a baby. This morning, she'd been on top of the world; now she didn't know if she could sink much lower. Sandra Marie returned with a glass of ice and a bottle of ginger ale. She filled the glass and handed it to her.

"Sip it slowly," she instructed.

Lauren took a few sips, grateful for the woman's care. "I have to confess, I don't think I've ever been this embarrassed."

"It's fine, truly. As I said, you're not the first to get sick after a ride with Derek."

"Why is he still a driver?" she asked, even though it was none of her business.

"Because he's Mr. G's best friend. He was a stock-car driver in his day."

Lauren laughed. "That explains it then."

"He's testing these new electric cars now. I think Mr. G will ride his ass over this trip."

"No, please, I don't want to get the guy into trouble; he could lose his job. I would feel terrible."

Sandra Marie chuckled. "No, his job is secure. Let's just make sure you have another driver while you're here."

The thought of getting into another vehicle right now almost made her sick again. "That's probably a good idea." She took a few more sips of her ginger ale and felt much better. "I'll get dressed, see what I can do with this mess." She touched the towel on top of her head.

"I'll step out, let you dress."

Lauren slipped into a pair of yellow panties and a matching lace bra. Not her style, but who cared at this point. She pulled the silky stockings over her pale legs, then stepped into the dress. It fit her perfectly. Sandra Marie had a good eye for sizing. The shoes were half a size too small, but she managed. When she stepped into the main area of the ladies' room—locker room, spa, she wasn't sure what to call it—Sandra Marie was there waiting for her, along with another woman, who was much younger.

"Lauren, this is Olivia: she's going to do your hair for you. If that's all right."

Relief washed over her. "Hey, Olivia. I can't thank you two enough."

"No worries," Olivia said. "If you'll sit here, I'll get to work on your hair."

She sat on a small stool while Olivia combed out her long hair, then used a powerful blow-dryer to style it. "I think this is perfect, don't you?" she said to Lauren.

"It is," she agreed, though she thought she looked more sophisticated with her hair up. But after what these two women had done for her, she didn't care if her hair was in pigtails.

"If you want some cosmetics, we have a full drawer of them," Olivia said, opening and closing drawers before she found what she wanted. "Mascara, blush, and a few tubes of lipstick. I can't imagine you would need any more than that."

"This is fine, thanks." She really could use a complete do-over, given the day so far, but she felt a lot better after showering and drinking a glass of ginger ale. She opened the new tube of mascara, loaded her pale lashes, then added the color back to her skin with the blush. "Would there be a toothbrush around here?" she asked before putting on lipstick. She'd rinsed her mouth in the shower, but she needed to brush her teeth, badly.

"Here you go," Sandra Marie said. "I was waiting for you to ask."

"You two are awesome. I can't believe you have all of these things here."

"It's Globalgoods.com. We have to have everything one would need in any given situation. Our motto in and out of the office."

Lauren used the sink at the end of the counter to brush her teeth, and finally, she once again felt like a human being. She added the lipstick and looked at her image in the mirror. "Not too bad, given that ride I was on."

Olivia spoke. "Mr. G needs to forbid that man from driving. He's a danger to the passengers and the people on the road." She had a slight accent, though Lauren couldn't identify what it was.

"I'm going to have Lucas have a talk with him," Sandra Marie said. "He still thinks he's driving stock cars."

"Lauren, Olivia is engaged to Lucas; she's the one who makes us all presentable if we're on television or a video conference."

Lauren smiled. "Well, you did a fantastic job with this." She patted her smooth, clean hair. "It's so exciting to know things like this are real; does that make sense?"

She felt out of her depth, but in reality, with a business the size of this one, she should have known they would have a staff to cater to every need imaginable.

"It does," Olivia said. "I was like you when I started working here six years ago. Mr. G, he's the best boss, but you wait and form your own opinion."

Lauren nodded. "I'm ready to meet him if he still wants to go through with this interview."

"He is, and said to send you up as soon as you felt comfortable."

"Then let's get this show on the road," Lauren said, amazed that she actually felt human again.

Chapter 22

Lauren was nervous as she took the elevator to the tenth floor. She had her bag, her computer, her notes. She knew how to conduct an interview. She'd done this before. She wrote best-selling books.

She was madly in love.

She smiled, and the elevator doors opened. She stepped into a lavish lobby, the red G prominently displayed at the back of a semicircular reception area. She expected to find a swarm of computers, and dozens of people taking orders and rushing around to make sure they filled their next-day-delivery promise. She reminded herself that this was the corporate office, not the warehouses, which were scattered all over the world. This was the home of the company's founder. His personal office.

"You must be Lauren," came a gruff voice. She knew

who he was before he introduced himself. "I'm John; most people just call me Mr. G."

"Mr. G, it's an honor to meet you." She shook his hand. He was tall and built well for a man his age. His skin was tanned in a natural way, he had a full head of white hair, and when he smiled, she saw the resemblance to John.

"Come on back here, and let's get to know one another."

"Of course," she said, walking beside him. She didn't want to cower behind, that would not make a good impression. She'd read enough self-help books to know that. "Confidence," Angela had said. "Always show your confidence in yourself without being too overconfident."

Two hours ago, that would have been impossible.

They walked down a long, carpeted hall and stopped when they reached a pair of wooden double doors. Lauren wasn't sure what kind of wood, but it was striking.

"I like to stay away from the other offices; it keeps me out of trouble," he said, opening the door for her.

Lauren stepped inside, expecting his office to be as lavish as his airplane, but it wasn't. Though luxurious, it wasn't an in-your-face kind of luxury. Gray, black, and, of course, the company's signature red could be seen throughout. A gray sofa, gray lounge chairs, shiny black tables, the red G embossed in the tabletops, but not in a distasteful manner. It was a professional office and nothing more. Mr. G's desk was quite large and was centered in front of the floor-to-ceiling windows that faced the Space Needle.

He must have seen where her eyes traveled because he said, "Don't need a lot of extra décor with that as a backdrop." He nodded in the direction of the Space Needle.

"This is perfect," she said, and meant it.

"Thanks. I hear you met Derek, and in the worst way. Please allow me to tell you how sorry I am. I've suspended him for a few days, the old cuss. He means well."

"It was quite an experience," she said, wanting to forget that it ever happened. She was just grateful he hadn't witnessed her embarrassment.

"John called me last night," he said.

Oh no. Not a good way to start. Surely, he hadn't spilled the beans, or whatever one called it these days.

"He told me he spied on you at your store."

She didn't know what to say, so again she smiled and let him talk.

"I knew he had gone to North Carolina. I just didn't know why. Tells me he found a few music boxes in your store, bought them all."

"He did. Each is handmade by some of the best artisans in the state. He has good taste," she said.

"He does. I want to apologize for his sneakiness."

"There's nothing to apologize for. He's watching out for his family; I get that. In his position, I might have done the same."

"That offer you made, the one I refused when I talked to Ms. Winters, you still considering that?"

She took a deep breath and felt light-headed all over again. "I thought it was off the table."

"I wanted to meet you first. You have quite the reputation, and when you offered a deal, I knew you were the perfect author to write my biography. The deal's still good, if and when you're ready."

She couldn't help but grin. "I'll keep that in mind."

For the next hour, they made small talk, getting to know one another. Lauren thought him extremely likable, exactly as his employees said. He had a light lunch delivered to the office, for which she was grateful. Turkey sandwiches, with fruit salad, and more ginger ale.

"You feeling better?" he asked when she drained her glass.

"Much, thank you."

"You gonna be able to tell my story in six weeks?" he asked out of the blue.

"Yes, I'm sure I can, but do you mind if I ask why?" She hoped he wasn't dying and wanted her to write his final good-bye to the world.

"I always said I'd have a bio by the time I was seventy. I'm seventy-two, and late."

She laughed. "Seriously?"

"Yes. I'm the kind of guy who likes to keep his word, though I am late on this. I'm thinking that at least now I have a couple more years' worth of stories to tell you."

"Then it all worked out for the best," she agreed.

They spent the next three hours going over the high points of his life. He told her how he had to work three jobs to put himself through college. His parents had died young. He wanted to make them proud, even though they weren't around to witness his success. Lauren took notes, using a pencil and a steno pad.

"Kind of old style," he remarked.

"It is, and I'll transcribe my notes later. My dad is old style, too." She told him her father's story, how his father and grandfather worked, opening the general store, then how the big-box stores forced them to sell pieces the big stores didn't want, hence their exclusive Christmas pieces.

"He's an entrepreneur, then. Sounds like he and I'll get along just fine."

Lauren panicked. "What do you mean?" she asked, feeling silly, but she had to know.

"If we're going to work together, I want to meet the man. I try to meet as many of our suppliers as I can. It's not always possible, but this, well, I'll let you talk to him first. I know he's not too thrilled about jumping on the Internet bandwagon, but I think I can change his mind. Now, I want to ask you something, and you'll tell me if I'm out of line?"

"Of course."

"John is smitten with you." He chuckled. "Though he didn't use that word, it's what us old guys call more than a casual date; I think those are the words he used."

Shit.

Where to start? What to say?

"He's a great guy. I think we hit it off."

At least that was true. Not knowing what John had told his father, she didn't want to say more for fear of assuming too much in the sense that she'd decided he was definitely the guy who'd knocked her socks off, took the wind from her sails, whatever.

"He said the same about you, though he led me to believe you two might end up being more than just friends."

Her heart filled with joy. Yes, they were on the same page. She knew he'd felt what she had. She gave Mr. G her first real genuine smile of the day. "He's probably right."

"Yep, I could tell. So you'll have dinner with us tonight? At the house, and we can talk more about the book, and I can watch you and my son together."

He wasn't asking, but she was good with this. "I would love to," she said, and meant it. "Something light." She added, fearing a repeat of this morning.

"I'll keep that in mind when I order up the groceries."

"Really? You use your service?"

"Heck yes, I do. All that traffic, I don't want to drive in it unless it's absolutely necessary. Helping to keep my employees employed."

"So you're making dinner yourself?" The words flew out of her mouth.

"Always. I like tinkering around in the kitchen. John does too. We've been our own family for so long, and as he got older, it seemed we spent a lot of our quality time together while we made dinner."

Lauren thought this would make an excellent addition to the bio, yet she knew there was much more to be learned. He wanted this bio completed in six weeks, so she would need to focus her undivided attention on every detail in order to make this a best seller. It wasn't so much the money the worldwide business made that her readers liked; it was the in-between, the everyday details that made them want to turn the page.

She glanced at her watch. It was after 4:00.

"We'll have dinner at eight; that sound good to you?"

"That's perfect," she agreed. It would give her time to unwind, maybe soak in the luxurious bathtub, transcribe her notes.

"Then that's what we'll do. I'll arrange for your ride back to the penthouse, so you can rest up. Could be a late night," he said, and winked. So this is where John had picked up the habit.

She dreaded the thought of getting in another vehicle, especially since she'd learned that Seattle traffic was a nightmare. She'd pop one of the Dramamine tablets Sandra Marie had discreetly tucked inside her bag.

Mr. G walked over to his desk, picked up the phone, and spoke into it, though she couldn't hear what he said.

"Your ride will be here in ten minutes," he announced, a sly grin on his face. "You'll need these," he said, reaching inside a drawer and handing her a pair of headsets.

She put them in her bag.

"You'll need those for the ride. I'm having the chopper take you back to the penthouse. I don't want you getting carsick again. You're good with a helicopter ride?"

Her stomach twisted, her fear of flying kicked up. "Honestly, I've never been in a helicopter."

"I always say there is a first time for everything. You'll want to put those on so you can talk with the pilot, keep down the noise."

Lauren seriously doubted she'd be in any shape to carry on a conversation, but she would keep those thoughts to herself. "Sure," she said.

"I'll let Sandra Marie know you're ready, and she'll walk you up to the heliport."

Lauren nodded. Living a life of luxury did have its share of perks. *It wouldn't be too much of a leap to get used to this*, she thought. *Traveling in a helicopter . . .* Hopefully, it was a short flight to the penthouse.

"Then I'll see you tonight?"

"I'll have the chopper pick you up at seven forty-five."

The office door opened, and Sandra Marie entered the room. "Chopper's six minutes out, G. You want me to bring anything tonight?"

"Just yourself," he said, winking at his assistant's assistant.

"Later, G," she said, and led Lauren down the hall to a flight of stairs.

"We've got an elevator to the roof, but it's only a couple of flights up. You're looking much better, I have to say," she said.

"I feel better, and thanks for everything. I feel so silly and embarrassed."

"As I said, you're not the first one, though I hope you'll be the last. Derek needs to learn how to drive like a human being." She took a card from her pocket, scanned it, and the door to the heliport opened.

"Put that headset on now," she instructed.

Lauren took it from her bag, pulled her hair behind her ears, then placed it over her ears. A long cord with a silver plug at the end dangled from the left-ear side of the headset.

"The pilot will hook it up for you," Sandra Marie said, pointing to a chopper headed in their direction. She cupped her hands together and shouted, "I'll see you at dinner tonight."

The loud whirring of the helicopter startled Lauren, even with the headset on. She waved at Sandra Marie, curious as to what her relationship with Mr. G, or just G, was. She hoped they were a couple, because didn't everybody need to be loved by somebody?

Chapter 23

Lauren clutched her Chloé bag close to her body as she made her way to the helicopter. Even though she was short and the blades were barely spinning, she ducked when she reached the chopper. A girl about Charlotte's age helped her inside, buckled her in, then plugged her headset into the jack. "I'm Evelyn. That better?" she asked, a grin revealing a mouthful of braces.

"Yes, I can hear you. A female pilot, awesome," Lauren said, thinking she was quite young. This was going to be fun.

"I'm not a pilot yet, but I hope to be someday," Evelyn said. "I'm just getting some hours in."

Lauren had no clue what she meant, but nodded. Evelyn slid into the front of the chopper and disappeared. Never having seen the inside of one before, Lauren sat there, waiting to find out what happened next. She had a death grip on her bag when the chopper's blades whirred into action, and seconds later, they were hovering above the rooftop, then slowly gliding away from the building.

This was fantastic!

She peered out the window, amazed. The traffic really was insane. She was clueless as to what roads went where, but from her vantage point, it looked as though it wouldn't matter which road you took. One could plan on spending time just sitting in traffic. Now she understood why Mr. G had suggested this mode of transportation. All thoughts of her fears were gone as they soared above the traffic, the buildings, passing the Space Needle. She wanted to go there, and if she didn't this trip, maybe another time. *This is going to be my best book yet*, she thought, because she was experiencing Mr. G's life in real time.

She wanted to call her family, Madison, Charlotte, Ruby, and Louise, and tell them how magnificent she felt right now, but couldn't because they wouldn't be able to hear a word she said. As soon as she was back in the penthouse, she'd at least call her mother, check on the kitties, and see how sales were at the store. Maybe she'd even tell Dad about Mr. G's interest in the offer she'd made, the offer he had no clue about. It didn't matter; she'd figure out the details, play it by ear. It seemed her carefully orchestrated life had culminated in this one moment, hovering above an exciting city where world changes were happening as she flew above massive skyscrapers, Puget Sound, headquarters for Microsoft and Global Goods. She truly did feel like Dorothy when she had first entered the Land of Oz, and was it coincidence that Seattle was also known as the Emerald City? She had never believed in coincidence, but that could change.

Static came through her headset, and she adjusted the volume, making sure she had the earpieces properly secured. She checked the receptacle where Evelyn had plugged the headset into the jack. It looked good to her.

"You doing okay back there?" asked a familiar voice.

She leaned forward, trying to see if she was imagining things; after all, she was in the Emerald City. Before she answered, she saw a hand slide open the panel that separated the passenger from the pilot.

"You sneaky thing, you!" she said. "Your dad didn't tell me *you* were flying this chopper!" Breathless with excitement, Lauren leaned forward, trying to get a glimpse of John, Mr. Hunk.

"I bet you didn't think to ask, either," he joked. "Evelyn is training to be a chopper pilot and needed to get in a few hours, so I asked her to come with me."

"Evelyn, can you hear me?" she asked.

A girlish voice came through her headset. "I can; can you hear me okay?" Her voice was sweet, and it reminded Lauren of Charlotte's.

"Perfectly."

"We're going to be landing in three minutes, so make sure you're buckled in tight," John said.

Lauren tightened the seat belt as much as she could without cutting off her circulation. "I think it's tight enough."

"Good girl," he said, and even though she could only see the back of his head, she knew he was grinning from the sound of his oh-so-sexy voice.

Lauren peered out the small window as John lowered the chopper onto a white helipad with the now-familiar red G in its center. Seconds later, the loud whir of the blades lessened. She unhooked her seat belt and removed the headset. Lauren kept it, knowing she would need it for the ride to Mr. G's house later.

John got out of the pilot's seat and came around to her side. "Better than an electric car?" he teased.

She let him help her out of the chopper. Smoothing her hair, she laughed. "Sounds like you've heard about my ride with Derek."

"Lucas called me. If it makes you feel any better, you're not the first person to barf after riding with him."

Lauren felt her cheeks flush. "Good to know."

"I'll show you the way to the penthouse, then I've got to let Evelyn fly for a while, and I'll pick you up at seven-thirty."

She nodded.

"I don't mean to sound as if I'm ordering you around. Do I come off that way?"

"No, not at all; tells me you're relaxed in my company," she said, and it was true.

"I am. Very much."

"Me too," she said, as he opened another door, using the same kind of card Sandra Marie had used.

He must have seen her watching him. "Security is pretty tight around here. These cards are changed out daily, but you'll learn all this after you've been around a while."

"Of course, it would have to be," she said. Actually, having seen the corporate offices, now that it was brought to her attention, she realized security must be out of sight. She'd only seen Sandra Marie use the card to unlock the steel door on the roof.

He led her down three flights of stairs, then he waved another card in front of yet another steel door and entered the penthouse.

She had that country-bumpkin feeling again.

"Something wrong?" John asked.

Lauren was amazed at how in tune he was with her emotions.

She placed her bag on the floor beside the door. "No, I was thinking about the security. I guess I expected guards at the doors, I don't know."

She walked across the room, used the remote to open the shades. "This is the most amazing view," she said.

"Almost as amazing as your Blue Ridge Mountains."

"Have you seen them in the fall?" she asked.

"Many times."

She turned to face him. "So this wasn't your first trip to North Carolina?"

He led her to the sofa, where they could share the view of the Space Needle and the city lights dotting the sky-line.

"No, I have a place in Asheville, close to the Bilt-more."

She remembered him telling her he was staying at the Biltmore. "You're weren't at the Biltmore, then?"

"Actually, I was. My place was being decorated for Christmas. And all those music boxes are in my home. You'll get to see it soon, I hope."

This man was totally out of this world. Easy to be with, and they'd barely kissed.

"If I stay a second longer, Evelyn might fly off in the chopper, and I'll be in big trouble. I'll leave, but I'll be back to take you to Dad's for dinner." He wrapped his arms around her waist, lifting her so that they were eye to eye, then he kissed her, so gently, slowly, that spirals of desire went racing through her body. Then he lowered her back to the ground. He took a deep breath, and said, "You're perfect for me, Lauren."

She just stood there, drugged with desire, and stared up at him. All she could say was, "Me too."

"I'll see you soon," he said, and gave her another kiss, though this time on her cheek.

"I'll be here," was all she said as she watched him leave through the steel door.

She literally dropped down onto the cushy sofa, closed her eyes, and admitted to herself that even though she'd just met this handsome, kind, sexy man and barely knew him, what she did know for certain was that she was head over heels in love with him.

She could have spent hours thinking about John and staring out at the view, but she wanted to type up her notes about her experience with Mr. G while it was still fresh in her mind. She'd leave out the part about her falling in love with his son, and especially his kisses.

Wanting to slip into comfortable clothes, she went to the master bedroom. She'd pulled her luggage into the walk-in closet to keep it out of sight. She switched on the light and saw that her Chanel suit was hanging up, and her Stuart Weitzman pumps were sparkling like Dorothy's red slippers. On a shelf were her cleaned stockings and underclothes, neatly folded beside them. "Unreal." She found her leggings and University of Florida sweatshirt still inside her luggage. She slipped out of the borrowed clothes, hung the dress next to her Chanel dress, kept the underclothes on, but took off the stockings and the borrowed shoes, which were a bit small but had certainly saved the day.

She took her laptop out of her bag, along with the steno pad with her notes, and sat at the counter for the next hour, working on transcribing her notes about what she'd observed. She wrote about security, but this was for her eyes only. No way was she going to even hint at this because she could jeopardize many people, plus she honestly didn't have a clue what kind of security they had—just knew it had to be the most high-tech on the market. She knew Global Goods had offices all over the world, and this wasn't small stuff. She would tell Mr. G's story and forget about his security for now. If he wanted her to know, he would tell her.

She'd plugged her phone into the charger before she started typing up her notes. It was now fully charged. She called the house, but no one answered. She looked at the clock. It was 6:00 here, so that meant it was 9:00 at home. Her parents never went out this late unless they were visiting Grandpa. She dialed Razzle Dazzle, just in case they'd stayed late. No answer there, either. She didn't bother leaving a message on the machine. Concerned that maybe the little kittens were ill, she wondered if she should call the vet. But they didn't have a veterinarian yet, only Dr. Melloh, who volunteered at the shelter, and the shelter would be closed as well.

Not wanting to, but having no choice since neither parent had a cell phone, she dialed Brent's number. He answered on the first ring. "Lauren, what's up? You calling to check on the kitties I delivered?"

"No, but thanks for taking them to the house. Mom and Dad seem to be getting a kick out of them."

"Oh, they are going to spoil them rotten, no doubt in my mind. Your dad was beside himself."

"Good, I thought he would be. Brent, did you notice how much better he's moving around?"

"I did. Your mother told me about the medication and

the depression. He'll get through this. He's a tough old dude. She also told me about the book you're working on. That's a fantastic opportunity for you. Global Goods."

"I hope it works out, but I need another favor." She hated to ask but didn't know what else to do.

"Anything," he said in that tone he used with her when he told her how he felt about her.

She rolled her eyes, then felt ashamed of herself. Brent was a great friend. And that's all he would ever be. "I tried calling the house and the store, and I can't seem to find them. Anything going on that you know of?"

"They're probably at the tree-lighting ceremony downtown; it started around eight o'clock."

Lauren breathed a sigh of relief. "I forgot all about that. Then I'm sure that's where they are."

"You want me to take a ride downtown, bring them in for curfew violation?"

She chuckled. "No, though it would be hilarious. I can just see the look on Mom's face. Busted." Lauren dissolved in laughter. "She's so proper."

Brent laughed with her. "Yes, they're old-fashioned, but good people."

"I think so," she said.

"Just like their daughter."

"Brent, please," she said, knowing where the conversation would go if she didn't stop it now.

"So, how is Seattle?" he asked.

Glad he changed the topic, she said, "It's beautiful. I'm looking at the Space Needle as we speak. The view from the penthouse I'm staying in is out of this world; you should see it."

"Maybe I will someday. With you."

"Maybe," she said, then decided to steer their conversation in a totally different direction. "Brent, do you remember Lee Hessinger? We went to high school with her."

"Absolutely. She's a knockout, works at the post office, though I haven't seen her there in a while. Why do you ask?"

"She has a fifteen-year-old daughter, Charlotte. I've sort of taken her under my wing. Lee has leukemia, and she's in the hospital waiting to have a bone-marrow transplant."

"Damn, I'm sorry. I didn't realize she was sick, but it explains why I haven't seen her at the post office. So, is she on a transplant waiting list?"

"Her daughter's a match. I don't have all the details, but Charlotte has to stay in the hospital for a few days, just to make sure she isn't sick or has the flu, something like that."

"What can I do to help?"

This is the Brent she adored, always quick to step in when he was needed. Obviously, he was the sheriff, so helping people was part of his DNA, as it was of her own.

What did she want him to do? "I may be out of town a few days longer than I'd originally planned. I wanted to see Charlotte before she went into the cancer-center hospital in Chapel Hill where they'll do the transplant, but once she's there, she'll be in isolation for a few weeks. I don't know how you feel about this, but I want someone to know, in case—well, in case something were to happen to me."

"Lauren, don't talk that way; you're fine."

"I know, but I need you to know this. Madison and Scott know, but I want you to know as well. Lee's insurance doesn't cover her bone-marrow transplant. It's crap insurance; we'll just leave it at that. Remember James Crawford? He's a neurologist in town. He told me about a fund hospitals have; he called it an indigent fund. Long story, but he's managed to get this fund applied toward Lee's transplant costs. It won't cover the entire hospital bill, and I told James I would cover whatever is left."

"What? Where in the world are you going to come up with that kind of money?"

Again, she couldn't help herself. She rolled her eyes. "Brent, I know we don't discuss finances often, if ever. But believe me, I am fully capable of covering this. I've transferred money into an account I set up in Charlotte's name. She doesn't even know about it. You know how I hate flying? Doomsday talk and all that? Before I left, I went online and set this up. If something were to happen to me—which I know it won't, but just in case—I want someone to make sure Charlotte knows the money is there for the transplant."

"That's big stuff, Lauren. Big stuff."

"I know. I'll e-mail you the bank-account numbers, everything you need to know, if you're okay doing this."

"I'm okay with it, but I'm not okay with you and your doomsday crap. You're going to be fine flying home. I heard you got to fly on the corporate jet, so maybe they'll fly you home. You arrived safely."

She wasn't sure she wanted to go into details about her experience, for fear she'd reveal her feelings for John. It was too soon. "It was a fancy flight, I can tell you that. They served raw oysters, salmon, all the stuff I love but never seem to make when I'm home. It was a nice flight."

"I'm impressed. Are they flying you home, too?"

"I think so," she said, though she truly wasn't one hundred percent sure if they would.

"If you do, sneak around and snap a few pictures, so us regular folks can get a glimpse of what it's like to be a billionaire."

"I don't think that's allowed. Kind of like certain things aren't allowed on Air Force One. I'm sure you could go online and find something there." She was not going to snoop around and take pictures of an airplane that probably had security out the wazoo, and even if it didn't, it wasn't her style.

"Probably can, but take a couple pictures for me anyway. I can say I knew you when," he added.

This was a part of her life she normally did not discuss with Brent. She'd made a lot of money through her books and investing. It was her way, and she wouldn't change.

"Look, check your e-mail tonight. I'll send you all the banking info, but promise you'll take care of this if something were to happen?"

"I promise."

"Thanks, Brent. I knew I could count on you. I'll get that info to you tonight, and remember, there's a three-hour time difference. I'm going to call Mom later; if she isn't home, I'll give you a call, if that's okay."

"Of course it is, but I'm sure they're at the tree-lighting ceremony. They go every year."

"You're right. Talk soon," she said, then clicked the END button.

Why she had that doomsday feeling again bothered her. She'd felt that way yesterday and had hastily opened the account for Charlotte, just in case. Probably guilt, she thought. She hadn't wanted to share her Seattle experience with Brent, felt like it was an invasion of her privacy, so letting him in on what she'd planned for Charlotte seemed to soften the blow he was bound to get when she told him about John. Also, telling him about Lee's illness would push him toward her, just as she and Madison had discussed.

She felt guilty for having these thoughts. She felt sad, then decided she had enough time left to take a hot bath before John arrived. It made her smile. She made a promise to herself: she was not going to feel sorry for Brent because she wasn't in love with him. She was thirty-five years old, and he was too. He would have to deal with reality and accept the fact she would always be his friend, and nothing more, no matter what.

In the bathroom, she filled the tub with hot water and took her razor from her toiletry kit. She planned to use the items provided by Mr. G. She took a bath bomb and a bottle of body lotion from the artfully arranged grouping beside the sink. When the tub was full, she dropped the bath bomb in, stripped off, and lowered herself into the warm water. Sighing, she couldn't remember when she'd felt so relaxed. She couldn't allow herself to get sleepy or she'd miss the dinner with John and his father. She soaked for ten minutes, gave herself a good scrub, shaved her legs, then stepped out of the tub. She slipped her nightshirt on while she did her hair and makeup. Olivia had given her a great blow-dry, and she wasn't going to mess with that. She had enough hair for three people, and it was a lot of work to take care of. She added a dark shade of brown shadow to her eyes, and with her hand now steady, she applied a winged liner, adding just a touch beneath her eyes, too. A smoky look. She contoured, highlighted, and added a powder blush, then outlined her lips with a soft brown lip liner, filling them in with her favorite lip gloss. She examined herself in the mirror. She didn't want to appear to be trying too hard, and she wasn't. This was her style when she went out for a night on the town, which was rare, but anyone who knew her wouldn't find it odd that she'd spiffed up. And who in their right mind wouldn't want to make herself glamorous for a night with John, Mr. Hunk?

She was glad she had thought to pack a dressy casual outfit, though. Obviously, when she'd added it to her luggage. she hadn't entertained the idea she'd be having dinner with Mr. G and a man she'd fallen madly in love with. She smiled, saw she had a bit of lip gloss on her teeth, and wiped it off with a tissue. She wore black Paige jeans with a cashmere sweater, and it just so happened to be red. She added a pair of black-leather booties to wear with these jeans. She'd only packed her long dress coat, so she brought this with her, then went back to the closet, remembering she had added her red Chloé purse. In the living room, she took a few necessities from her bag and added them to her smaller purse, along with a tube of lipstick.

While she waited for John, she tried calling her mother again. She answered on the third ring.

"Hey, Mom."

"Lauren, dear, we just walked through the door. Dad's warming milk for the kitties, as a treat. And they're all doing just fine; Daisy too. Looks like they're satisfied with their place in the den. I think they like the fireplace, but don't worry, you know how careful we are."

Lauren laughed. "I trust the kitties are fine. I can't wait to see them. How was the tree-lighting ceremony?"

"Heavenly, as always. This year the city used all purple LED lights. Different from what they've done in the past, but the purple is for the Alzheimer's Awareness Association, which I thought was a wonderful way to bring awareness to this sad illness."

"I didn't realize they were doing that. No one mentioned anything at the last chamber meeting." That was the place where this type of thing was discussed.

"Seems it was last-minute. Mayor Thurman's father was just diagnosed with Alzheimer's."

"I'm sorry to hear that."

"How are you faring in Seattle?"

"Mom, I'm staying in Mr. Giampalo's penthouse apartment. I have a perfect view of the Space Needle and the city. It's way more amazing than I'd imagined."

"Sounds pretty fancy to me, but I bet you'll enjoy being in a new city. I'm kind of jealous," her mother said.

"Mom, stop! It's not like you and Dad can't hop on a plane and visit Seattle, or anywhere else for that matter."

"I know, and I do want to plan a trip after the holidays."

"Mom, real quick"—her mother could get very long-winded if she let her—"how were sales at Razzle Dazzle today?"

"Not very good. I sold one of those hand-painted sweatshirts."

"Ugh, that's not good. Listen, Mom, and I'm serious, when I come home, I want to talk to you and Dad about creating an online version of Razzle Dazzle. Promise me you'll keep an open mind. You can't imagine what I've learned about online sales today. Shops like yours too. They still have their stores, but with the online sales, they're able to do so much more. Promise me you'll talk to Dad, and we'll discuss this? This is really important to me."

"All right, I give you my word."

"Good, I'll try to check in tomorrow. I'm not exactly sure how many more days I'll be here yet, so don't worry. Just love the kitties and talk to Dad."

"Good night, dear."

"Night," she said.

Lauren was beyond tired but couldn't wait to ride in the helicopter at night. She looked at her watch. It was after 7:00. She left the blinds open but turned the lights off so she could admire the view. She was about to drift off when her cell phone dinged with a text message.

HEADING YOUR WAY. I'LL SEND FOR YOU.

OK.

Her heart rate doubling, she ran to the bathroom and checked herself one last time before returning to the living room to wait for someone to knock at the door.

Ten minutes later, she heard the chopper land on the roof, and two minutes after that, there was a knock on the door. She opened it, surprised when she saw Sandra Marie.

"What a surprise," Lauren said, opening the door.

"You'll learn all about me tonight. Let's not keep that chopper waiting."

Lauren grabbed the headset from the table near the door, closed the door behind her, and even though she had no key, no card, she heard the lock click into place.

Following the older woman up the stairs, Lauren prayed she would be in this good a shape when she was older. Though she wasn't sure of Sandra Marie's age, she guessed she was older than she looked.

The blades whirled on the giant helicopter, and Lauren was sure this was not the same chopper she'd flown in earlier. This one was twice the size. Sandra Marie opened a sliding door and stood aside for her to climb aboard. As soon as they were buckled in, Lauren placed the headset over her ears and plugged into the jack in front of her.

"Can you hear me?" she asked Sandra Marie.

"Loud and clear," she responded.

"And so can your pilot," John said. She was able to see him in this chopper.

"How many of these things do you have?" she asked, truly interested.

"San, how many?"

"Ten," she said.

"Oh." Lauren was shocked. *Who needs ten helicopters?*

"That's worldwide," Sandra Marie said.

Lauren nodded. "I see."

"Just the one airplane, though," John said.

"That's not true, John Anthony."

"We have one commercial aircraft."

"And a dozen or more Learjets."

"Okay, we have a lot of smaller aircraft."

Lauren didn't want to appear awestruck, but she couldn't help herself.

"You'll get used to it, honey," Sandra Marie said. "It sounds lavish, but we use the airplanes for the business. G can fill you in on the details if he wants this info in the book. By the way, I've read all of your biographies. You're very good."

"Thank you. It's the style of writing I enjoy. The research, the people I get to meet. Though Mr. G is by far the most famous entrepreneur I've had the pleasure to meet. And the most interesting." It was true.

"I don't know, I think Albert Grossman is pretty impressive," Sandra Marie said.

He was the founder of Shout Out, a social-media must-have for anyone who had a cell phone or any kind of notebook or computer. He'd opened the door for people all over the world to communicate.

"He was a lot of work, that's all I'll say." Lauren was loyal to her subjects. If she knew bits and pieces through her research and the interview process that the public didn't need to know, she kept them to herself.

"We're preparing to land," John said. "It's a bit windy, so hang on."

Again, they hovered over yet another helipad, though Lauren didn't see the trademark G.

The whir of the blades died, then John removed his headset. The ride couldn't have been more than ten minutes. Briefly, Lauren wondered why Mr. G had a home so close to the penthouse apartment she stayed in but figured he'd tell her if she asked. And she would.

"Okay, ladies, let's see what Dad's got cooking."

John helped Sandra Marie off the chopper, then he held out his hand to Lauren, though he didn't let go as they made their way to the entrance. Again, a card was scanned, a red light flashed, and the door slid open.

"One more," John said. They took an elevator to the floor below them. "Security," John explained.

Another scan, though this time John stood in front of a lens, a green light moved from side to side, then a red light flashed three times, and the door opened.

"That's a retinal scan," John explained. "Crazy world requires this now."

She had heard of these types of scans—they weren't all that uncommon—but she'd never witnessed one in action.

Mr. G himself greeted them as soon as John walked into a giant room similar to the penthouse.

"I see my son delivered my guests without any problems."

"Nothing to it," John said. "So, Dad, I'm starved. What's for dinner?"

Lauren felt out of place for a minute, then Mr. G took her by the hand. "I want to show you this new gadget in the kitchen first," he said, and again gave her a sheepish wink. "Come on, San, you need to see this, too."

"G, you and your gadgets."

Lauren was expecting something out of this world, or a robot making table-side Caesar salads.

"Watch this," Mr. G said, picking up a bottle of red wine and placing his gadget on the bottle; then he took out the latest model of cell phone created by Global Goods and touched the screen. The cork flew off the bottle of wine.

"So, what do you think?" he asked them.

"Dad, you have too much money," John said.

"I like it," Sandra Marie said. "Let's save a bottle for later." She leaned in and gave him a kiss on the cheek.

"All right, Lauren, I'm ashamed of myself. I didn't have a lot of time to prepare something extravagant, but I make a killer meat loaf and mashed potatoes, so I hope you're okay with this? I use a turkey-chicken mix."

She couldn't help herself. She laughed out loud. "I love meat loaf and mashed potatoes." She'd been prepared for anything but this. Something fancy that she'd have to pretend to like.

"Are you sure?"

"One hundred percent. Meat loaf is the best staple meal in the world. At least, that's what I think. I'll have to give you my recipe. I make it for my dad once in a while. I use fresh tomatoes, and instead of crackers or bread crumbs, I use crushed-up potato chips. Not the healthiest meal in the world, but it's still delicious."

"That restaurant in Fallen Springs, Ruby's. I'd like to get my hands on her recipe for yeast rolls. Those were some of the best I've ever had."

Lauren couldn't believe how normal they were, though she wouldn't admit it. "You'll never get it, either. Half the town has tried for years. She'll threaten you with that giant butcher knife she keeps tucked away. I have a recipe that's close to hers that I'll give you."

John lifted her up and kissed her right in front of Mr. G and Sandra Marie.

"See, I told you this fella was smitten."

Lauren normally would have been a little embarrassed by such a crazy show of affection, but she wasn't in the least bit bothered by John's actions. In fact, she wished he'd do it again.

Mr. G had a table in the kitchen, set for four. Nothing fancy, just what any family would have. The dishes were Fiesta Ware, and, of course, they were red, and the flatware didn't appear to be anything one couldn't purchase at any department store. The napkins were white and had the trademark G in one corner, but nothing over the top. The dinner was served family-style, not much different from the way her family meals were served.

"Lauren, you okay with saying grace?" Mr. G asked.

"I would be honored," she said, her heart filled with such joy she thought it would burst. "Bless this food, this home, and the wonderful family and friends as we share this bounty before us."

"Thank you," Mr. G said. "I'm always grateful that I have the ability to make a meal, and even more so when I can share it with others."

"Then let's dig in," John said.

Lauren took a chunk of meat loaf, passed the serving dish to Sandra Marie, took the potatoes from John, loaded her plate because she adored mashed potatoes, handed those to Mr. G, then added a heap of green beans to her plate. A platter of sliced tomatoes and scallions was passed around last.

"Mr. G, you have Southern roots, right?" Lauren asked between bites.

"I do, though not too many people know that. North Carolina. I was born in a small town, Bethania, just north of Winston-Salem."

"I know of it; not sure if I've been there," Lauren said.

They chatted throughout the meal, as any normal family would. When Lauren excused herself, saying she would bust if she ate another bite, they all laughed, remembering the ride with Derek.

"I'm still embarrassed," she said, as she and Sandra Marie began clearing away the dishes.

The guys made themselves scarce while they washed up.

"Don't be, kiddo. G's out there having a cigar now, and they're on the balcony, so they can't hear us. He wanted to get the Christmas tree set up, but there wasn't enough time. We usually drive to one of the tree farms, pick out several, and have them cut and delivered. I know it sounds a bit over the top, but you should see this place, the offices, and John's mountain home when they're decorated. I think they'd give the Biltmore estate a run for its money as far as the decorating goes. We've got the best team of tree trimmers in the Northwest."

Lauren pulled her hair away from her face. "Sandra Marie, can I ask you a personal question? It's fine to say no."

"Ask away," she said, drying her hands with a tea towel.

"Tell me about your name," she asked her. From the look on her face, it was not the question she had expected.

"It's my full name. My father always used my middle name when I was growing up, didn't matter what the situation was. I was Sandra Marie, and it stuck. Everyone calls me this as though it's one name, and it's fine. The guys don't always. You've probably heard them call me San, and that's okay, too. I'll answer to just about anything."

"Another question. Are you comfortable telling me about your relationship with Mr. G?" Lauren knew this was very personal, but they had all made her feel so included, as though she were part of the family, so she didn't feel as though she was being too intrusive.

"Of course. As you might have observed at the office, we're polite and professional because that's what works for us. G is down-to-earth, but he's a true genius. Has an image to maintain, so we're close friends at work, but outside of work, G and I have been together for twenty-one years."

Lauren's jaw actually dropped.

Sandra Marie laughed. "Caught you by surprise?"

"A little bit. I knew there was something between you two; I didn't expect the time span. You've been with him since the beginning then?"

"Yes, and let me tell you, we have had our share of ups and downs, inside-outs, but I wouldn't trade one minute of our life together. Forget the money, the airplanes, the cars, houses. None of that matters if you're not truly and madly in love with your partner."

"My parents are like that, though they're beyond old-fashioned. Dad doesn't have the Internet or a cell phone. We still use a credit-card machine that requires a swipe of the card; remember the ones with the carbon paper?"

Sandra Marie nodded.

"That's what we use at Razzle Dazzle. Dad's against online shopping. If he can't see it, touch it, or smell it, he says, why buy it. It's worked for a while, but between us, the store is just a few months away from having to declare bankruptcy. He'd have a fit if he knew I was telling this to a stranger." Lauren held her hand out. "I didn't mean it that way. A stranger to him. I've added funds to cover the place for a couple of months just because that store is his life, his father's life, so on and so forth. I would hate to see it fail, but his stubbornness will most likely be its downfall."

Sandra Marie didn't say anything. Lauren had let herself get too relaxed and revealed too many details that should have remained in the family. They were out now, and she wished she could take them back. She'd made her father sound backward and ignorant.

"We need to get G down there, talk to him. Show him the ropes. Get some of your merchandise online. Do you think he'd be willing to listen to G? Sometimes, men don't want to hear or see what's right in their face. Family traditions are very important to G and me; John, too. I'm sure G wouldn't mind sharing a few tricks of the trade, though your dad would have to be willing to hear him out. G's a talker, a wheeler and dealer, in a good way. He's as honest as they come. I think you should ask him to step in, help your family."

Lauren hated that sappy tears were rivering down her cheeks. Her makeup was ruined. Sandra Marie handed her a tissue. “Don’t cry, sweetie. I’m sure there’s something we can do to help out.”

Lauren blotted her eyes with the napkin. “You really are the real deal, aren’t you?” she asked. “My parents are fine financially. They’ve made good investments, but Dad won’t step into the twenty-first century. However, he might listen to Mr. G. Dad’s a man’s man. He’s a good person. I feel like I’ve just bad-mouthed him, but I don’t want to see Razzle Dazzle fail any more than he does. I think he just hates hearing it from me.”

Mr. G came in from the terrace, a cherry-smelling smoke emanating from his clothes. John was right behind him. “You two get all cleaned up?”

“We did,” Sandra Marie said, “and I want to talk to you about a new business opportunity.”

Friday night, December 6, would be a night to remember for Lauren because it was the night that the Giampalo family became her second family.

Chapter 24

The next several weeks went by in a flash. After Lauren returned from Seattle, they managed to get through the holidays. When Lauren could take time off from her writing, she and her mother baked, shopped, and decorated, and did all their usual traditional care packages for several local charities. Her mother and father purchased dozens of toys for those less fortunate. Mr. G matched their donations tenfold.

After the holidays, when Lauren settled down in earnest to write her biography of the founder and CEO of Global Goods, Mr. Giampalo made a special trip to Fallen Springs to thank her father personally for giving Lauren time away from her job at the store to complete a first draft of his biography in the six weeks she'd promised.

The two men meshed like peas in a pod. For weeks afterward, her father spoke to Mr. G on the phone, sent letters through the post office, and became impatient when he didn't receive a speedy enough response from Mr. G, who was still at the helm of the biggest online retail business in the world. But he did send answers to all of her father's letters, handwritten by him personally.

One day, a package from Global Goods arrived for her father via FedEx. He opened it but was completely clueless as to what it contained. However, there was a yellow slip of paper with the instruction PUSH THIS BUTTON. Her father pushed the button, and Mr. G himself appeared on the screen of the Global Goods digital notebook that Mr. G had sent.

"Al, listen, I've got a business proposition for you, and I can't discuss it over the phone, and letters take too long. I want you to read the instructions I've personally handwritten, and I want you to follow them exactly."

When he followed the instructions, the screen on the notebook lit up to display a website. "What?" her father said, seeing a picture of the outside of Razzle Dazzle Décor. Continuing to follow the instructions, he scrolled through a mock website of the store. A replica of the store, the decorations they sold, even the old cash register appeared onscreen, and when he saw the old NCR antique, he tapped the screen, and the cha-ching sound the register made when the drawer opened was exactly the same as the sound made by the register at the store.

"Lauren, look at this," he said. "Is this for real?"

She scanned through the website as though she'd never laid eyes on it. He didn't need to know that she was the prime mover behind making sure the website looked exactly like the store.

Lauren touched the screen a few times, acting as though she were as surprised as he was. "This is identical to the store." She winked at her mother, who'd been helping out on the sidelines and was watching her husband and daughter, delighted with what she was seeing. Ilene had been a big supporter when Mr. G had approached Lauren with this idea for propelling her father into the twenty-first century, but her father would never learn of that. It was their secret.

"It's a website. Looks like Mr. G wants you to work with him and Global Goods." Lauren and her mother knew that in order for this endeavor to be successful, it had to appear as though it was entirely Mr. G's idea. Her dad liked and respected him and wasn't the least bit intimidated by the fact that he was the richest man in the United States, possibly the world.

Fortunately, Razzle Dazzle had made it through the season; it actually made a tiny profit, helped enormously by John's purchase of the music boxes. But a tiny profit was not enough to keep the doors open. Without the money she'd had Roger transfer to the business account, the store would have had to close for good.

Once the holidays were over, they had been lucky, on any given day, to have a single customer come in, let alone make a sale. It was at that time that she and her mother gave Mr. G the go-ahead to approach her father as though he wanted to make a business deal.

"I think we need to do this, Ilene. G says it's time to look at this online stuff."

Lauren almost cried when she heard her father agree to Mr. G's proposal.

Once the website was up and running, preorders started coming in faster than their artisans could fill them. They hired dozens more, but her father insisted they had to be from the state of North Carolina. Lauren agreed, and sales continued to skyrocket.

Throughout that period, Lauren and John saw each other as much as time and distance allowed. It was apparent to anyone who spent any time with them that they were totally in love with one another.

Her parents were so thrilled that she'd met someone who "knocked her socks off and blew her away."

On the first of July, Madison gave birth to a healthy ten-pound, three-ounce baby girl. Lauren was asked to be godmother to Julie Anne Murphy, named for the month of her birth.

On the Fourth of July, Fallen Springs had its annual parade. There were floats and beauty pageants, the high-school marching band belted out tune after tune, and many local businesses decorated fancy convertibles in which local beauty-pageant contestants who had qualified to enter the Miss North Carolina Pageant rode, on the backs of the cars. In their fancy dresses, they waved at the crowds gathered along the sidewalks. There were hot dog stands, burgers, Carolina barbecue, and roasted corn on the cob. Locals sold jams, jellies, pies, and cakes.

Lauren viewed all this and knew how lucky she was to live there and experience life in a small town. Later that night, they all watched the fireworks. Her parents, Mr. G, and Sandra Marie were there, too, as they'd all become like family. And, of course, John was there. She couldn't remember ever being so happy. Her life was as close to perfect as could be.

Angela had called the day before, telling her that Mr. Giampalo's biography would hit the stores in November, and preorders would most certainly guarantee this would be another best seller under her belt. Lauren kept this to herself because she didn't want her news to overshadow the holiday and Madison's giving birth to Julie.

Later that night, when she and John were alone, he asked her to marry him.

"You've made me the happiest man alive, Lauren. I don't care where we marry or live; the details will work themselves out. I just want you. Forever and always." It was so unexpected that she burst into happy tears and said yes so many times, he finally brought his mouth to hers to seal the deal.

He kissed her again, and she felt desire so strong, so intense, she'd didn't think she could stand being away from this sexy, kind, perfect Mr. Hunk much longer.

She told him about the nickname she had bestowed on him when she had first seen him.

"And I remember thinking you were the most beautiful woman I'd ever seen. Though I didn't have a nickname for you."

They were married in October at the church where she had been baptized, then held the reception at John's stunning home in Asheville. The jewel-toned colors of the Blue Ridge Mountains were an extraordinary backdrop of brilliant reds, yellows, and shades of orange. The weather was cool and crisp. Ruby and Louise catered the reception, making a traditional Thanksgiving dinner, even though the holiday was still over a month away. The yeast rolls went so fast that Ruby cried because she hadn't made enough but promised that anyone who came to the diner could take home a dozen, on the house. The diner's business picked up so much that she had to hire two waitresses so she and Louise could focus on cooking food for people to enjoy.

The year flew by so fast, and Lauren had so many good memories, that she couldn't imagine her life being any more perfect than it was.

Epilogue

Black Friday, 2020

If Lauren had been asked a year ago about the probability of Razzle Dazzle's stepping into the twenty-first century, she would have laughed. In a million years, no way was her father going to break the Montgomery tradition.

Yet here they were. Shoppers began forming a line at 5:00 A.M. outside Razzle Dazzle Décor for the first big sale of the holiday season. Sales were expected to be off the charts for the first time in years. Al and Ilene, with Lauren's help, had chosen the most exclusive Christmas decorations their artisans made. They had begun ordering in early May so they would have enough for today's grand reopening.

Nothing had changed. The store hadn't been redecorated, the gas fireplace still worked, the old wooden floors still squeaked if you stepped on them in just the right way, the window display was still an artificial Christmas tree trimmed with ornaments made exclusively for today's big event. Lauren and her mother had spent hours going over old photographs of trees they'd had in the past. They had picked their favorite ornaments from the pictures and had them re-created. Some were delicate as a bird's wing, others glassblown; many were hand-sculpted, each as unique as the artisans themselves.

Twelve music boxes were displayed on a glass shelf they had purchased secondhand from Wilbur at the drugstore. Lauren thought it was a good idea to keep these out of reach. Small hands could do big damage.

Lauren and her parents had made the decision to hire a few part-timers for the Christmas season. Charlotte, Lacey, and Kiley were excited about their new jobs. Lauren, Beth, and Lee had taken the girls to a spa in Asheville for a weekend once Lee's doctor's gave her a clean bill of health. The bone-marrow transplant had been totally successful, and Lee had returned to her job at the post office. Three weeks ago, Brent Ludmore gave Lee a diamond ring, announcing their plans to marry in the spring. Madison secretly took credit for their engagement.

"Are you feeling all right, dear?" her mother asked Lauren.

"I've had too much coffee. Why?"

"Just asking," her mother said, turning her attention to the three girls. "If I run into a problem with this newfangled credit-card machine, you'll help me out?"

"It's super easy, Mrs. Montgomery, but one of us will give you a hand if you need it," Charlotte said.

"It's time to open the doors. Christmas 2020, here we

go." Her father turned the OPEN sign over, Lauren hit the remote that turned on the lights in the display window, and the rush began.

Locals and out-of-towners filled the store until late afternoon, by which time they'd sold out of just about everything. Luckily, they had enough stock to carry them through the month and would continue selling their unique Christmas decorations year-round.

Later, when the doors were locked, the floors cleaned, and the shelves tidied, Lauren asked her parents if they'd have a cup of tea with her before she and John went to the guest house for the night. They were all worn-out, and a cup of tea was welcome. Charlotte, Kiley, and Lacey went to Beth's house, as they'd planned a sleepover.

"You look worn-out, sweetie," John said, as he wrapped his arms around her.

"I think we're all ready to call it a day," her father said. He was his old self again, his depression completely under control, and she couldn't be happier.

Her mother made the tea, handing them each a mug, and sat next to her husband on the sagging sofa. John took a seat in the desk chair, and Lauren sat on his lap.

"I have an early Christmas present I'd like to share with you all," Lauren said.

"I thought you didn't like getting or giving gifts early," John said, surprised. She'd told him about Eric and her distaste for his eagerness.

"This is a gift for all of us, and it doesn't matter if I give it to you a bit early," Lauren said.

She had their undivided attention.

"John, Mom, Dad, I'm going to have a baby."

"Oh my gosh." John kissed her so long and hard, she felt herself blush.

"I knew it," her mother said. "You have that look. Oh, honey, you and John have given us the best gift ever, a grandchild."

Lauren looked at her father. Tears were rolling down his face. "You two, well, you've just given me the brightest star of all."

Ruby's Yeast Rolls

½ cup whole milk
½ cup granulated sugar
¼ cup melted butter
1½ teaspoons of salt
½ cup water (105–115 degrees)
2 packages of any active dry yeast
2 eggs, slightly beaten
4½ cups all-purpose flour

1. Place the milk in a small saucepan and bring it to a light boil. Remove from heat, then add the sugar, butter, and salt. Let this cool to a lukewarm temperature, about 110–115 degrees.
2. Combine the warm water and the yeast. Allow this to sit a few minutes.
3. Pour the yeast mixture into whatever kind of mixing bowl you have for an electric mixer. Add the milk mixture, the eggs, and 2 cups of the flour. Beat with a paddle attachment until mixed.
4. Beat in the remaining 2½ cups of flour.
5. Knead the dough with a dough hook on the electric mixer. You may knead the dough on a lightly floured surface. Beat on low speed for 5–10 minutes.
6. Place the dough in a medium-sized buttered bowl, turning the dough through the butter, allowing the butter to be thoroughly distributed onto the dough. Cover the bowl with a tea towel or plastic wrap. Place the bowl in a warm area and allow the dough to rise for 1 hour.

7. Punch the dough down, then divide it into balls of about 2–3 tablespoons each. Place the balls of dough in a 9- by 13-inch greased pan. Cover and let them rise for 1 more hour.

8. Preheat the oven to 375 degrees F.

9. Bake for 20–25 minutes, until lightly browned. Brush melted butter on top of the rolls before serving.

Enjoy!

Keep reading for a sneak peek at

SANTA CRUISE

The latest holiday novel from

Fern Michaels

Available now from

Kensington Books

Wherever books are sold

Chapter One

June
Ridgewood, New Jersey

The big banner read WELCOME RIDGEWOOD HIGH CLASSMATES! For some, it was a frightening experience. For others, it was an opportunity to show off how far they had come in the fifteen years since leaving high school.

Francesca (Frankie) Cappella was on the fence. She had built an excellent reputation in the publishing industry, marketing books for authors and publishers, but her love of music and the desire to perform had never left her. After graduating from a top music school, she had spent six years in New York City, auditioning for every part for which she thought she was suited. She had a "big voice" with a lot of nuance, but the producers were looking for a big *nasal* voice, something that made her cringe. Sure, she could sing that way if she had to, but she hated it. Why would she want to do something she hates? It took all the pleasure out of singing for her. Eventually, every singer sounded the same. She had spent too many years working on her own sound. Taking matters into her own hands, she found a producer and cut a few tracks. She got some radio airplay, but without the backing of a big record company, she could only go so far. During the years she had spent following her dream, to pay the rent she had worked as a temp for a number of large corporations, eventually taking a full-time job with a publisher of comic books. Her parents knew that working in corporate America wasn't in her heart, but it was a living, and living in New York was challenging enough.

She eventually worked her way up to the top at a major publishing house, but she never felt as if she was a success, especially after the incident at the last reunion, when Drew Aikens said something right to her face. "Gee, Frankie, you were such a good singer. Too bad you never made it." Those crushing words almost kept her from coming to this reunion, which included several classes besides hers. Still feeling the sting of those hurtful words, she thought to herself, *Maybe that creep won't show up.*

Frankie knew that some would be envious of her position as a vice president of a successful publisher. Her life was interesting and filled with a lot of professional events, but she still felt that a piece was missing. A lover, a partner, a friend. Sure, she could have three different men, but what she really wanted was a man who was all three. *Yeah. Good luck with that.*

She took one more glance at her reflection in the glass of the hotel artwork. *Hair?* Jet black, slicked, and pulled into a long ponytail. *Dress?* Figure-flattering little black dress that showed off her well-toned calves. *Lipstick?* Bright. She then had the horrifying thought she might have lipstick on her teeth. Next came the angst of her eye-liner running. But before she had the chance to pull out a small mirror, the squeals of Nina Hunter were heard across the lobby.

"Frankie! Oh baby." Nina Hunter pushed through the crowd and gave her friend a huge, crushing hug.

Nina was five feet eight inches tall, towering over Frankie's five-foot-four-inch frame. In high school, Nina had been in every school play, community-theater production, and summer-camp program. That's where she and Frankie had bonded. Frankie was the singer; Nina was the actress. Nina's love was acting, and she was particularly good at it, so much so that she had landed a part on a television sitcom after attending the University of Southern California. She wasn't the star of the show but had enough screen time to make her a fan favorite. Her long brown curly hair, big brown eyes, and long legs were hard to miss.

"Nee-Na," Frankie howled back, making sure her makeup didn't smudge on Nina's silk dress. "I wasn't expecting to see you here!" Frankie was surprised but also tickled pink.

"I have an audition in the city in a few days, so I thought I'd return to our old haunts."

"You mean Shut Up and Eat?" Frankie joked, referring to the local diner where they would hang out after football games or other school events. Only the coolest kids would go there.

"Is it still there?" Nina asked.

"It is. Butch Anderson organizes breakfasts there several times a year," Frankie replied. "I've been to a few; but to be honest, I don't feel I have anything in common with them anymore."

"I think I know what you mean." Nina put her arm around her friend. "It's married couples talking about either their latest renovation or bragging about their kids." Nina made a snoring sound, causing Frankie to burst out laughing.

"Oh my goodness. You are *so* right." Frankie nodded in agreement. "I feel like the only thing I talk about is work or some function I've attended. They look at me as if I'm some kind of snob. Or weirdo."

"I totally get it. If I'm not surrounded by Mr. and Mrs. Whoever, it's someone in the biz blowing smoke about their latest script, treatment, and who *might* be reading it next. I mean, it *is* Hollywood, but it can be so superficial."

"I can only imagine," Frankie said. "I had a small taste of it when I was trying out for musicals. Funny thing, though, publishing isn't all that different. It's a sliver of show business. Besides, most of the publishing companies are owned by big conglomerates. But enough of that. Tell me about you. Besides your acting success, what else keeps you out of trouble?" Frankie chuckled.

"My dog." Nina smiled. "He's a big Bernese mountain dog named Winston. We go for hikes in the hills. He makes me feel safe on the trails even though he's really a mush."

"I assume you live in a house?" Frankie asked.

"Oh yeah. I cannot imagine Winston in an apartment. It would be like a bull in a china shop!" Nina chuckled. "I rent a small house in Topanga Canyon. It's just far enough from the hustle that I can drain my brain after long days of shooting."

Glancing at the posters covered in student photos, Frankie said, "You're probably the most successful graduate."

"Oh, I don't know about that. Yes, I am incredibly lucky to have landed this part, and I mean *incredibly lucky*. It's really about being in the right place at the right time."

"Speaking of being in the right place, I think I may need to go to the bar and get a little something to soothe my nerves." Frankie linked her arm through Nina's.

"Nervous? You?" Nina was surprised. "You were the ringleader, party thrower, class president, lead singer in a band, *and* captain of the gymnastics team."

"That was *before* I knew anything about life." Frankie laughed. "Back then, I thought if you went for something and gave it your all, you'd be rewarded. And if you tried really hard but made a mistake, all would be forgiven, and you would get another chance. Nope. You make one mistake, and it goes into your permanent record." Frankie used air quotes for "permanent record." "This grown-up stuff isn't easy."

Nina burst out laughing. "Kinda like you make one creepy low-budget film to try to get exposure, and you're pegged as 'Oh yeah, that Nina Hunter. Didn't she play a disembodied creature in that hack movie?' "

The women howled and continued making their way toward the bar. As they waited in line to be served, Frankie whispered to Nina, "Who *are* these people?"

Nina let out a guffaw, then whispered in return, "I think we went to high school with most of them." She ordered a gin and tonic for herself. "Frankie? What are you having?"

"Hemlock?" Frankie chortled.

"Ha! Wine? Or a stronger adult beverage?"

"I'll have what you're having," Frankie replied, and Nina held up two fingers to the bartender.

Frankie lowered her voice further. "They all look so frumpy! Sure, you would expect that of the people who graduated a few years before us, but even our own classmates! Most of them look like they gave up caring years ago." She nodded to a woman wearing clogs. Nina almost spit out her drink.

"Oh my gosh. That's Amy Blanchard. She hasn't changed a bit." Before either of them had an opportunity to say hello to Amy, a loud cry came from the throng.

"Ladies!" It was Rachael Newmark, one of their old pals, doing a little rumba dance in their direction.

"Honey!" Nina gave her a one-arm hug, trying not to spill her drink. "You look great! Still dancing, I see?"

Rachael Newmark was the shortest and most petite of the three, with a brown pixie haircut, turned-up nose, and green eyes. "*Chicas!* So good to see you. You both look fabulous."

They immediately huddled and joked that they were not old enough to be at the reunion.

Amy caught a glimpse of the three women and started in their direction. "Well, if it isn't the unholy trinity," Amy teased.

Frankie bit her lip, Nina was taken aback, and Rachael couldn't help but blurt out, "I see the fashion police haven't been here yet."

Amy blinked. "Oh these?" She pointed to her feet. "I broke my toe and, quite frankly, I don't give a darn."

"When did you ever?" Rachael said, with a touch of sarcasm.

"Good point," Amy agreed. "But I'll have you know that it's quite the geek fashion statement now." She took a bow.

All four women laughed. Amy had been the geek,

dweeb, nerd of the group. She was president of the science club in school but had a lot of team spirit and would always sign up to be the stage manager for the plays. She would often get teased because she was much more the intellect than most of her classmates, but Nina, Rachael, and Frankie always included her. They would refer to Amy as "the brains of the operation." She still wore the same big black-rimmed glasses. Her ash-blond hair was adorned with a pink headband that matched her maxi dress. She had a pretty, round face with a milky complexion and rosy cheeks. There was a spunk and youthfulness about her that belied her age of thirty-three.

Nina took the lead. "Well, ladies, perhaps we should grab a table before we're forced to sit with some creep from biology class." They all laughed, recalling Billy Gwyer chasing the girls around with a garden snake.

"Do you think he might be here?" Frankie surveyed the room.

"The big question is, is he as cute as he used to be?" Rachael snickered.

"You were always boy-crazy." Amy poked at her.

"And look where I am now," Rachael replied. "I got married because my parents didn't want me running all over the world chasing men. And how did that turn out? Well, now I'm divorced."

"But are you still chasing men?" Nina joked.

"I've given up." Rachael sighed.

"*You?*" they mocked in unison.

"It's slim pickings out there, girls. Even old Slim Pickens himself is no longer available."

The women hooted. "I hear you loud and clear." Frankie joined in. "I haven't had a date—I mean a *real* date—in probably three years."

"You can't be serious." Nina crowed. "Look at you. You're stunning and successful."

"Thanks, but that doesn't seem to make for a great date, let alone girlfriend. My friend Ken once told me that I'm very intimidating." Frankie shook her head. "I don't get it. I'm so charming." She smiled wryly.

"Honey, I'm in the same single boat," Nina confessed.

"But you're in the land of glamour and excitement," Amy protested.

"It's a lot of smoke and mirrors. Trust me," Nina replied. "If I were a high-powered producer or an agent, I'd have a new date every night. But unless you can do something for someone, you're not dating material."

"I don't believe it," Amy objected. "You, famous actress, can't get a date?"

"I'm not that famous," Nina said.

"Well, you are to us," Amy insisted.

"Yes, you are," Frankie added, and Rachael agreed.

All eyes were on Amy. "So? What about you? Have you found geek love?" Nina asked.

"Nah. Most of the guys I meet are asexual or indifferent."

"Funny how things change. When we were in high school, we had to beat the boys away with a stick." Frankie laughed.

"That's because *you* weren't so intimidating back then," Rachael said, poking fun at her friend.

They leaned conspiratorially toward each other, ignoring everything that was going on around them, and caught up on the past fifteen years.

After high school, Rachael Newmark had attended NYU. After she graduated, she had traveled to South America, where she met a suave but unemployed Paulo.

With her trust-fund maturity on the near horizon, her parents clamped down on her escapades, forcing her father to hire a private jet to bring her back home. Following weeks of pouting, Rachael realized that if she ever wanted the money left to her by her grandmother, she needed to think about settling down. The thought sent chills up her spine, but reality had set in. She took a job at a bank, working in their international department, and began dating one of the accountants. She wasn't madly, passionately in love with Greg, but he was steady and would be a good provider. Love was not her parents' main concern. Stability was. A year later, they got married.

Two years after getting married, they had a son, but being a stay-at-home mom just wasn't *her* thing. She was restless and needed a purpose, something Greg couldn't understand. Greg left the bank and went to work for an independent accounting firm. Rachael's parents thought it would "look better" for Greg in their social circle if he worked at a high-powered company. If she wanted, Rachael could be a local socialite, join the garden club or the Junior League. But Rachael's personality was not compatible with women who were prim, proper, and phony. Especially phony.

Before Ryan started school, Rachael would arrange playdates with other moms and kids, but after a period of time, she would get bored with the vacuous conversations and move on to another group.

By the time Ryan entered kindergarten, Rachael was ready to climb the walls, so she took a part-time job at the local dance studio. She had always been an excellent dancer and had taken lessons in jazz, ballroom, and a variety of other disciplines. By the time she was eight, her parents had her schedule completely filled. Dancing lessons, piano lessons, tennis lessons, and water skiing were planned. Tutoring in foreign languages was also on her calendar. It was no surprise that she had rebelled after graduating.

Of all the extracurricular activities, it was the dancing that made her feel alive. She could lose herself in the music and the moves. Plus, it was important to know how to dance, especially when you had to attend galas and fundraisers. It wasn't surprising that she was everyone's favorite dance partner.

Within two years of working at Salon de la Danse, her classes became so popular that there was a six-month waiting list if you wanted to learn to salsa, rumba, or swing. People of all ages were clamoring for Rachael's dancing excitement.

But when Rachael was home with Greg, the only excitement was the argument du jour. It became obvious that their marriage wasn't going to last, at least not without a lot of door slamming, yelling, and sulking.

Finally, after an uncomfortable dust-up at the country club, Rachael's family intervened and encouraged her to get a divorce. They could see the pain in their daughter's eyes whenever she and Greg would meet them at a social event or dinner. Her father took her aside and said, "Sweetheart, your mother and I have been talking." That sentence was always a warning signal, but this time it worked to her favor. "We can see how unhappy you are, Rachael. I know your mother and I pressured you into getting married and having a family. But we never expected it to make you this miserable. It's the last thing we want. We will help you with whatever resources you need, particularly a good lawyer."

Rachael was shocked and elated. Never in a million

years did she think her parents would approve of a divorce. *You made your miserable bed and now you have to lie in it* was a much better summation of their take on life. But getting married hadn't really been her choice. She *had* been pressured into it. Yes, her parents wanted stability for her, but they hadn't counted on the misery that went with it.

Aaron Newmark was a man of his word and provided Rachael the counsel of the best divorce attorney in the state, Lloyd Luttrell.

She and Greg tried to keep the divorce civilized, although Rachael was always seething when it came to Greg. Over the course of their marriage, Greg had spent a good chunk of Rachael's trust fund buying luxury cars and expensive designer clothes. That, too, caused a great deal of contention. He said it was important to look rich. No one was going to trust a poor-looking accountant. He had a point, but he had carried it much too far. He was supposed to be the breadwinner and she the dutiful wife, whose half-million-dollar bank account was at his disposal. As soon as the smell of divorce was in the air, Rachael's father and her lawyer tied up all of her assets so Greg could no longer treat them as his personal piggy bank. They sold the elaborate McMansion they had bought with part of Rachael's trust fund and put some of the money away for Ryan's college education. Greg was lucky to get out of the marriage with the fancy designer shirt on his back.

To that day, Rachael had never had a total grasp on how much of her money he had milked. She knew she was complicit by not paying attention. But still. It was not *his* money to spend.

Once the divorce was final, Rachael used the rest of

the money from the sale of the house to buy the dance studio from its owner. She renovated the space and hired more instructors, and the studio doubled its clientele in less than a year. It helped that she was located near a senior-citizen community with most residents only in their mid-fifties. Part of the studio's service was planning dance parties for organizations. Rachael had finally hit her stride.

The women stared at Rachael. Nina was the first to speak. "Wow, he really took advantage of your family's money."

"Oh, that's not all." Rachael tossed her head back. "He was cheating on me the whole time."

Screams of "What?" "Are you kidding?" "You can't be serious!" went around the table.

Rachael crossed her arms across her chest. "No, I'm not kidding, and yes, I am serious."

"Holy smokes!" Amy broke in. "How did you find out?"

"It all came out after the divorce. A few people knew about it, but no one had ever told me. And frankly, I do not care. I had no physical interest in him at all." She paused. "Probably ever." She burst out laughing. "Talk about stupid choices."

Frankie chimed in and lifted her glass. "What doesn't kill you makes you stronger!" The rest followed suit, uttering words of cheer.

It was now Frankie's turn to catch the women up on her escapades. She had moved to New York after graduating from the University of Miami. She auditioned for musicals and got a few small parts in Off-Broadway shows, but that and temp work paid very little, forcing her to live with a variety of roommates, two to three people at a time. One summer, Frankie rented a bedroom in a large two-bedroom apartment on the Upper West Side. They had divided it up so that Dave and Laura would have the living room as their space, Marilyn would have the other bedroom, and they shared a ridiculously small kitchenette. It wasn't ideal, but it was doable for the few months she was there.

Finding a suitable place to live was a full-time job. She eventually moved into a duplex with a work associate and stayed for several years until she was able to afford a modest studio apartment in Gramercy Park.

Frankie and Rachael had stayed in touch and met for lunch a couple of times a year, so they were familiar with each other's horror stories. Rachael was getting impatient and urged Frankie, "Cut to the chase. We want to hear your stories. I *know* you have a few lulus."

Frankie took a deep breath. "Are you sure you want to hear the gory details?" Nina and Amy urged her on. Frankie confessed that she had been through a boatload of relationships, affairs, heartbreaks, and deceptions. New York. Lots of men. It was easy to meet someone at a bar, club, event, or concert. Learning about someone was another story, especially with most New Yorkers her age coming from all parts of the country and the rest of the world. She often thought it was ironic that someone could be in the biggest city in the country and still feel lonely and isolated. That's probably why she was eager to have something meaningful with someone. Too bad she had made a lot of lousy choices in her pursuits. Frankie continued, "Then there was the medical intern who had not one but two other girlfriends."

"Two?" Amy gasped.

"Yes, two." Frankie took a sip of her drink.

"How did you find out?" Amy was curious.

"I had spent the night at his apartment. The next morning, he left before me. I opened the door to the linen closet to get a towel."

"Oh sure. You were spying." Rachael poked her.

"No. Honestly," Frankie continued. "I was getting a towel and noticed a small container on one of the shelves." She took a sip of her drink. "It was a diaphragm." Another sip, waiting for a reaction from her friends.

"A what?" Amy blurted.

Nina patted her hand. "Oh, honey. It's one of those contraceptive contraptions that women use so they don't get pregnant."

"I know what a diaphragm is. Duh," Amy shot back. "I was kidding."

Nina patted her hand again and turned to Frankie. "So what did you do?"

"I did what any other red-blooded woman would do. I took it with me and threw it in a dumpster several blocks away."

The women were doubled over in hysterics. Frankie continued, "I never said a word to him. I figured he would be squirming enough when she went looking for it."

Nina was laughing so hard, tears were streaming down her face.

"Did he call you?" Rachael tilted her head.

"Yes, he did." Frankie played with the small straw in her glass.

"Spill, girl!" Amy was almost shouting. "What happened?"

"I didn't answer the phone but he left me a voice mail saying how immature it was of me to take someone else's property."

Amy's mouth was agape. "He said what?"

"You heard me. But, I must say, I got a lot of satisfaction out of that call. He was so pissed. Too bad, too sad. Such a jerk."

"So how did you know he had been seeing two other women?" Amy asked curiously.

"A friend of mine. One could say it was a coincidence, but think about this. New York City has a population of eight million people, and over ten thousand doctors."

Nina pushed, "Get to the good part!"

"As I was saying, a friend of mine was introduced to him at a hospital function. He was with a woman named Victoria. Well, while they were chitchatting, a woman named Michelle walked up to him and slapped him in the face." Frankie sat back in her chair with a wry smile.

"Wow." Nina gasped. "Well, at least he got the slap he deserved."

"Yeah, too bad it wasn't from me." Frankie chuckled. "I felt vindicated without having to do anything except dispose of something gross. It's funny. Odd, I mean. I wasn't angry. I was stunned. But when I tossed that thing in the garbage, I felt elated just thinking about how he was going to talk his way out of its absence."

"He sounds like a real piece of work," Nina observed.

"Yes, indeed. I pity his patients. Now he's a psychiatrist."

The women almost spit out their drinks. "Seriously?" Amy barked.

"Yep." Frankie nodded. "I feel like I dodged a bullet with that one. And several others, I suppose."

Silence fell across the table.

Frankie's eyes twinkled. "I have an idea."

"Uh-oh," Amy said.

"I know we all hate Internet dating . . ."

Nina held up her hand. "I am going to stop you right there, girl. There is a NO DIVING sign at the dating pool." The women laughed.

"Seriously. Listen," Frankie went on. "Let's make a pact. I know this is probably something we swore we would never do. But"—she took a deep breath—"if none of us have dates for New Year's Eve by this Thanksgiving, we'll go on a singles cruise together."

"What?" Nina's eyes almost bugged out.

"Huh?" came from Amy.

"Count me in," Rachael said, jumping at the idea.

"Really. What's the worst that can happen? We'll have fun, get a tan, and come home with some duty-free perfume," Frankie assured them.

"That could be fun," Nina agreed. "It's only June now, so we have plenty of time to either ruin our lives again with a man or get ourselves into bathing-suit shape."

A groan went around the table. "OK. So we'll wear sarongs," Nina added.

"And cover-ups," Amy said.

"And big hats," Frankie suggested.

"Let's not forget the dark sunglasses." Rachael put her two cents in.

"Caribbean?" Frankie asked. "We can meet up in Miami and take one of those four-or-five-day singles cruises. Come on! Like I said, the worst that can happen is we get a tan."

"Or tossed in the drink for being too rowdy." Nina chuckled.

Rachael clapped. "I love it!"

"Don't get too excited there, missy. We'll keep you on a tight leash," Nina said.

"Ha. Isn't the whole point to have some fun?" Rachael protested.

"Absolutely!" Frankie was pleased with her idea, and her friends were enthusiastic about it, too. "It will be like *The Love Boat* with eggnog."

The women reached across the table and grabbed each other's hands. "Pinky swear!" They locked fingers the same way they had in high school when they set out to accomplish something.

Frankie surveyed the room. "I think our work here is done. Are any of you staying here at this hotel?"

"I'm at my folks'," Amy replied.

"I'm at a B and B off Henshaw Drive," Rachael said.

"I'm at the Courtyard," Nina put in.

"Oh good. So am I. I couldn't get a room here, which is fine. I don't know if I want to keep running into people I don't remember," Frankie said almost apologetically. "Let's go over to the Courtyard and hang out. I don't see anyone or anything worth pursuing here." She giggled.

"Splendid idea," Nina agreed.

"Pajama party?" Amy almost begged.

"I have two beds in my room. You can join me, but won't your mother be upset?" Frankie asked.

"You mean my mother and Mister Charm? Nah. They're at the club. I'll send her a text so she won't worry."

Rachael frowned for a moment. "Can I come and play, too?"

Nina put her arm around Rachael. "Sure thing, babe. I also have an extra bed."

In unison, they high-fived each other, grabbed their purses, and headed toward the door when a loud voice came over the speaker. "Let's all say hello to the famous Nina Hunter!"

Hoots and applause filled the room.

"Uh-oh. I thought we could make a quick getaway," Nina said with clenched teeth, feigning a smile. "Hello, everyone!" She made her way up to the podium while the three other women waited near the exit.

"It's so nice to see all these familiar faces," Nina lied, with a big, bright smile. Frankie was stifling a laugh. Then Nina said, "Let's have a round of applause for the reunion committee. Didn't they do a great job?" Lots of clapping, whistling, and cheers filled the room. Once the noise subsided, Nina ended her impromptu appearance with, "I trust everyone tunes in on Thursday night for a half hour of laughs and crazy family fun! See you on the boob tube! Enjoy the evening! Be safe!" She gave a wave and stepped away from the microphone as the group gave her the appropriate applause. She hustled toward her friends to make a quick getaway in case other people wanted to talk to her. In spite of her big personality and her love for theater and acting, Nina was basically shy. She said it was her acting skills that helped her deal with people.

As the four women exited the hotel, Frankie pulled up her Uber app and ordered a car to pick them up. When they got to the Courtyard, they raided the minibars in their rooms, settled in, and made plans for their seafaring adventure.